Roger Palm

Miami F___

1950

P

MB

BEYOND DEFEAT

BEYOND DEFEAT

BY

HANS WERNER RICHTER

TRANSLATED BY ROBERT KEE

G. P. PUTNAM'S SONS

NEW YORK

TO MY FOUR BROTHERS, *who opposed this war and were soldiers in it, who hated a system and yet had to fight for it, and who betrayed neither themselves, their beliefs, nor their country.*

BEYOND DEFEAT

I

THEY drove into the town. Unarmed Italian soldiers were streaming past them to the rear.

"War finished," they shouted. "*Alles kaput.* Everything finished."

They drove past the silent guns that had been meant to defend the town. Konz and Beijerke were sitting sunning themselves in the front garden of a house. Gühler wrenched open the door of the truck.

"What's wrong?"

"Nothing. Everything's fine," said Beijerke.

"What about the wops?"

"Surrendered."

"What's this place?"

"Nettuno."

"What have they got you doing?"

"Security," said Beijerke, grinning.

They sat on the steps and waved to him. The sea was visible between the houses behind them. Konz had propped his elbows on one of the steps. He rocked his

3

knees. Beijerke sat on his ammunition boxes. The machine gun and their helmets lay close by.

Gühler drove his truck into the town. The truck ahead of him stopped in front of some barracks. Men and women were standing in the narrow street shouting.

"Supply barracks," said Breutzmann, the driver of the other truck.

The bowlegged *Feldwebel* who looked like a cavalry general went into the barracks. He had been in charge of the column since the day before.

"Go in with him," said Breutzmann. "Maybe there's something worth getting hold of."

Gühler followed the *Feldwebel* into the barracks. He found a bottle of olive oil and brought it out.

"Right. Now it's my turn," said Breutzmann.

He came back with a round cheese and some tins of mule meat.

"Your turn again," he said.

They went into the barracks alternately and loaded everything onto their trucks.

The *Feldwebel* with the bowlegs came back out of the barracks.

"He's all right," said Breutzmann. "A little cracked, but otherwise all right."

"Do you know him?"

"I was in Russia with him. Name's Buschmann."

The *Feldwebel* came up to them. He had little mouse-gray eyes which always seemed to be smiling.

"Stay here with the trucks," he said.

"How come?" said Breutzmann.

"You two stay here. We're taking over coastal defense."

"Very good, *Herr Feldwebel*," said Breutzmann.

4

The *Feldwebel* laughed. The rest of the platoon filed past the truck and marched on down the street.

"A nice hole to get stuck in," said Breutzmann. He looked at the tall miserable houses.

They sat in their trucks and made a meal of the cheese and tinned meat.

"Tastes like rotten fish," said Breutzmann.

Half-dressed women were standing round the truck. They lifted their hands begging.

Gühler took one of the tins of meat and threw it to them.

"Just whores," said Breutzmann.

A woman climbed up on the truck. She was tall and thin and had a pointed face. She bent down toward the tins of meat.

"This evening," she whispered in broken German, "come this evening. Third house up the street. I'll be waiting. And bring something with you."

Gühler saw the flat breasts under her bright red dress.

"Whores, all whores," shouted Breutzmann again from the other truck.

Gühler turned away. The smell of the begging women seemed suddenly unbearable.

"Beat it," he said.

He gave the woman a push in the bottom with his knee.

"Hungry," she said, "hungry, sir."

He took one of the tins and threw it to her. The woman's face disintegrated. She wept. The tears made streaks down the white powder on her face. The others were standing round the truck shouting. Breutzmann sat on the truck and cut off thin slices of cheese. He held

5

each slice up, let the women jump for it, and then threw it into the street.

"Cut it out," said Gühler.

"Just tarts," said Breutzmann. "Nothing but tarts."

Gühler said nothing. He looked down at the women and was silent.

"War finished. *Krieg kaput*. We're all brothers," said one of the women.

There were deep lines round her mouth. Gühler looked at her red-painted mouth. He took a tin of meat and threw it to her. The woman smiled.

"She'd make a nice one," said Breutzmann.

Gühler suddenly understood the longing of the women, a longing for life, a longing for peace. He took all the tins and threw them to the women. A motorcycle came round the corner.

"What's going on here?" said Sergeant Hahnemann.

Breutzmann laughed.

"*Mensch*," he said, "nothing but whores."

Gühler threw one tin after the other out of the truck. Hahnemann said:

"What the hell are you doing?"

"They're hungry."

"You must be nuts. For every tin you could lay one of them."

Hahnemann's broad fleshy face beamed.

"Do what we do," he said, and showed them two bottles of olive oil in his pocket. "A bottle a lay."

Gühler looked at Hahnemann and said nothing. He took the remaining tins and threw them down to the women.

"Give me the cheese," Hahnemann said. "I can use it."

"So can I," said Gühler.

"That's an order," said Hahnemann. "*Los*. Give me the cheese."

The women pressed round the motorcycle. Hahnemann took the cheese and put it down in front of him on the gas tank.

"You can have a whole night for that, you idiot," he said.

The women snatched at the cheese.

"Damned rabble," said Hahnemann. He pushed the motorcycle through the crowd. Then he took out his pistol and fired it into the air. The women fell back.

The motorcycle drove slowly down the street.

"What a swine," said Breutzmann.

Gühler's eyes followed the motorcycle. He had known Hahnemann since France.

"He's gone nuts," he thought.

"*Tedeschi kaput*," shouted one of the women suddenly. She raised her hands and ran toward the barracks. The other women followed her.

"*Tedeschi kaput, Tedeschi kaput*," they all shouted.

The sentry on the door of the barracks raised his rifle. The women swarmed down on him and knocked him over. They ran through the door into the barracks.

"They'll loot the whole damn barracks," said Breutzmann.

"Yes," said Gühler.

But they stayed sitting in their trucks and watched the women looting. The women tore their booty out of each other's hands and started fighting among themselves. More and more women came out of the houses.

An Italian police car drove into the street. The police

leveled their machine gun at the women. The women screamed at them.

"*Maledette fascisti! Maledette fascisti!*"

The machine gun began firing.

"We've put the swine back again already," said Gühler.

The women shrieked. They threw themselves down in the street and ran into the houses.

"Stop that!" Gühler shouted at the police.

The machine gun went on firing. The women lay under the barrack walls shouting "*Maledette fascisti, maledette fascisti!*"

The police jumped from their truck and ran toward the women. Tins rolled out of their pockets onto the road.

"Damned clever, those whores," said Breutzmann.

The women ran into the houses. Slowly the street emptied. One of the women was left lying on the pavement. She was screaming. A red spot was forming on her pale green dress, spreading over her thigh. She pulled her dress up. Her jerking thighs stood out white against the stones.

"She's had it," said Breutzmann.

Gühler watched the blood flowing over the pavement. The woman pulled her pants down from her hips. She pressed her hands to her stomach. The blood welled through her fingers. It ran between her legs onto the road.

"In the belly," said Breutzmann.

"Yes. Stomach wound," Gühler murmured.

But they stayed sitting on their trucks and didn't move. The woman gave a piercing scream, whimpered, and was silent. The Italian police picked her up and car-

8

ried her into the house, leaving a thick trail of blood behind them. Then all was quiet in the street.

In the evening they drove into the market place. Some Italian officers were standing in front of the town hall. They were officers from the Artillery School and from the division which had been stationed in the town.

"You're to take the officers back to Frascati and deliver them to the German command post there," said Lieutenant Woltmann, who was in charge of the company. He was thin and pale and looked like a schoolteacher. He wasn't liked. But in the first action against the Italians he had stood up and fired at the Italian tanks. Since then they laughed about him good-naturedly.

The Italian officers climbed up onto the trucks. Gühler walked round his truck, tested the tires, and fastened the tail board behind the officers.

"There are thirteen of them," said Breutzmann. "Have you counted?"

"Thirteen on each truck?"

"Yes," said Breutzmann.

"Unlucky number. What if one of them escapes?"

"Then you'll only have twelve."

"And who's responsible?"

"You, of course. Who else? Each man's responsible for his own thirteen."

"No guards?"

"No," said Breutzmann. "We've got to drive behind each other, and watch the truck in front."

They climbed into the trucks. Gühler took his pistol out and laid it on the seat beside him.

"I'll let them all go," he thought. But he picked up his pistol and looked to see if it was loaded.

9

Hahnemann came and looked into the truck.

"Well, how are all the girls?" he said.

"Cut it out. How far is it to Frascati?"

"Eighty kilometers," said Hahnemann.

He slammed the door of the truck. They drove slowly out of the town. Night was already crouching on the road. Gühler stared fixedly at the red taillights of the truck ahead. He thought, "Mine is the last truck. If I stop now and let them out, they're free."

But he looked down at his pistol.

"If I let them go, they'll go home. Somewhere their wives will be waiting for them."

The moon rose up over the maize fields. Its half disc floated out over the fields.

"What's the difference?" he went on thinking. "Thirteen Italian officers jumped out of my truck, thirteen officers with no significance whatever."

The red taillights of the truck in front receded and then came back again.

"And no guard. They jumped out of the truck and ran off into the field and I never noticed."

But he fumbled for the pistol in the darkness and felt the barrel between his fingers.

Then the red taillights in front of him disappeared. A gray night mist crept over the road. The light from the headlights was caught and blunted in the mist.

"Drive slower," he thought, but he pressed the accelerator down harder. Fear sat suddenly beside him, a senseless fear. The truck shot forward, but the red lights in front of him did not reappear. A few houses slipped by, then a bridge, then some more houses. He was suddenly overcome by the feeling that he was alone. He thought, "Now you can let them go. All of them."

He drove more slowly. He drove to the side of the road and stopped the truck. He picked up his pistol, took off the safety catch, and jumped into the road.

The officers sat jammed close together, asleep. Their patent-leather boots shone in the light of the moon which now hung orange-yellow between the houses in the fields. He counted them over.

"Still thirteen," he thought. "No one's missing."

He shook one of the officers.

"Anyone here speak German?" he asked.

"Yes," said the officer, "I do."

"How do I get to Frascati?"

"Back a bit. The other road," said the officer.

The other officers woke up. They talked among themselves for a little and then fell silent again.

"Now," thought Gühler, "they'll get up, push me out of the way, and run off into the fields."

But they didn't move.

"Come up front with me," he said to the officer who spoke German.

He turned the truck round and drove back.

"Left," said the officer, when they came to a crossing. Gühler drove down the other road.

"Are we going to prison?" said the officer after a while.

"Don't know," said Gühler.

"The war is over," said the officer again.

Gühler looked at him and said, "For you, yes. Not for us."

They were both silent. The truck drove over a few craters.

"American bombs," said the officer.

"Yes," said Gühler, "American bombs."

"America has much aircraft."

"Yes," said Gühler.

"You'll lose the war."

"I know," said Gühler. And he watched the road to avoid the big bomb craters.

"Why did you fight against us? Why didn't you stop too?"

"It's not so simple as with you."

"Are you anti-Hitler?"

"Yes," muttered Gühler.

"Why are you fighting against us then?"

"In this war one's always on the wrong side."

The taillights of the other truck appeared in front of them.

"We're in Frascati," said the officer.

He drove close up behind the other truck, which had stopped in the road in front of him. Breutzmann was standing in the road.

"We can't go into the town," he said.

"Why not?"

"Danger of plague. The Americans have wrecked the place."

"To hell with it," said Gühler. "Come on, we'll go in."

They walked past the truck. The Italian officers sat cowering together asleep. They walked past tall heaps of rubble, and round huge bomb craters. A soldier stood in front of what was left of some sort of façade. He looked lost in the night among the ruins.

"Hey, you! Where's the German command post?" said Breutzmann.

"There ain't no German command post any more."

"What do you mean?"

"Gone," said the guard.

"What do you mean, gone?"

"They beat it. Everybody beat it."

He looked indifferently at Breutzmann.

"We've got a hundred and thirty Italian officers in the trucks," said Breutzmann. "We're supposed to deliver them here."

"There are two hundred and fifty in the cellar behind me. We don't need any more."

"Isn't anybody left in town?"

"There's a *Feldwebel* running around somewhere. You'll have to find him."

They walked on farther into the town. As they approached the market place the mountains of ruins became higher and higher.

"They say there are four thousand bodies still under the ruins," whispered Breutzmann.

Water was dripping from the ruins in the market place.

"What's the time?"

"Almost one."

"Why are you whispering?"

"Am I whispering?"

They stopped in front of a ruined café. Broken chairs were strewn chaotically over the terrace.

"This is where the women used to sit in the summertime," whispered Breutzmann.

"Let's go," said Gühler out loud.

"Are you afraid?"

"It gives me the creeps," said Gühler.

They heard the water dripping through the ruins. Breutzmann said, "The women. Where are they now?"

"Come on," said Gühler.

13

"They used to be lovely. You've never seen anything like it."

"That was a long time ago," said Gühler.

'Yes," said Breutzmann, "four weeks."

They walked down the avenue. Crater after crater yawned in front of them. They found the *Feldwebel* sitting on a bench.

"What are you doing here?" he said.

"We've got a hundred and thirty Italian prisoners on our trucks. We're supposed to deliver them here," said Breutzmann.

"That's bad," said the *Feldwebel*. "Very bad. We've got enough already."

He walked back through the town with them. The trucks were still standing on the road. The drivers and the officers were asleep. They woke up the drivers and drove back through the town. It took an endless time. The bomb craters kept holding them up. They drew up in front of a castle which stood on a hill on the other side of the town.

"How many are there?" asked the *Feldwebel*.

"A hundred and thirty."

The *Feldwebel* opened the main gate of the castle. The officers climbed off the trucks. They looked sleepy and tired. One after the other they went through the gateway. Their patent-leather boots gleamed in the bright moonlight.

Breutzmann said, "Isn't anyone going to count them?"

The *Feldwebel* raised his hand and wearily let it fall again.

"What's the point?" he said.

"We could have let them go," said Gühler.

14

The *Feldwebel* said nothing. The insignia of the military police shone on his chest.

The officer with whom Gühler had talked went past. Gühler nodded to him.

"*Auf wiedersehen*," said the officer.

Gühler didn't answer. He turned round and said, "What'll happen to them now?"

"I don't know," said the *Feldwebel*. He pushed the great doors together and closed them.

"You should have sent them all home," said the *Feldwebel*.

"*We* should?" said Breutzmann. "We had orders to deliver them here."

Gühler looked at the *Feldwebel*, whose face was old and tired. He thought, "I should have let them go."

"What am I going to do with them?" asked the *Feldwebel* again.

"Send them home," said Gühler.

"It's not as easy as that. I've got orders to lock them up here."

They climbed into their trucks. The moon hung above the castle. It was bright as day. Gühler said, "We should have let them go."

"Yes," said Breutzmann, "if I'd known."

The headlights quivered over the lawn.

Gühler picked up his pistol which lay on the seat. The safety catch was still off. He pushed it on and put the pistol in his pocket.

"*Sheissding*," he muttered.

They drove back through the night.

II

THE column was moving southward again between huge fields of dried-up maize, down country roads that were hot and dusty. The dust caked on their uniforms and sifted into their eyes. Black herds of oxen moved past them going northward. The oxen trotted along indifferently, their heavy heads sunk toward the ground. "Like us," thought Gühler.

Toward evening they came to the sea again. One truck after another dropped behind.

"They're splitting up again."

"What does that mean?" asked Grundmann.

"Probably coastal defense," said Beijerke.

They stopped on the edge of a town. The gardens in front of the houses were full of fruit trees but looked deserted and desolate. There was no sign of anyone in the houses.

Buschmann came by.

"Get ready. Our platoon's occupying the town."

"Very good, *Herr Feldwebel*," said Grundmann.

16

"You and your very good *Herr Feldwebel*. Stick it," said Gühler.

Grundmann reddened and said nothing. He was a bulky young noncom who had come up recently as a replacement. A massive head set directly atop his uniform gave him the look of a charging bull, but his eyes were watery gray and childlike.

The inhabitants had left the town. Silence crouched in the palacelike villas by the sea. Fountains splashed in the gardens but the fruit hung withered and rotten on the trees. The doors of the villas stood open or had been broken in. Ants crawled over the marble flagstones.

"You're taking over a gun in the southern part of the town," said Buschmann.

They moved along the harbor, dragging their machine guns and the boxes behind them, tired and irritable. Hahnemann came past on his motorcycle.

"Konz is going to be the *Feldwebel's* orderly," he said.

"Great," said Beijerke. "Two machine guns and one coastal gun for three men."

The gun was built into the rock directly overlooking the sea. They went up to a house near the rock. They put down their boxes and their machine guns and went inside. In the kitchen they found a pot of lard, a piece of bacon and, in the corner, a heap of potatoes. Gühler began to peel the potatoes.

"Christ, am I hungry," he said.

Grundmann poked around in the fire, trying to stir it up.

"Gühler, man, it's swarming with ants."

"Let it swarm," said Gühler.

Beijerke climbed up to the second floor. The house was flimsily built and they could hear his heavy nailed boots above them. The sound of a croaking gramophone came from upstairs. It was an American swing record.

"Hell," said Gühler, "Beijerke's going modern."

He cut up the potatoes in small pieces and shook them into the frying pan. Beijerke came clattering down.

"Jesus! That upstairs is really something!"

"What do you mean?"

"White beds, eiderdowns. The whole place stinks like a brothel."

"What of it?" said Gühler.

They ate the fried potatoes out of the pan. The ants ran over their boots. Beijerke struck at them with his fork.

"Filthy little bastards," he said.

They went up and threw themselves on the beds. The beds were soft and white and smelled sweet and enticing. Gühler got up, pulled off his boots, and threw himself down on the bed again.

"Almost like home," he said.

Beijerke sat in front of the open window. Outside lay the sea, leaden and dead. Twilight shadows stood on the horizon and came creeping slowly over the water. Beijerke had the gramophone in front of him. He played the same American swing record over and over again.

Grundmann was on the bed next to Gühler. He lay for a while without speaking. Then he said suddenly, "Do you think we'll win the war?"

Gühler said nothing.

"Tell me, do you think we'll win the war?" he began again.

"I don't think anything," said Gühler.

"They all talk so much, first about Stalingrad and then about Tunis. They say the Americans will overrun us."

"Who says so?"

"The folks back home."

"Maybe they're right."

Grundmann half sat up and tried to look Gühler in the eye.

"Look," he said, "do you think that too?"

"Yes," said Gühler, "I think that too."

"Then you're against Hitler?"

"Yes, I'm against Hitler."

"And yet you fight for him."

"No," said Gühler, "I'm only a cog in a machine, one that can't get out."

"Why not?"

"Well," said Gühler, "court martial, firing squad, you know the story."

"Are you afraid of that?"

"Yes," said Gühler.

Grundmann said nothing. It was completely quiet in the room. Beijerke had stopped playing his gramophone. His silhouette stood out in the dusk against the open window.

"Then you'd like the others to win?" began Grundmann again.

"It'd be better for us."

"Yet you fight against them?"

"Yes. That's the hell of it."

They both fell silent. Beijerke was raking around in the cupboards. He pulled everything out and threw it onto the floor: shoes, powder puffs, bottles, underclothes. He pulled out a pink nightgown and held it up in front of Gühler's nose.

"Just get a stink of that."

"Let's go to sleep. It's late," said Gühler.

He turned on his side. Beijerke spread out the night-dress.

"A woman, a real woman, can you imagine it?"

He went over to Grundmann and pushed the night-gown into his face.

"A whore," said Grundmann, "maybe it was a whore's."

"What do you know about whores, baby face?" said Beijerke.

He sat down at the window again. It was quiet in the room. They heard nothing but the sea rubbing against the harbor wall.

Gühler smelled the strong sweet smell that came from the pillow.

"A woman," he thought, "my God, a woman."

Next to him Grundmann was breathing deeply and heavily.

"Perhaps she was beautiful," thought Gühler, "beau‧tiful like the women on the corso at Frascati, who now lie under the ruins."

"The ants," whispered Grundmann. "Do you notice anything?"

"Perhaps a few days ago she was lying here, and her legs were young and slender."

"The ants," said Grundmann. "Do you hear, Gühler, the ants are coming."

"Perhaps she was alone," he thought, "and her husband was one of the prisoners I drove away."

"The ants!" shouted Grundmann.

"Who?" said Gühler, drunk with sleep.

He jumped up. The ants were running over his body. He felt them all over him, in his arm pits, on his chest,

20

between his legs. Watery moonlight bathed the room. He looked at the bed and it was black with ants.

"Out of here! *Raus!*" shouted Grundmann.

He ran down the stairs with his boots in his hand.

Beijerke still sat in front of the window.

"Yes," he said, "out with you."

Gühler ran down the stairs behind Grundmann. He ran down to the harbor and pulled off his clothes.

"Into the water. *Los!* Into the water," said Grundmann.

They undressed and threw their clothes on the ground.

"It's cold," said Gühler. But his skin burned. They jumped into the water and swam out a little way. The moonlight lay in a broad yellow band across the sea.

"It's incredible," said Grundmann. "Where did all these ants come from?"

"Out of the ground."

"I don't know. Beijerke shouldn't have pulled out that nightdress."

"What do you mean, the nightdress?"

"I don't know," said Grundmann. "Perhaps . . ."

"Don't be superstitious," said Gühler.

He lay on his back and pushed the water away with his legs. The white drops danced in the moonlight. They swam back, shook out their clothes, and dressed again. Then they sat down on the harbor wall and looked at the sea. They could see long shadows moving out there.

"English submarines?" whispered Grundmann.

"Nonsense, where would they come from?"

"Just the same, you can't tell," said Grundmann.

From the window above them came the soft rhythm of the swing record. Beijerke was playing it unceasingly.

"What's the matter with Beijerke?"

"Perhaps he's homesick," said Gühler.

"And the ants?"

"He doesn't notice them."

They heard Hahnemann's voice behind them.

"What the hell are you doing there?"

"Sunning ourselves," said Gühler.

"Don't you see anything out there?"

"Yes," said Gühler.

"Get the machine gun out then. Quick."

They ran into the house and got the machine gun.

"Beijerke!" they shouted up the stairs, "Beijerke!"

They heard the gramophone stop and Beijerke's heavy footsteps.

"What is it?" he said, halfway down the stairs.

"*Los!*" said Grundmann. "U-boats!"

They ran along the quay behind Hahnemann. Out to sea the dark shadows slipped on toward the south.

"Shh," said Hahnemann.

They came out on the road which ran directly along the sea south of the town. They stole along behind each other with the shadows creeping southward just ahead of them. Filusch, the butcher from Upper Silesia, joined them. He walked next to Hahnemann, carrying a machine gun and swearing continually.

"Never any peace. Always the same old shit."

They bumped into a sentry from another platoon.

"Those are German boats," said the sentry. "They go past here every night."

"That's what I thought," said Hahnemann.

Gühler laughed. He looked at Hahnemann and laughed. Hahnemann gave him a push in the ribs and said, "I don't like that dirty laugh of yours."

"Supplies for the front," said the sentry.

They returned, exhausted. The night collapsed about them and dissolved. Over the sea it grew lighter and lighter. They closed their eyes as they walked. Sleep sat on their shoulders and made them stumble forward unconsciously. Their boots moved, but they didn't notice that they were moving. Filusch was singing to himself.

"The night was not made for sleeping."

"Crackpots," muttered Hahnemann.

"Ants," thought Gühler. "Millions of ants crawling over the earth. . . ."

In the morning they went inside the rock and looked at their gun. It was an Italian model and looked small and neglected standing there on a platform in the rock. There were no sights left on it. A rope led from the firing lever down over the platform. The barrel peeped out to sea through a narrow opening in the rock. Grundmann said, "We ought to fire it to see if the thing works."

"Without any sights?" said Gühler.

"It's important to fire it. It must be fired," said Grundmann.

There was a whole mountain of shells near the gun. Grundmann picked up a shell and prepared to load.

"What are we going to shoot at?"

"We only want to test it out."

"But we must shoot somewhere," said Gühler.

"Just out to sea," said Beijerke, "straight out there."

They climbed down the ladder and examined the rope, which was almost as thin as string. They looked out to sea again.

"Who's going to fire it?" asked Grundmann.

"I'll see that the road's clear," said Beijerke.

"What do you mean, 'see that the road's clear'? There isn't a soul in the town."

"You can't be too sure," said Beijerke. He was out of the rock in a flash. They heard him walking along the road.

"He's scared," said Grundmann.

They examined the rope again and looked at each other.

"Who's going to pull it?"

"I'll observe the fire," said Grundmann.

"Oh, sure. That's very important," said Gühler.

He was alone. Grundmann sat down outside on the quay. The sea was calm. The sun lay full on the water and the air sparkled so that sea and horizon seemed to melt into one another. Not a sound came from the harbor. The town lay dead, extinct, as if it had never known life.

Gühler stood inside the rock and held the rope in his hand.

"All clear on the road," yelled Beijerke.

"Fire!" shouted Grundmann.

"Idiots," thought Gühler.

He hung onto the rope and began to pull. But nothing moved. He pulled himself up on the rope and felt it cutting into his hands. But still the firing lever didn't move. Then he let go of the rope and ran down onto the road.

"Hi, Grundmann! Come up here."

"Don't you want to do it?"

"We'll both have to pull," said Gühler. They both hung onto the rope and pulled themselves up on it. Their faces went red and sweat broke out on them. Then they fell to the ground with a bump. The rock heaved.

24

"Bastardly thing," said Gühler.

"The results!" cried Grundmann and ran out. Gühler jumped up and ran out after him. Far out to sea they saw a fountain of water leap up.

"Bull's eye!" shouted Beijerke from the road.

They ran back inside the rock. They climbed up the ladder and began to load the gun again.

Shot after shot rolled out across the harbor. The thudding and booming echoed through the dead town. "Bull's eye," shouted Beijerke every time the fountains of water went up out at sea, and "Fire!" shouted Grundmann before the gun went off. They pulled at the rope and shouted and laughed every time they fell. They clapped each other on the back with pleasure as the white foaming fountains of water spouted up time and time again. There were no sights and they shot straight out to sea.

Then Hahnemann came riding up on his motorcycle looking flushed and excited. He jumped off and came running up into the rock shouting, "You men gone crazy?"

They were in the process of cooling the red-hot barrel with a rag soaked in water.

"A good gun," said Beijerke.

"Are you all nuts, for Christ's sake!"

"What do you mean?"

"Making that goddam racket!"

"Guns must be fired," said Beijerke. "There's a war on."

"Stop it at once," shouted Hahnemann, "at once!"

He snatched a shell out of Grundmann's hand and threw it onto the pile with the others.

"Too bad," said Beijerke.

25

They climbed down the ladder and walked onto the road.

"And without sights, you half-wits."

They all pushed the motorcycle. Hahnemann sat firmly and broadly on the seat and let them push.

"And out there are English submarines watching every move we make," he said.

"What an ass he's got," said Beijerke.

Hahnemann turned round. "Shut your trap, Beijerke."

The motorcycle started up. They watched him ride along the harbor, and then went back to their rock, climbed up the ladder, and sat down on the gun.

"They never let a man have any fun," said Beijerke.

In the town, it was again deathly still.

In the evening Gühler was detached to take over the guarding of a grain warehouse at the station. Filusch was supposed to be there waiting for him. He went out through the empty streets to the station, which lay in the northern part of the town.

"*Mensch*, Gühler," said Filusch, who was standing in front of the granary door, "we've got it good here." He gave Gühler the key and they went inside. There was a smell of wheat in the vast hall.

"It's to be loaded up and sent to Germany."

"Who's doing the loading?"

"We are. Tomorrow some Italian workers are coming from the mountains."

They went back into the yard. Dark banks of clouds were collecting above the mountains behind the town.

"Listen," said Filusch suddenly. "They're coming."

26

They stopped and listened to the sky.

Suddenly there were two red and yellow balls of fire hanging above them in the air.

"*Los!*" said Filusch. "This is no place for us."

They ran across the yard, shut the gate behind them, and ran down the road. They heard a dull explosion and ran faster. Then all round them it was bright as day. They ran across the station and threw themselves down beside a freight car. Gühler shouted, "We can't stay here."

The yellow balls of fire hung above them like giant lanterns. They pressed themselves flat against the tracks. Then the earth began to shake. The sound of the exploding bombs came nearer and nearer.

"Get away from here," yelled Gühler. But it was as if no sound came out when he opened his mouth.

"The station," he thought, "they'll bomb the station."

Between explosions he heard the sound of the planes' engines as they made their bombing runs again and again. The explosions became more and more frequent.

"You can't stay here," he thought, "can't keep lying here."

The tracks began to tremble.

"Filusch!" he shouted, "Filusch!"

But he didn't hear his own words. It was still as bright as day all round him. He saw Filusch on the other side of the freight car, lying on his stomach flat on the ground with his arms stretched out wide.

Gühler jumped up and ran over the rails. The dazzling light pierced his eyes. He felt that he could be seen by everyone, as if he were alone in the world, alone in this unearthly brightness. He saw Filusch running beside him. They jumped into a ditch and ran into the fields. A high fence rose up in front of them.

"Go on," panted Filusch, "over it."

They climbed up the fence and jumped down on the other side. It seemed to them as if the bombs were running after them. They jumped over hedges and ditches. Then they came to a tunnel.

"In here," shouted Gühler.

They ran into the tunnel and threw themselves down on the ground. The ground heaved. Their throats were dry and empty. Their breath came in quick gasps.

"Christ!" said Gühler, "Christ!" He writhed around on the ground.

The air still droned around them as they pressed themselves into the earth.

Then all round them it was suddenly quiet. It was so quiet that they held their breath. They lay and listened to the stillness. The dark night hung in front of the tunnel mouth. Then they heard the rain coming. It fell splashing onto the vine leaves outside.

"Rain," said Gühler.

"Yes," said Filusch, "it's raining."

They fell silent again. They sat against the wall of the tunnel with drawn-up knees, looking out at the rain. In the morning they went back. They walked over the rails past the station. They went along the street and came to the grain warehouse. Everything was still standing just as they had left it. Nothing had changed.

"I thought all this would be blown to hell," said Filusch.

Above the mountains on the other side of the town

the clouds broke up. They went into the warehouse yard and looked around. The freight cars were still standing over by the station. This was where they had lain the evening before. It seemed an eternity since then. Beyond the tracks the fields steamed as the early morning mist rose off them. They heard the clatter of the motorcycle and went over to the gate.

"Well," said Buschmann, "everybody survive all right?"

He sat with his bowlegs round the motorcycle and laughed at them. They said nothing.

"You started something with that gun of yours."

"With our gun?" said Gühler.

"Go down and have a look. Everything's in ruins."

"Our gun?" Gühler said again.

"Yeah. They must have thought that new batteries had come into position. Now they've kicked hell out of the place."

"Only that one spot?"

"A hundred square yards, crater after crater."

"And Beijerke?"

"You were lucky," said the *Feldwebel*. "I'd have cut your balls off if anybody'd got hurt."

"And Grundmann?" asked Gühler again.

"They all beat it in time. But the gun's still standing in the rock."

Buschmann started up the motorcycle and drove out of the gate. His bowlegs encircled the motorcycle as if it were the belly of a horse. Gühler shook his head.

"You and your gunnery," said Filusch. "Another night up the creek."

They went across the yard, found a little house nearby

with two beds, and set themselves up in it. They threw themselves down on the beds, exhausted.

"We're supposed to guard the station, too," said Filusch.

"The station can guard itself," said Gühler.

III

THE Italian workers from the mountains arrived the next morning and began to load up the wheat. With the workers came the women. They came in the evening, and stood in front of the gate begging for wheat. They brought eggs, chickens, and wine. The freight cars stood in the station all the time but were never full. At night the workers stole the sacks of wheat they had loaded during the day. The station master reappeared and sat in his office. At night he fetched himself one sack of wheat after the other. Gühler and Filusch paid no attention. They roasted the chickens, ate the eggs, and drank the wine which the women brought in exchange for the wheat. One day a train came from the north. It brought a whole troop of women with suitcases and baskets.

"You can't go into the town," said Filusch. "No one's allowed in the town."

They stood on the station warding off the women who tried to rush them. A few women ran across the tracks into the town. "Shall I shoot?" said Filusch.

31

"Let them go," said Gühler.

At night the women sat in the little waiting room and sang. They had their baskets full of wheat beside them and Gühler sat with them. It was cosy and warm in the little room. The women sat on the benches and lay on the floor. They sang all night long.

One evening a woman appeared at the gate. It was late and the crowd had already gone. The woman said nothing. She stood there looking into the yard. Gühler went up to her.

"Well?" he said.

The woman didn't answer. She looked at him and said nothing.

"What do you want?" he said again.

The woman didn't answer. Gühler looked at her. He saw a young face with two hungry eyes burning in it.

"Are you hungry?" he asked.

"Yes," she whispered.

He took her by the arm.

"Come on," he said.

He went with her into the warehouse, took her bag and filled it with wheat.

"Thank you," said the woman.

He went back across the yard with her.

"Where do you live?"

"There," she said, pointing into the fields.

They went down the road and into the fields.

"You speak German," he said.

"Yes, my mother comes from Merano."

"From Merano," he said.

They went farther into the fields. The night was still and clear. They came to a hut which lay small and squat among the fields. "This is where I live," she said.

32

She leaned against the low doorway and looked at him.

"She's lovely," he thought.

Suddenly he found what he had intended to do here ridiculous.

"Well, when will you be wanting more wheat?"

"Tomorrow?" she asked.

"All right, tomorrow."

"*Auf wiedersehen,*" she whispered.

He turned round and went into the fields.

"To forget the whole rotten mess for one hour, just one hour. . . ." he thought.

He stood still and then went slowly back to the house. It stood there darkly hidden among the vines. He stopped again on the path and looked at the house. The little windows were hung with curtains.

"Come here," he heard a whisper in front of him.

She still stood leaning against the doorpost as he had left her.

"Come in," she said.

He went close to her. Her face stood out palely in the darkness of the doorway.

"You've come back?"

"Yes."

"Why?"

He didn't answer. He looked at her, glanced at the fields, and said nothing. Then he began to talk.

"Yes," he said. "The war. You play soldier day after day, and you're always alone. . . ."

"I know."

"Yes, it could soon be over."

"For us it's never over."

She sat down in the doorway, clasped her knees, and looked into the night.

"My husband was killed in Africa," she said. "My brothers are somewhere or other, my parents are in Merano. I used to live in Rome. When the Germans came I fled here for fear of the bombs."

"There are enough bombs here."

"But where shall I go to?"

"I don't know. Into the mountains perhaps."

"The war is everywhere," she whispered. "Everywhere."

"Yes. The father of all things," he said. He laughed roughly, but his hands clasped the doorpost against which he was leaning.

"Why do you say that?" she said.

"Because it isn't true."

"No," she said, "it isn't true."

They were both silent. From far away out at sea came the distant droning of airplane engines.

"Can you hear it?" she said.

"Yes. That's the war."

"But here, here with us there's peace."

"And if they come, those up there?"

"They won't come. Tonight they won't come."

They both fell silent again. The rising and falling sound over the sea came nearer and nearer.

"Let's stay here. They'll fly over."

"Yes," he said. "They'll fly over."

"I've been cowering in my house so long. I was afraid of all of you. But I went today because another woman showed me her wheat and told me about you."

"About me?" he said.

"They say you're good. You know how to laugh."

"Do they say that?"

34

"And they say you give away everything, the wheat and the oats, everything in the warehouse."

"It belongs to them."

"It belongs to you now," she whispered. "And the others will come and then it will belong to them."

"The others?"

"Yes, those from the other side."

"Do you think they'll come?"

"You'll lose the war. You'll lose everything, just as we lost everything."

"We've lost everything already."

He sat down beside her in the doorway. The night wind came across the sea and touched the leaves on the trees behind the house.

"I knew it," she whispered.

"What did you know?"

"That you thought like that."

"How?"

"The women who bring you the chickens all say so, the ones who come down out of the mountains in the morning and go back at night."

"I've never said a word."

"They sense it," she whispered.

The sound of engines was directly above them. They saw the dark shadows under the stars. A white flare unfurled itself.

"Quick," she said, "let's get into the house."

"That's too dangerous."

A second and third flare jumped out of the dark sky above them.

"We'll go into the fields," he said.

They ran out into the fields. The vines looked white and milky in the piercing light.

"Faster," he said.

She ran in front of him with easy, supple movements. Her hair streamed down her neck. She had thrown her head back and bent her arms like a long-distance runner. She threw herself down on the grass under a tree. Her breath came quickly and heavily. They heard the bombs exploding but they sounded a long way off as if they were on the other side of the town.

"I'm afraid," she whispered.

He felt her body trembling beside him, but said nothing.

"I've known so much fear lately," she began again. "I was all alone."

"We ran out into the fields somewhere around here," he said.

"Yes," she said, "so close."

The flares in the sky went out. The explosions came nearer and went away again. When the sound of the exploding bombs was close to them, he felt her body shaking against him.

"Hold me tight," she whispered.

"Yes," he said.

"I'm afraid."

"Nothing will happen to you."

"Not now that you're there," she said.

The last flare went out on the distant horizon, as if it had fallen into the sea. They saw the stars come out behind the branches of a tree. They came out one after the other as if jumping back out of the brightness into the night. He lay on his back and looked at the sky.

"They've flown over," he said.

"I knew they would."

She sat up and looked at him. He saw her face above him.

"How small her mouth is," he thought.

"Gühler!" came a sudden shout across the night. "Gühler! Gühler!"

"What is it?" she said, raising her head.

"That's Filusch," he said, jumping to his feet.

"Coming!" he shouted, "coming!"

Gühler took her hand.

"Tomorrow," he said, "tomorrow." He ran into the fields.

"The old man's here," said Filusch.

Lieutenant Woltmann stood in the yard.

"Where have you been?" he said to Gühler.

"In the fields, *Herr Leutnant!*"

"What were you doing there?"

"Some wheat had been stolen and I went after the people."

"In future you'll stay at the station. The whole town's swarming with women."

"Yes, *Herr Leutnant*."

"Good night."

"Good night, *Herr Leutnant*," they both said together.

They remained standing in the yard and watched the Lieutenant go through the gate into the street.

"Where'd he come from?" asked Gühler.

"Christ only knows," answered Filusch.

The next morning a few fighters flew across the yard. They flew low firing their guns. The Italian workers ran out into the road and scattered. Alexandro, the Italian interpreter, shouted that he was wounded, but he had only torn his knee on the hard surface of the yard. In the afternoon Filusch came and said that Alexandro had rounded up a couple of women from the mountains for the night. He drove into the town with Alexandro. They brought back a case of champagne, and sat there in the yard drinking it in the middle of the afternoon. Filusch opened bottle after bottle and drank them all down at a few gulps.

"We'll fetch some more tomorrow," he said. "If we don't lap it up somebody else'll only steal it."

"It's from a good cellar," said Gühler.

"You need a nose for this sort of thing."

Filusch took an empty champagne bottle and threw it across the yard. Gühler carried a couple of bottles into the cellar.

"For this evening," he said.

"Yes, yes, for the women. That'll be something."

"Oh, yes, the women."

The Italian workers who had run into the field that morning never returned. Gühler thought of the fields, of the squat house among the vines, and of the evening. Alexandro sat leaning against the wall, talking nonsense to himself. He had drunk too much champagne. Gühler asked, "Do you think the old man will come again this evening?"

"Why?"

"I was just wondering."

"Ach," said Filusch, "you want to go looking for stolen wheat again."

"Only a walk."

"Oh, sure! Just a walk."

A couple of women came into the yard. They spoke excitedly to Alexandro. One of them was very young.

38

She looked almost like a child and was crying. Filusch
went over and stammered a few words in broken Italian.
He came back and sat down with Gühler again.

"Someone's been at her."

"Who?"

"The little one over there."

"Who's been at her?"

"Some son of a bitch. One of ours. For a couple of
tins of rations."

Gühler looked at the girl. She had long black pigtails
and seemed very young. He thought of the evening, of
the champagne bottles in the cellar, and said nothing.
Filusch got up again and went over to the women. He
filled their bags up with wheat.

"Compensation for war damage," he said when he
came back.

"A dirty business."

"Our turn this evening," said Filusch.

"I won't be here. I'm clearing out."

Filusch looked sideways at Gühler. He had small
black eyes in which the pupils changed size rapidly.

"And what do I do with the women?"

"I don't care."

"Two at once. A little too much."

"For you?" said Gühler.

Filusch took a bottle of champagne, twisted the wire
off, and let the cork pop into the yard.

"Well, we'll see," he said. He leaned backward and
poured the champagne down his throat.

"Don't drink so much."

"Why not?"

"Suppose the old man shows up."

"He won't come, pal, he won't come," said Filusch.

He stood up, tightened his belt, and went over to the station.

"Gotta see what's going on," he said.

Gühler went over to Alexandro and sent him off to the station after Filusch. Then he sat down on his box again and looked out into the late afternoon.

"Perhaps she'll come now," he thought.

Alexandro came back and reported that Filusch was being sick. Gühler had an idea. With Alexandro's help he began to fill up two sacks of wheat. They loaded the two sacks onto a donkey cart. Gühler described the little house in the fields to Alexandro and sent him there with the donkey cart. The donkey bucked in the road and lashed out with its legs.

"Get on with you," shouted Alexandro and beat the donkey.

Gühler thought of the night before, of the flares over the house, and wondered if tonight would be quiet.

"How firm her breasts were," he thought.

Then he heard the sound of trucks arriving. They were the trucks of his platoon. Beijerke, Konz, Grundmann and the rest were sitting in them.

"Hop to it, Gühler," shouted Konz, "we're moving again."

The others laughed. Buschmann came up to him and said, "You must hand over your little nest here."

"Very good," said Gühler. "Very good, *Herr Feldwebel.*"

A strange noncom was standing beside Buschmann. He was from another unit. Filusch came across the yard.

"*Mensch,*" he said, "the women are here."

"To hell with them," said Gühler.

"That dame of yours is here too."

40

"Which dame?"

"Yours from yesterday, of course," said Filusch.

Gühler went across to the station with the noncom.

"Must hand over the station," said Buschmann.

Filusch came up behind him. He reeled and stumbled.

"Filusch is pissed to the ears," shouted Konz.

"*So eine scheiss*," Filusch was saying. "A man hardly gets himself fixed up somewhere when they rout him the hell out again."

Two women were sitting in the station. They were fat and shapeless.

"There they are," said Filusch. "Peaches and cream, eh?"

He laughed and told the noncom about the women and the champagne.

"Lovely," said the noncom. "Great."

Filusch gave the noncom a nudge and said, "That's the way we do things."

They went into the station, informed the station-master, and came out again. Gühler saw her standing there and went up to her. He would have liked to take her hands in his, but he didn't dare. The strange noncom looked across curiously. Filusch whispered something to him. The two women sat on a pile of wood laughing.

She looked at him. "You've got to go?" she asked.

"Yes."

"I would have waited for you tonight."

She spoke very softly. Her lips hardly moved.

"I know," he said.

Neither of them said anything. Filusch was talking to the women. They both shrieked with laughter.

"Where are you going?" she began again.

"I don't know. To the front, perhaps."

They were both silent again. Gühler was suddenly unable to think of anything to say.

"I'd like to give you something," she said.

She pulled a little card out of her bag, took out a pencil, and turned to the wall. She wrote a short sentence on the back of the card. It was in Italian.

"Can't read it," said Gühler.

"You don't need to."

He took the card. It was a little picture of the Madonna. He looked at it quickly and put it away in the pocket of his tunic.

"Thank you," he said.

She looked at him again. He had the feeling that the station was suddenly receding from him.

"I'd like to kiss you," he said.

Behind him he could hear Filusch talking to the noncom.

"First-class dames, eh?"

"Tonight," said the noncom. "Tonight's the night."

"Transferred according to regulations."

"Signed, sealed, and delivered."

He heard them laugh.

"Go on," she said, "go now."

Gühler looked at her. Her eyes were quite still.

"I had two bottles of champagne," he said. "I wanted to bring them for this evening."

"For this evening," she said.

"Got a pair of asses on them like truck horses," they heard Filusch say behind them. The noncom laughed again.

"Go," she said.

Konz came running into the station.

"Gühler, Filusch, *los!*" he yelled.

42

"What's it matter?" thought Gühler.

He took her hand and wanted to pull her toward him but she turned away.

"*Los,* Gühler!" shouted Konz again, "get moving."

"Go," she said, and pushed him away with her hands

"A pity," he said, "it's a pity."

"*So eine scheiss,*" he heard Filusch say behind him.

"I ought to just stay here," he said and then stopped and looked at her.

"It's nothing," she said, "nothing at all."

"*Mensch,* Gühler," shouted Konz, "what's wrong with you?"

"I'm coming," said Gühler.

He turned around and walked across the station. Konz, Filusch, and the noncom walked beside him. As they went past the two women he looked into their fat, flat faces. They sat there laughing.

"I wouldn't take them as a gift."

"What?" said Filusch. "That's sugar, pure sugar." He smacked his tongue and pretended to suck his finger.

"Where in hell have you been?" shouted Buschmann.

"Handing over the station," said Gühler.

He climbed on the truck and sat beside Grundmann.

"Was she beautiful?" said Grundmann.

"I don't know," he said, "I don't know if she was beautiful or not."

Buschmann shouted some orders across the yard. The trucks rolled out of the gate. When the trucks were out in the street Gühler turned around. He saw Alexandro coming up the road with the donkey cart. The cart was empty.

"Thank God," he thought.

Then at the far end of the street he saw a woman walking away. She grew smaller and smaller until she was only a black point in the distance. Beijerke said, "What are you gawking at?"

"Nothing," said Gühler.

"You and your women," said Beijerke.

Grundmann was silent. He looked at Gühler and said nothing. The truck drove southward out of the town and into the mountains.

"Where are we going, do you know?"

"Up forward."

"Probably Cassino," said Grundmann, "and then the front."

"So that's it," said Gühler.

IV

IN the morning they awoke on a high plateau near Cassino. They lay under olive trees in the damp mist which moved up the mountains out of the morning. Over the mountains came the sullen mutter of the front. The whole company was assembled there, made up to strength, refitted and ready for action again. They had looted gramophones with them, which screamed into the morning in gay confusion. They sat under the olive trees, half drunk with looted schnapps, and watched the air battles going on above the mountains. Whenever one of the circling aircraft came plunging down from the sun in flames they cheered wildly, and it didn't matter whether it was one of theirs or one of the others'. When two parachutes slid away from a shot-down aircraft, and glided over the mountains toward the south they shouted "*Auf wiedersehen in Kanada*"—"See you in Canada!" * In the early hours of the night they drove

* In the early years of the war, before American participation, prisoner-of-war camps were set up by the British in Canada. The German soldiers were aware of this; therefore, whenever captivity seemed possible they said to one another, "Well, chum, I'll be seeing you in Canada." This

past Cassino, already half destroyed, and passed through a valley which they were later to call the Valley of Death. They drove up the road leading to the pass which ran through the high chain of mountains on the other side of the valley. The trucks stopped under cover of the pass.

"*Los!*" said Buschmann, "up into the mountains." They walked in single file along the edge of the road toward the pass. The mountains rose steep and sheer beside them.

"Got the dynamite and the picks?" Hahnemann asked.

"Everything," answered Beijerke.

They left the road and went up into the mountains.

"We're occupying the mountains on both sides of the road," they heard Buschmann say to Hahnemann. "We've got to hold the pass."

From the forward slope of the mountain they looked down into a broad valley stretching southward to the horizon. The moon hung full and clear above the open plain. Buschmann went with them and showed them where in the rock to blow the foxholes.

"You two come right to the top," he said to Beijerke and Gühler. They climbed up almost to the summit of the mountain. Buschmann halted on a little promontory of rock.

"Here you are," he said. "Clear field of fire all round." In front of the promontory the mountain fell straight down into the valley. Far below them they saw the road winding down into the plain.

"You can keep the whole road under fire from here."

---

became a cynical catch phrase, the "Canada" reference remaining even after most of the prison camps were in the U. S.

"I'd like it better on the other side of the mountain," muttered Gühler.

"Me too," said Grundmann.

"Start blowing tomorrow morning. You've got plenty of time to dig yourselves in good." Buschmann climbed down the mountain again.

"Let's hit the sack," said Beijerke.

They lay down on the ground and went to sleep. Gühler lay on his back and felt the stones digging into the small of his back. The moon shone straight into his face. Rocky pinnacles loomed stark in the moonlight.

"Hell of a mess," said Grundmann, who lay just above Gühler. Gühler began to drowse off, when suddenly he heard the rattling of stones and the slipping of nailed boots over the rock.

"Alert!" said someone. He came creeping across the rock doubled over.

"He's nuts," said Grundmann.

"*Los!* On the double! Everybody on the trucks in ten minutes. Bring all your junk with you."

They gathered up their picks, the machine gun, and the dynamite and climbed down the mountain. "Like a lot of goddam mules," said Beijerke. They found the truck waiting on the road.

"You and your lousy alert," said Filusch to Hahnemann.

"The Americans have landed behind us on the west coast."

"That's a lot of crap. Just another excuse for pushing us around."

"Shut your trap, Filusch," said Hahnemann.

The trucks were turning into position on the narrow road. The noncoms and the drivers cursed.

47

"*Los, los,*" said Buschmann. "Hurry it up!"

They threw their picks and shovels and machine guns onto the truck. "No noise!" Buschmann yelled.

"But he shouts as if he was on a drill ground," said Gühler.

They wrapped themselves up in their blankets, huddled close to each other, and fell asleep. The trucks drove down out of the mountains. Toward morning they came to the coast again.

"Not an American in sight," said Beijerke.

"Just an excuse to push us around, that's all," began Filusch again. Some fighters suddenly came swooping over the fields toward them. They jumped down from the truck and threw themselves into the ditch beside the road. The fighters raked the trucks with their machine guns. "Pretty fireworks," said Beijerke.

They ran to the road. The driver of their truck was hanging out of the open door.

"What's eating him?" said Filusch.

"Had it," said Beijerke.

A few drops of blood dripped from the driver's forehead. They took him out of his seat and laid him in the ditch. The fighters came back. They were like huge graceful swallows flying over the fields of withered maize.

"They'll shoot up the whole lot of us," shouted Beijerke. They ran into the fields leaving the truck where it was, Buschmann running ahead on his bowlegs. They came to a house standing alone in the fields and stopped panting behind the wall.

"The bastards," said Buschmann.

The fighters flew in again and again. Beijerke went

48

into the house and came out with a pot containing half a boiled chicken.

"There you are," he said. "Straight from market."

They went into the kitchen, put the pot on the stove, and sat down round the table.

"Let 'em shoot," said Beijerke.

Heavy bombers passed over the house, flying high toward the north. The fighters came in low over the roof and shot up the trucks on the road.

"They'll knock hell out of the whole damn column," said Filusch.

They tore the chicken apart and each of them took a piece and bit into it.

"Rather tough," said Gühler.

"Yeh," said Filusch, "tough as a sergeant's heart."

On the road all was suddenly quiet. They returned to their truck which was standing empty in the sun. Breutzmann came, small and fat, and took charge of it. They dug a shallow hole in the maize field and laid the driver in it. Then they quickly shoveled the sand back on top of him.

"*Los!*" shouted Buschmann from the road. "Hurry it up."

They drove down close to the coast and took up a prepared position in a wood.

"No Americans," said Filusch.

"Maybe they're on their way," answered Hahnemann.

They lay waiting in the woods all night. In the morning they went up the road with Buschmann. They found a small farm, empty and deserted, in which they set themselves up. In the stable they found a couple of half-grown chickens.

"We'll have them," said Buschmann.

49

The chickens fluttered through the stable and ran out across the yard with Buschmann after them, his shirt flapping behind. They drove the chickens back into the stable and wrung their necks. Then they set about cooking in the middle of the yard.

During the morning Italian volunteers from the Fascist militia were assigned to their company. Grundmann and Gühler lay in the straw which they had collected for the night. One of the volunteers lay beside them. Gühler said, "Why don't you go home?"

"Italy is great," he said. "Italy will win."

"Well, well!" said Gühler.

"Italy more culture than all."

"You don't say," said Grundmann.

"Oh, Italy old culture. All big towns, Florence, Milan, Venice, Rome. . . ."

"And what about us?" said Grundmann.

"You only Berlin, France only Paris. Poor countries."

"What about Mussolini?" said Gühler.

"Oh, Mussolini great man. He will win."

"Still?" said Gühler.

Filusch came over and said, "Your job is to get the coffee."

"Me?" asked the Fascist volunteer. "I no get coffee."

"*Los,*" said Filusch. "Get going."

"I no get coffee."

Filusch gave him a push and said, "*Los, los.*" The Fascist stood up and swung at Filusch.

"Who'd have thought it?" said Filusch. He grabbed the Italian, who was like a beanstalk beside him, and threw him to the ground. "You and your Mussolini," he said.

Gühler and Grundmann jumped up and broke them

apart. Hahnemann came over and asked the Fascist what was going on.

"He hit me."

Filusch stood there grinning. "Balls," he said.

"See it doesn't happen again, Filusch." Hahnemann gave Filusch a nudge and said softly, "You bastard."

In the evening they lay on the straw and looked at the sky. There was a continuous humming sound above them. On the horizon they could hear the thundering of the front. Gühler listened to the sound of the artillery and the exploding shells. Toward morning a fine rain began.

"Form a circle around me," said Buschmann the next morning. They stood around him and looked at him. The rain drizzled down grayly out of an overcast sky.

"All right now," said Buschmann, "get this." He cleared his throat and said, "Now then: anyone who voluntarily lets himself be taken prisoner will be court-martialed. In fact, anyone who's taken prisoner will be court-martialed, regardless. Every case will be taken up individually at the end of the war."

"Too late then," muttered Gühler.

"What's that, Gühler?" asked the *Feldwebel*.

"Nothing, *Herr Feldwebel*," said Gühler.

"Right. And anyone who picks up leaflets dropped by enemy aircraft and passes them on will be shot."

"Anything else?" muttered Gühler.

"What's Gühler jabbering about?"

"I only said about those leaflets—all lies."

"Right," said Buschmann. "Nothing but lies."

"Keep your trap shut, Gühler," said Hahnemann.

"Remember about being taken prisoner," began

Buschmann again. "You can only be taken prisoner if the situation's hopeless, and that means no ammunition left and retreat impossible. Don't forget about the court-martial."

"*Auf wiedersehen in Kanada,*" whispered Filusch.

Hahnemann turned around, furious. "Shut your goddam mouth!" he said.

That afternoon they moved into an olive grove. The rain came down in thin streaks. They put up their tents and crawled inside. The water ran into their tents. They dug drains and ditches and banked them up with earth. Hahnemann brought a gramophone from the truck and they played one record after another. They were American swing records.

"What's the nigger music for?" said Buschmann once as he was passing.

"Just a little foretaste," said Gühler.

"Careful," said Buschmann, "careful."

They stayed in their tents until the next day, took turns at guard duty and submitted themselves to the drizzling rain. Then the weather cleared again.

In the evening they drove back. The fighters came flying over the maize fields again in the late twilight. They threw themselves into the ditches, ran across the fields, and left the trucks where they stood on the road.

Then they drove up into the mountains.

They lay in another olive grove near San Pietro. The morning rose gray and misty out of the woods. They heard the roaring detonation of shells in the trees ahead of them. The explosions came regularly and without interruption.

"Long-range guns," said Grundmann.

It began to rain again. The clouds hung low over the olive grove.

"*Verfluchte scheiss*," said Beijerke.

"Steady, boy," said Filusch. "Steady."

When daylight came the shelling stopped. They loaded up their trucks with boards and heavy railway ties. A dozen mules stood in the olive groves, their heads drooping.

"Beijerke and Konz, you bring up the mules," said Buschmann.

They climbed on their trucks and drove up into the mountains. It rained continuously. The trucks became jammed in the narrows of the pass. The drivers unloaded the boards and the ties, then turned and drove back down the hairpin bends. Gühler and Grundmann climbed up the mountain with Filusch to the site that Buschmann had shown them a few days before.

"Wait! You're in the movies!" Hahnemann shouted to them from where he stood in the road. They turned around.

"Newsreel," said Grundmann.

A man stood there with a camera taking pictures of them.

"That's right," he shouted. "Keep on like that. A little more to the left, and quite naturally, please, quite naturally.... Let the machine gun hang quite free please, quite free."

They stood staring at him. Filusch thrust one leg forward and stuck his hand inside his coat.

"Maybe my old woman'll see me."

"They'd photograph you at a mass burial," said Gühler.

"Keep on please, just continue as you were," the photographer shouted up at them. "Just be natural."

"Are we in a war or a lousy film studio?" said Grundmann.

"As long as those boys are around," answered Gühler, "you can bet the war's a long way off."

They found that their dugout had already been blown, but it was small and narrow and they could only sit in it with their knees drawn up. They sat down on the rock and watched the road. Below them the trucks drove back and forth bringing up boards and railroad ties. They saw Beijerke and Konz coming up the road with their mules. They were each riding a mule, sitting in the saddles as if they had never done anything else. Beijerke came up the mountain with two big, powerful-looking mules. He had lashed a couple of ties onto them and drove one ahead of the other.

"I picked the best ones," he said.

"Nice animals," said Filusch. "I could use them at home."

Buschmann came clambering across the mountain.

"Well," he said, "all set?"

"The hole's a bit small," said Gühler.

"Small holes are good. Keep you warm." He turned to Beijerke. "Come along and help me with my dugout." Beijerke went off with him to the rear slope of the mountain.

"And you get going," he shouted back at Gühler. "The quicker the better. There isn't much time."

Gühler took over the mules and went down the mountain with them. The mules trotted in front, making their way down surely and easily over the rocks. On the road, Gühler lashed two ties to each of them, tried to make

54

them balance on either side, and then drove the mules up the mountain again. Beijerke met him halfway up.

"Buschmann, first," he said.

"What about us?" said Gühler. "When do we build ours?"

"Later. After us," said Beijerke. He unloaded the ties at Buschmann's dugout and went down with the mules again. Konz, Beijerke, and Filusch were building Buschmann's dugout. Grundmann stood alone on the tongue of rock and tried to pull the heavy ties over the hole. All day long Gühler went up and down the mountain with the two mules. The rain had stopped. One of the mules started to go lame. He became bad tempered and began kicking. Gühler had to let him go, but the mule continued plodding up and down the mountain behind him, only without the ties. Toward evening Gühler stabled both mules in a cave on the farther side of the mountain. Buschmann came from the company command post which lay in a bit of dead ground at the back of the mountain.

"Damn little time," he said. "They could be here by tomorrow."

Gühler went over to Grundmann. Twilight lay over the mountain. The clouds had disappeared. Four ties lay atop the hole they were in. This was cut slantwise into the mountain, and it looked as if the ties would slide off it and down into the valley at any moment.

"It doesn't exactly inspire confidence," said Gühler. Grundmann shrugged. He looked tired. "It's the best we can do," he said. "It'll hold when we pile some stones on there." They lay down on the rock. They were tired and didn't feel the hardness of the stones on which they lay. The moon came out behind the ridges of rock. All

55

around them it was bright and still. Not a shot, not an explosion, disturbed the silence of the night.

"It's spooky, this silence," said Grundmann. Gühler pushed a stone with his foot and let it roll down the mountain. They heard it bouncing from rock to rock.

"Everything must be moving up," he said.

"Yes," said Grundmann, "they're advancing."

"You'll see, they'll be here tomorrow."

"It's pure insanity trying to hold this pass with a handful of men like us," said Grundmann. They fell silent again. Far below in the valley they heard a truck moving.

"America," whispered Gühler.

"What about America?"

"Just America," said Gühler. "A free country."

"Our enemy. If we can't handle them, we're done for."

"Our enemies are behind us, in our own country," said Gühler.

"What can you do about it?"

"Nothing. Come on, let's go to sleep."

During the night Konz came climbing over the rock. Gühler saw him suddenly sit down beside him.

"I almost didn't find you," he said.

"What's the matter?"

"The Americans are close," he whispered.

"Well?" said Gühler.

"A whole division. Mountain troops. An élite division."

"It won't be so bad."

"You ought to have a sentry out," whispered Konz again.

"It's all right," said Gühler. "I'm awake."

Konz stole away. The rock rose another hundred

meters to the ridge. Gühler watched Konz climb up and then disappear behind the great crest of rock. The moon gradually grew paler. The black of the sky turned into a transparent blue. There was a streak of misty red all round the horizon. "It'll be a hot day," said Grundmann.

Beijerke and Filusch came creeping out of the dugout where they had been sleeping with their knees drawn up. They stood there stiffly, heavy with sleep, trying to rouse themselves.

Grundmann laughed. "Idiots," he said. "You should have laid down outside."

"You can't be too careful," said Beijerke.

Gühler went over to his mules. They were still standing in the cave where he had left them the evening before. He led the mule that was almost as big as a horse down the mountain. Konz came running after him.

"Hi, I need a mule to get coffee."

"Take the other one," said Gühler.

"He's lame."

"He's good enough to haul coffee."

Konz took the lame mule and went off. Gühler watched him climbing down the valley on the road to San Pietro. He had slung two canisters across the mule's back and was pulling it along behind him. Gühler loaded a couple of ties on his mule and went up the mountain with it. Grundmann and Beijerke took the ties off and laid them across the hole. Then he went down the mountain again with the mule.

Filusch came to meet him. "All ties go to the *Feldwebel*," he said.

"God damn it!"

"Buschmann says one dugout at a time."

"Yes, one dugout at a time. Everything nice and

57

orderly, strictly according to rank. And in the meantime the Americans come and we're sitting out in the open air."

"We're all up the creek here," said Filusch.

Konz came back with the coffee, the mule limping up the mountain behind him. They poured the hot coffee into their canteens and drank it where they stood. Two fighter bombers came up the valley behind them, flew over the mountain, and circled in the plain in front of them. Buschmann followed them with his eyes.

"German," he said.

"A miracle," said Gühler. "Are there really some left?"

They watched the bombs fall on the plain and the little black mushrooms of smoke that rose up.

"They're not far off now," said Buschmann.

The smoke moved slowly across the plain.

"Giddap," said Gühler, and drove his mule down the mountain again.

V

GERMAN soldiers were sitting on the road. They sat on the piles of ties, in the ditch, and on the rocks. They sat there with their coats open and sweat running down their faces. Their uniforms were torn and filthy. They looked wild and desperate. New units kept coming up the road out of the plain.

"You'll never hold 'em," one of them said.

"Who?" asked Gühler.

"The Amis," he said.

"Why?"

"Too damn much artillery."

Gühler left his mule standing and sat down with them.

"They shell you deaf, dumb, and blind," one of them said. "Then they come and pull you out of your hole like a piece of shit."

More troops came past. They were half naked and carried their coats under their arms.

"*Los*," they said to the others. "We're the last."

A squadron of heavy bombers flew over. The men scattered among the rocks and threw themselves down on the stones. Gühler's mule stood deserted in the road-way.

"*Mensch*," said one of them huddling with Gühler behind a clump of rocks. "Go home."

"Easier said than done."

"They'll knock the living hell out of you."

The bombs fell into the valley behind them.

"Come on! *Los!*" they shouted and ran off along the road and down the other side of the mountain.

"Have a good time in Canada," one of them said.

"Is anyone behind you?"

"A couple of beat-up assault guns. That's all."

Gühler watched them move off toward the north. Some limped and walked with sticks. They straggled along without their weapons, as fast as they could and without looking back. Several assault guns came up the road. They went into position on a small open space at the side of the road.

"There's nothing more behind us," said one of the drivers.

"Only the Amis," said another.

Gühler took his mule and drove it up the mountain. The ties dragged heavily on the ground. The girth broke, and they fell to the ground. Konz came down the mountain.

"Let them lay," he said. "It's too late."

"Where are you going?"

"To get rations," said Konz. Then he added, "Give me the beast. You won't need it any more."

Gühler took the black mule that had gone lame and gave Konz his brown one in exchange. Konz mounted and rode down the mountain toward the north. Gühler sat on a rock and watched him go. His mule stood beside him snuffling at his arm. He watched guns of the motorized infantry getting into position down below on either side of the road. He saw them driving in and out of the stunted trees and point their barrels to the south. In the valley all was still and quiet.

"They're holding their breath," he thought.

Suddenly he fell from the rock to the ground, skidded over the stones a piece, and lay still. The black mule reared up and ran off down the mountain. Some stones came rattling down beside Gühler. Above him billowed a thick white column of smoke.

"They're finding the range," he thought.

He jumped to his feet and ran up the mountain. Far below he saw a second white spout of smoke rising, then a third, close to the road. The black mule was standing placidly beside the infantry guns.

Gühler leapt from rock to rock. "I must get to Grundmann," he thought.

When he got to the top he looked back. The white clouds of smoke were scattered all across the mountain. They spurted up, stood like candles, and then disintegrated. There were flashes down below beside the assault guns. Then came the sound of the shots, one after the other. A black mushroom of smoke rose up on the road beside the guns. "It's starting," he thought.

Hahnemann came toward him from behind some twisted scrub. He was in his shirt with his sleeves rolled up. The gramophone was playing inside his foxhole. "Christ," he said, "they were damn quick finding the range."

They looked down to the assault guns. Black fountains of dirt were now rising from their position in the little

61

clearing. The crack of firing and the noise of exploding shells reverberated from the mountain walls.

"They won't take long," said Gühler.

The gramophone ran down with a thin, scraping sound.

A cloud of black smoke rose up a little distance away. They threw themselves to the rock and pressed their bodies hard upon the stones.

"Into the hole," yelled Hahnemann.

Gühler jumped up and ran across the rocks.

"I've got to get to Grundmann," he shouted back. Hahnemann disappeared into the hole behind the scrub. He ran along the mountain ridge among the stunted bushes and heard the shells exploding behind him. He threw himself on the ground and jumped up again. The shells were bursting more frequently with every step he took. He climbed higher, and then ran down the forward slope of the mountain toward their dugout. He saw Grundmann lying beside it looking down through a telescope at the assault guns. Gühler threw himself down among the stones and lay still. He pressed his head flat against the stones and felt his breath hot on his hands.

"Here, Gühler," shouted Grundmann.

He crawled over and lay down beside him. The assault guns were still flashing but the black mushrooms on the road and on the clearing were rapidly intensifying.

"They're pulling out," said Grundmann.

They watched the guns reverse, turn around, and creep slowly up the road.

"Let's have a look," said Gühler. He took the telescope and looked down to the clearing. The little trees lay uprooted on the ground and shell after shell was bursting among them. The mushrooms merged into one another and reappeared again separately. He saw the assault guns vanish among the mountains. "Done for," he said and gave back the telescope.

Suddenly all was deathly still. The shelling stopped.

"What's happening?"

"They're coming," said Gühler.

Grundmann looked down into the plain with the telescope. "Nothing," he said. "All quiet."

Beijerke and Filusch came crawling out of the hole. They lay flat on the ground.

"What about the machine gun?" said Grundmann.

"What about it?" answered Beijerke.

They lay there looking into the valley, but nothing moved. The road below lay empty and deserted in the glare of the midday sun.

"Do you see anything over there?"

"Where?"

"Over there on the ridge," said Gühler.

Grundmann turned the telescope and looked across.

"*Mensch*," he said. "Somebody's running upright over the ridge."

"Americans?"

"Possible," said Grundmann.

They heard the deep rattling bursts of German machine guns.

"That's the first platoon," said Beijerke.

Now, with the naked eye, they could see men running along the ridge. There seemed to be no end to them.

"That's them," said Gühler.

"Nervy bastards," said Grundmann. "Standing up like that without cover."

They heard hand grenades exploding and then the quick rattle of German machine guns again.

"They're throwing hand grenades down from the ridge."

"Let's see," said Gühler.

Grundmann gave him the telescope. He watched the hand grenades exploding on the bottom part of the ridge. On the ridge itself the Americans were leaping in single file, over the rocks. American artillery started up again. They heard the guns firing in the plain.

"That's for us," said Gühler.

The black mushrooms sprouted on the road again and spread slowly up the mountain. The men slipped into their hole and hunched close against each other. All around the dugout the shells came crunching down. Grundmann had weighted the beams above them with stones and these began to rattle. Then the shell bursts wandered away down the mountain again.

"They're feeling their way," said Gühler.

They crept out again, lay on the ground, and looked across. The artillery was now firing only sporadically and in salvos. From the ridge came the sound of bursting hand grenades and the rattle of machine guns. A stone was dislodged above them. They started and listened to it rolling all the way down the mountain. Hahnemann came crawling down between the rocks.

"*Los!* Get ready. The Americans are breaking through over there."

Gühler felt the fear that sat suddenly in his stomach.

"Have we got to go over there?"

"Yes," said Hahnemann. "All hell's broken loose." He crawled on to a hole about thirty yards away from them, higher up the rock.

"Come on," said Grundmann, "the machine gun."

"Both machine guns," said Filusch.

"Everything," said Grundmann.

They took the machine guns and the ammunition boxes and crawled up the mountain. They crawled yard by yard between the rocks. Gühler was beside Grundmann whose face was pale and sweaty with agitation, as if he were feverish.

"They'll catch us before we get there," he said.

Behind them they heard the shells bursting. They pressed themselves against the rocks, breathing heavily.

"Madness," said Grundmann.

"Yes," said Gühler. "They can see us from all sides."

They crawled on again. Beijerke and Filusch writhed along behind them. Again they heard the artillery below in the valley. They saw the shells bursting in the front of them on the ridge.

"*Scheiss*," said Filusch.

They reached the ridge and ran in single file through the low scrub to the cover of the rear side of the mountain. They joined Hahnemann's section, which he had routed out of the other hole.

"Woltmann's lost both legs," one of them said.

"Frank caught it too," said another.

Hahnemann came up from behind and said as he passed, "We're counterattacking."

Gühler said nothing. A dull, empty feeling of fear rose up inside him. A few shells burst in front of them on the ridge. They threw themselves among the bushes and then leaped up again.

"With these few men," said Gühler to Hahnemann, as if the answer had only just occurred to him.

"And what's left of the first and the second platoons."

They came out into the clearing where Buschmann's dugout lay in a square grass-covered patch. The sound of bursting hand grenades, German machine guns, and American Tommy guns came closer and closer. Buschmann came running toward them, his bowlegs working like a machine.

"Grundmann and Gühler, go back," he shouted at them. They stopped and looked at him. It suddenly seemed to Gühler as if the machine gun had become light and weightless on his shoulder.

"Grundmann and Gühler?" Hahnemann shouted.

"Yes, back to the dugout with the machine gun."

"Lucky bastards," said Filusch.

"Oh well," muttered Beijerke.

They went on without turning around. Grundmann and Gühler stared after them. "Thank God," said Grundmann.

They both looked at each other, laughed, and climbed back up the mountain. Then they crawled down the forward slope, lay down near their hole, and looked across to the other side. Over by the wall of rock the sound of hand grenades suddenly stopped. The machine guns fell silent. It became utterly quiet. The afternoon sat broiling in the narrow kettle of stone beyond the road. Then they heard the guns beginning to fire again down in the valley, one after the other in rapid succession.

"They're crossing the road," said Grundmann.

"They must be crazy."

"Instead of going round at the bottom."

"Probably no time," said Gühler.

The black mushrooms leapt up beside the road, close together. Grundmann looked down at the road with the telescope.

"Can you see them?" whispered Gühler.

"They're jumping around like lunatics," said Grundmann.

The artillery was quiet again.

"Now we're going to get it, wait and see," said Gühler.

A fat little airplane was suddenly just above them. It seemed to be almost standing still in the air. It droned quietly and stuck in the sky as if someone had hung it there.

"*Los!* Into the hole," whispered Gühler.

He slipped into the hole without getting up. Grundmann came in after him.

"What's the matter?" he said.

"Observation plane," said Gühler.

They drew up their knees and lay so that they could see out of the opening. The plane hovered motionless above them.

"If he spots us, we might as well pack up," said Gühler.

Far down in the valley they heard the guns starting up again. They sounded farther away, but deeper and heavier.

"New batteries," said Grundmann.

"They're bringing up plenty," answered Gühler.

The shells were crashing into their mountain. The cracking and bursting came closer to them, went away, and then crept back again.

"They've noticed something," said Grundmann. "They want to cut off reinforcements."

Suddenly it was as if their mountain began to heave. The beams above them shifted and sand and stones came pouring through the opening. They crawled to the

67

farthest corner of the dugout and held their helmets in front of their faces.

"That's meant for us," said Gühler.

The shells receded again and wandered off down the mountain. Everything was once more quiet. They crept to the opening and looked out. The plane was no longer there. They slipped the upper part of their bodies out of the hole and looked over the edge. From a long way behind the mountain they heard three guns fire. Dark columns of smoke went up with a roar by the wall of rock across from them.

"German artillery preparation for the counterattack," said Grundmann.

After the three shots it was quiet again.

"Is that all?" said Gühler.

They heard the furious barking of German machine guns. American Tommy guns replied. Hand grenades began bursting again. Little white clouds suddenly appeared above the mountain. They burst with a crack and left a black puff of smoke behind.

"They're using shrapnel," said Grundmann.

The observation plane flew over the mountain. It hung like a great buzzing fly above the exploding shrapnel. The German machine guns could now be heard firing only one at a time. Then they were silent altogether. Shadows began to lengthen down in the valley.

"We've got to get ourselves something to eat," said Grundmann. Gühler took the mess kits and crept over the rocks up to the ridge. Twilight was setting in. Konz stood on the other side of the mountain giving out the food.

"Buschmann's waiting for you," he said.

"What's happening over there?"

"Don't know," said Konz. "Hell of a mess."

Gühler took the mess kits and went over to Buschmann's dugout.

"Take these three up forward with you," said Buschmann, "Pöhler's coming to you. Schneider and Gervin go to the other hole."

"There's no cover on it."

"Can't be helped," said Buschmann. "That's the way it's got to be."

The three crawled out of the hole and followed along behind Gühler.

"Watch yourselves when we come out on the other side," said Gühler.

They said nothing. They walked behind him in silence. He heard Pöhler, who seemed rather fat and misshapen, panting. They crawled down the forward slope, Gühler and Pöhler carrying the mess kits. The guns were firing rapidly, one after the other.

"Cover," whispered Gühler, and threw himself down. Pöhler fell clumsily to the ground behind him. The mess kits struck the stones with a leaden sound. The shells exploded with a roar, but they fell beyond them almost on the ridge. Gühler jumped up.

"*Los!*" he said. "Hurry!"

Pöhler was kneeling and scratching among the stones with the mess kit.

"The jam," he said.

"To hell with the jam," said Gühler, and ran down the slope. Again the guns bellowed down in the valley.

"Pöhler!" he shouted. "Pöhler!"

He heard him panting behind him.

"I can't move so quick," he said.

69

They threw themselves down again and crawled to the hole.

"You're making one hell of a noise, man," said Grundmann.

"Replacements," said Gühler.

"For Beijerke and Filusch already?"

"Perhaps," said Gühler.

Pöhler lay shaking beside the hole.

"The jam," he said. "All gone."

Gühler crawled over with Gervin and Schneider to the hole which lay twenty yards away from theirs. It was a deep wedge-shaped hole with only a few beams over the top.

"Make yourselves at home," said Gühler.

"Yes," they whispered and crept into the hole.

VI

GÜHLER and Grundmann lay in front of the hole. They had laid the machine gun, the hand grenades, and Grundmann's submachine gun on the beams because there was no room for them inside. Pöhler had crawled inside, pulled a blanket over his head, and gone to sleep. They heard him snoring.

"No more peace for him," said Grundmann.

"He's a pastry cook from Berlin."

"A little thick in the head."

"And not exactly young," said Gühler.

They were silent again. Over on the mountain they heard a spade clink. Suddenly a series of green sparks flew in quick succession across the mountain. Red ones began flying toward them from the other direction. The shots echoed off the mountain walls more loudly than during the day.

"They're using tracers," said Grundmann.

The red and green sparks intermingled ever more thickly until they arched the mountain like a rainbow.

"It's starting up again," said Gühler.

The jerky bursts of the machine guns became inseparably mixed up with the slow tack-tack of American Tommy guns. It sounded so close in the night that it might have been taking place just beside them. They could hear every sound.

"Hands up!" shouted a deep voice in English.

"Do you hear?" said Grundmann.

Cries reached them from beyond, abrupt individual cries.

"Stretcher bearer!" a voice cried.

"Here, here," shouted another.

Slowly the cries increased. They rose to a yell, died down, and then swelled up again.

"*Mensch*," said Gühler, "it's enough to drive you crazy."

The red and green sparks clashed together under the reddish yellow moon.

"Like fireworks in Luna Park," said Grundmann.

Gühler sat on a stone and looked across. The cries were becoming more and more numerous. They were the cries of the wounded for help, the shrieks of the dying. He differentiated between the various cries and classified them.

"There," he thought, "that one's a goner." He saw himself sitting there classifying the cries and said to himself, "There's no feeling left in us. We're dead even before we die."

Something whistled past his ear.

"What's that?"

"Someone's shooting at us," said Grundmann.

They looked up to the ridge and then down into the valley in front of them. The humming sound came again.

"*Mensch*, ricochets!" shouted Grundmann.

"Let's get out of here!" said Gühler.

They crawled into their hole, drew up their knees so as to have enough room, and leaned against the wall.

"Ricochet from over there. What do you think of that?"

The firing slowly diminished.

"One of us must stay outside," said Grundmann.

"Yes," said Gühler. "I'll go."

He crawled out of the hole. The firing gradually stopped. Only the cries continued for a while. Then they stopped too. Only one cry was repeated again and again. It cut regularly into the silence of the night. At first it was "Stretcher bearer! Stretcher bearer!" and finally "*Mutter, Mutter.*"

Gühler sat in front of the hole and thought, "Where can she be, his mother? There aren't any mothers left any more."

"*Mutter!*" came the cry again from somewhere in front of him, and it echoed back from the mountain walls.

"He'll bleed to death," thought Gühler.

He lay down on his back and closed his eyes.

"Sleep," he thought, "sleep."

"Mother, help me," came the cry again.

"He ought to stop screaming," thought Gühler. "He ought to stop that."

He felt sleep coming over him.

"Mother," thought Gühler. He fell asleep.

He was awakened by the sound of steps above him. A few stones rolled down the mountain. A shadow came toward him. He jumped up and snatched the submachine gun.

"It's me—Beijerke!"

73

"Beijerke?" whispered Gühler.

"Yes," said Beijerke.

"Where have you come from?"

"There," said Beijerke, "over there."

"Where are the others?"

"Gone," said Beijerke.

"What do you mean, gone?"

"Don't know," answered Beijerke.

The cries kept coming again and again out of the night. Beijerke sat down on the stones.

"Filusch too?" asked Gühler.

"Yes, Filusch," said Beijerke.

He was silent for a moment, listened across to the mountain and said, "He's gone mad, that man out there."

"Why don't they bring him in?"

"No stretcher bearers."

"What about the others?"

"No one dares go out there," said Beijerke, and then, "Yes, Filusch. Filusch is over there."

"Over where?"

"With the Amis."

Beijerke was silent for a moment; then he said:

"It was murder. When we came to the mountain, there was Hahn from the first platoon. He lay in his hole shaking and saying he couldn't lead the counter-attack because he was sick. Hahnemann would have to do it. And Hahnemann came out of the hole red in the face and yelled 'What about our barrage?' Hahn crawled out after him and said he could telephone. So Hahnemann went to the phone, and the artillery lieutenant told him he could only give him three rounds. They only had twenty-five left altogether. Hahnemann

74

bawled into the phone, 'You can stuff your three rounds up your ass!' "

"But," said Gühler, "they did give you three."

"Yes, too little and too late. The stuff came down on top of us. Well, then Hahnemann said *'Los!'* and we picked up our machine guns and followed him. The Amis were firing away like hell. Our guys just lay there, huddling behind the rocks. But we followed Hahnemann. Then we caught a few Amis in a corner where they couldn't go backward or forward. Hahnemann said, 'We'll grab them.' We brought our machine gun into position and Hahnemann went up to them and said 'Hands up' in English and they put up their hands. One of them had half his face torn off. They were nothing but a bunch of wounded, anyway. They gave Hahnemann their chocolate and moved off down the hill. They carried their wounded with them, bleeding like pigs. Then the shrapnel came."

"And Hahnemann?" asked Gühler.

"Yes," said Beijerke. "He was just going back to get the others. But he got blown up and that's the last we saw of him. We flattened ourselves against the stones and behind us they were screaming. Once Filusch said his mouth was full of dirt and he wanted to say *scheiss* but he could only get as far as 'sh—, sh—' because his teeth were grinding in the dirt. Then some more Amis came up and let us have it with their Tommy guns. I said to Filusch 'Come on, man, let's do something,' but Filusch just lay there and shook his head. Then everything was quiet again and night came and we went on lying there without moving."

"Why? Why didn't you move?" said Gühler.

"The Amis were only about twenty yards in front of

us, and during the night they started using tracers. Just behind us our own paratroops had been sent in as replacements. We were caught between the two and Filusch said 'We'll never get out of here.' 'We've got to hold out,' I said, and Filusch took hold of the machine gun and said 'Throw the goddam thing down the mountain.' But I grabbed it and said 'Don't be a fool, Filusch' and he said, 'Haven't you had enough of this stinking war yet?' Then we stuck our faces into the dirt again because the Amis started firing like crazy in front of us. And then the screams started."

"Yes," said Gühler, "we heard them."

"But right in our ears, man," said Beijerke. "The Amis suddenly appeared right in front of us and shouted in German, 'Surrender, *Kameraden*.' Filusch said 'Throw the machine gun away, Beijerke' and I said 'Filusch, we've got to beat it.' But he pushed the machine gun over the edge of the rock with his leg and it went down with a crash. 'I've had enough,' he said. Suddenly he yelled, 'I'm through, Beijerke, I'm through' and the Amis shouted 'Throw your weapons away, *Kameraden*.' I began crawling back a little at a time but Filusch lay where he was. I saw him get up and crawl over to the Amis and I pushed myself farther and farther back, yard by yard. Then I jumped up and ran and they fired with their Tommy guns and I threw myself down. Then I ran on again. Around me they were screaming like maniacs. I fell over someone with both his legs torn off. It was *Oberfeldwebel* Hahn who hadn't wanted to lead the counterattack. But he got it just the same, right in front of his hole. I didn't see anyone else."

Beijerke stopped talking. The wounded man out on the mountain started yelling again.

"He's bleeding to death," said Gühler.

"Yes," said Beijerke. "And then I crawled down the mountain through the scrub—on my belly all the time, or they would have seen me. On the way I met Mahler, our medic. He was lying behind a rock shaking all over and saying, 'Nobody can go up there and live,' and a couple of paratroopers were lying there too and said 'That bastard, he keeps sending us up again' and I said 'Which bastard?' and they said 'Stein. Don't you know Stein?' And Mahler said that the despatch riders' dugout had had two direct hits and that Schmidt had got it."

"What, Schmidt?" said Gühler.

"Yes," said Beijerke. "And then I was with Buschmann. He was asleep and I woke him up and he said 'What's wrong, Beijerke?' and I said 'Nothing, *Feldwebel*, everything's in order,' and he said 'Where did you leave Filusch?' and I said 'The Amis took him.' 'Good' he said, and went to sleep again."

The wounded man started crying out again. It was a soft, rattling noise now.

"He's a goner for sure," said Beijerke.

The moon began to pale. Gühler looked up. "It's growing light," he said.

VII

THEY woke up when the barrage began. The coldness of the early morning made them shiver. The first guns that fired sounded quite close and fairly light, then the heavier ones followed farther away in the valley.

"It's starting," said Grundmann. They put on their helmets. The guns were now firing rapidly one after the other. All the shells burst on their mountain.

"They've brought up plenty," Gühler shouted. Grundmann nodded. Gühler crawled close to Grundmann so that they could talk to each other. Pöhler had pulled a blanket over his head and put his hands over his ears. The beams above them began to shake.

Beijerke's face went suddenly white and chalky. The shells were bursting closer and closer. Splinters of stone flew into the hole. Sand sifted down through the beams above them. They tore their helmets from their heads and held them in front of their faces. Their hands shook. They crawled up close to each other.

"It'll stop in a minute," thought Gühler. "Then they'll attack."

The shelling ceased for a moment. The silence was unbearable.

"*Los!*" said Grundmann. "Out of here."

"Balls," said Beijerke.

Gühler said nothing. He looked at the whiteness of Beijerke's face and thought, "He's afraid."

Beijerke shook his head and said, "Don't go out."

"What if they break through?"

"I don't give a goddam if they do," said Beijerke.

The guns started up again, one after the other in an unbroken hurricane of shelling.

"There you are," shouted Beijerke. He made himself into a ball, held his helmet in front of his face, and pulled his legs tight against his body. Pöhler wrapped himself up in his blanket.

"The blanket won't help you," shouted Grundmann.

Pöhler said nothing. The blanket, which also covered his face, cut him off from everything that was happening.

"They're afraid," shouted Grundmann.

"Aren't you?" asked Gühler.

"Yes, but . . ." said Grundmann.

The shell bursts came up the mountain like a typhoon. "The rocks are heaving," thought Gühler. "The rocks are heaving."

He pressed his face into his helmet. The beams above him shifted. The hole was filled with smoke and dust. There was a smell of scorched earth.

"They're using phosphorus shells," he thought.

The shell bursts raged across the mountain like a whirlwind. Thousands of shells went gurgling over them and exploded in the valley behind them. They followed one another like bursts from a machine gun. A continuous rushing sound filled the air. The number of explosions round their hole increased from hour to hour.

"It's got to stop some time," Grundmann shouted.

Gühler shook his head. But he said nothing. In a moment of silence he heard Pöhler praying. "Please let us get out of here again," he said. "Please let us get out of here again."

Then he was silent again. Their voices were drowned in the tornado of shells. The midday heat came creeping into their hole. Sweat stood on their faces.

Toward afternoon the barrage lifted. There was a sudden silence. Slowly they awoke from their numbness. They lifted their heads and looked at each other.

"Everybody still here?" asked Grundmann.

"Pöhler's gone to sleep," said Beijerke. Pöhler still sat motionless under his blanket.

"Yes," he whispered.

Gühler crept to the opening and looked out. The midday sun on the rocks was dazzling. Nothing moved. He heard a humming sound above them. He lay on his back and looked up. The observation plane was there again like an immovable dot in the sky. He slid into the hole.

"He's back again," he said.

They listened. The humming sounded soft and dangerous.

"My God," said Beijerke. "Maybe I'm not starving!"

"We haven't got anything," said Grundmann.

"No one can go now," said Gühler.

They squatted against the walls with their knees drawn up. Pöhler crawled out of his blanket.

"Thirsty," he said.

80

"Wait till this evening," said Gühler.

Grundmann lay on his back and looked out of the hole. "He's still up there," he said.

"The Amis are having a break for lunch," answered Gühler.

After a while they heard the guns begin again.

"It's starting again," said Gühler.

"The amount of stuff they've got—!" said Grundmann.

They sat there the whole afternoon, their knees drawn up and their helmets pressed against their faces. The barrage raged without interruption over the mountain. Dirt trickled down through the heaving beams above them. Stone fragments flew into the hole. Smoke hung beneath the roof. In spite of their helmets their eyes were pasted shut with dirt. When the shelling slackened toward evening, Pöhler began to whimper.

"I can't stand any more," he said.

The others looked at Pöhler and said nothing. Outside, night was beginning.

"Who's going?" said Grundmann.

No one said anything. They all looked straight ahead as if they hadn't heard the question.

"I can't," said Beijerke.

Gühler took his mess kit and said, "Give me your kits."

"Are you going?" asked Grundmann.

"Yes," Gühler answered.

"I'll come with you."

They gathered up the mess kits and crawled out of the hole. Flat on their bellies, they pushed themselves over to the other hole.

"Give us your mess kits," whispered Grundmann into the hole.

"Who's there?"

"It's us," said Gühler. "Hand over your mess kits. It'll be your turn tomorrow."

They writhed their way up the mountain. Whenever they dislodged a stone and sent it rolling down the slope they held their breath and pressed themselves flat against the ground. They did not stand up until they reached the other side.

"Konz isn't here yet," said Buschmann.

"When will he be back?"

"I don't know," said Buschmann.

They sat and waited in the hole with Buschmann. Once they crawled out to look for Konz.

"You're letting yourselves be seen," Buschmann yelled from inside.

They wriggled down into the hole. The shells burst just in front of the dugout, spurting dirt through the opening. "For Christ's sake!" Buschmann shouted, "watch what you're doing!"

They didn't say anything but looked at Buschmann. His eyes flickered.

"What's going on over there?" asked Gühler.

"Don't know," said Buschmann.

Again the shells began bursting all around the dugout. Konz slipped down into the hole.

"Where's the food?" asked Buschmann.

"With the Amis," said Konz.

"What do you mean—with the Amis?"

"The mule broke away and went over to the Amis with the canisters."

"You're crazy," shouted Buschmann.

"Crazy's the word, all right. You're all crazy. A pig couldn't hold out in this position any longer. The whole valley's been under fire all day long and now it's starting up again."

"Where's that mule?" asked Buschmann.

"With the Amis," shouted Konz. "I told you. It broke away. They can see us from all sides. I went down through the mountains but came back along the road. They saw that and started shooting. I threw myself into the ditch but the mule was hit somewhere. He reared up on his hind legs and went hell bent down the road to the Amis."

"With the canisters?" asked Grundmann.

"Yes, with the canisters," said Konz.

"What do we do for food now?"

"Nothing," said Konz, "nothing." He wiped the sweat from his forehead. The freckles on his nose looked like black dots in the pale light of the dugout lantern.

"Lauterbach's dead," he said. "The battalion command post got three direct hits. Everything smashed."

"But what do we do for chow?" Grundmann asked again.

"We'll take another shot at getting the rations," said Buschmann.

"Ha! Get the rations! Easy enough to say," cried Konz. "A pig couldn't get the rations any more. There's nothing left at battalion. And the main supplies are thirty kilometers back."

"So we starve," said Gühler. "And some of our people are dying of thirst besides."

"We'll leave the mess kits here," said Grundmann. They crawled out. The night was bright and clear.

"Careful," whispered Buschmann.

They wriggled over the grass on their bellies until they came to the cover of some small fir trees, where they lay down in the scrub.

"Let's catch our breath," said Grundmann.

They lay on their backs and stretched themselves out. Steep walls of rock rose above them.

"Nothing to eat and no artillery," said Grundmann.

"Three rounds," said Gühler.

They lay there listening to the night. Grundmann said, "No ammunition. And over there they squander acres of shells on this pass alone."

"They have to get this pass if they want Cassino," said Gühler.

"But why haven't we got any artillery support?" Grundmann began again.

"Because we're at the end of our rope."

"*Mensch*," whispered Grundmann, "I can't believe it."

"Stalingrad," said Gühler. "Tunis. And now Cassino."

"I believed in it all," Grundmann whispered again. Gühler laughed softly and cynically.

"Believed it?"

"Yes, and I still do."

"You've got a shock coming then."

"Maybe," said Grundmann, "maybe it was all lies."

"It was," said Gühler.

The heavy artillery began firing down in the valley.

"Now they're starting at night too," said Grundmann.

They lay flat. The heavy shells howled over them.

"They're cutting off all our supplies," said Gühler.

Giant fountains of dirt rose with a roar behind them in the valley. The woods below began to burn. The flames leaped from treetop to treetop.

84

"They're using phosphorus again," said Grundmann.

"Valley of Death," said Gühler.

The barrage rose to a raging crescendo.

"*Los!*" shouted Grundmann.

They ran through the low undergrowth and crawled down the slope of the mountain to their hole.

"Thank God," said Beijerke. "We thought they got you."

"We've got nothing to eat," said Grundmann. "The mule went over to the Amis with the canisters."

"*Scheiss,*" said Beijerke.

"And nothing to drink?" whispered Pöhler.

"No," said Grundmann, "nothing."

They crawled close to each other in the hole. Heavy shells labored over them hour after hour. During the night it began to rain. The water trickled through the beams, came running down the slope in little streams, and began to cover the bottom of the dugout.

"We've got to get out," said Gühler.

"What, with that going on?" shouted Beijerke.

The whole slope of the mountain lay under heavy fire. The rain poured down. More and more water seeped into the hole. They stood up, bent their heads, and held onto the beams. The water rose and ran into their boots.

"God damn this to hell," shouted Beijerke.

Pöhler pulled his soaked blanket over his head. "If I only had a nice piece of cake to eat, a piece of really good cake."

"You and your goddam cake," Beijerke shouted.

The rain stopped. They tried to bale the water out with their helmets. They kept bumping into each other in the narrow hole. They cursed and shouted and fell exhausted into the water.

85

Toward morning the heavy artillery stopped. They heard the last guns firing down in the valley. Then everything was quiet.

"I've had enough," said Beijerke. He collapsed and lay where he fell in the filthy water. Pöhler squatted on his haunches, went to sleep, and keeled over.

"They're finished," said Gühler.

"Yes," said Grundmann, "so am I."

They crawled out of the hole, lay down on their backs, and went to sleep. When the first booming of the renewed barrage began, they slid back into the hole. They fell into the water, which was seeping slowly away, snatched up their helmets, and pressed them close to their faces. The barrage swept over the mountain again.

"My birthday is on the tenth," said Gühler during a pause.

"That's a long way off."

"You'll see, we'll make it till then."

"You're just kidding yourself," said Beijerke.

"On the tenth we'll either be taken prisoner or . . ."

"Prisoner," said Grundmann. "Better to die here."

The beams above them began to shake again.

"We'll all be up the creek long before then," shouted Beijerke. Mud from the exploding shells splashed into the hole. The barrage kept up until the evening.

VIII

D AY after day the barrage started at five o'clock in the morning and covered the mountain until the late evening. During the night heavy shells flew over them into the Valley of Death. Rain came and the water ran down the mountain into their hole. At dusk they crawled over the rocks after rations. They seldom got any. Day and night they sat with their knees drawn up, their helmets held in front of their faces, waiting for the attack.

"If they'd only come!" they said. But they didn't come. Every morning and every night the valley ahead of them began spewing thousands of shells at their mountain. Their weapons rusted away on top of the beams and nobody bothered about them.

One night when there was no shelling Gühler crawled out of the hole. The smell of scorched earth hung over the mountains. Gühler sat on a stone against the rock wall and stared into the night.

"Maybe they'll come tomorrow," he thought.

He leaned against the wall and shut his eyes. Down in

the hole the others were snoring. Far down in the valley he could hear the sound of trucks moving. Then a few voices, shouts of command. Then the sound of trucks again.

"They're bringing up new batteries," he thought. "Still more batteries."

He heard a few stones rattling above him. They rolled a little way down the mountain and lay still. He jumped to his feet and looked up. In front of him to the left something moved. Some bushes there were swaying backward and forward.

"There weren't any bushes there before," he thought.

He squatted on the ground and edged his way back to the hole.

"Grundmann," he said.

"Yes?"

"Something's coming."

Grundmann crawled out of the hole. They both looked at the bushes which were now moving slowly toward them.

"That's them," whispered Grundmann.

He took the submachine gun off the roof. The bushes came nearer. Now they could see helmets and behind them the shadows of bodies.

"Shall I shoot?" said Grundmann.

"You must be crazy," Gühler whispered. He put his hand on the gun and said, "Give it to me."

"Why?"

"So you don't do anything silly," said Gühler.

The bushes came closer. The helmets were just in front of them.

"Amis," whispered Grundmann.

"Yes."

"Call to them."

Suddenly the bushes were standing in front of them. They recognized the shape of the steel helmets behind them. They were German.

"What do you want?" Gühler said.

They were German sappers. They jumped up and came over to Gühler and Grundmann.

"God damn it," said Grundmann, "don't let yourselves be seen."

One of them came forward. "Lieutenant Muller," he said.

"Yes," said Gühler, "what do you want?"

"Are you the noncom?"

"No."

They stood and looked at each other. Gühler felt fury rising inside him.

"Grundmann," he said, "he wants you."

Grundmann was silent and looked at him. Then he shrugged his shoulders and said, "Have you come to relieve us? You're the first officer we've seen out here."

"It wasn't easy," said the lieutenant.

"Well, relieve us then. We've been waiting to be relieved for a week."

"There won't be any relief," said the lieutenant.

"Why not?"

For a moment the lieutenant didn't say anything. Then he took Grundmann to one side and whispered.

"You've been written off already."

"So what do you want?"

"To lay mines in front of your dugout. Divisional order."

"Impossible," said Gühler. "We've been under a continuous barrage for days. They can see everything that moves here."

"It's an order," said the lieutenant. "You're to cover us with your machine gun."

"Cover from what? From the barrage?"

"I've brought a platoon with two machine guns for covering purposes. With yours that makes three machine guns. Nothing can happen. My men work like cats."

"You've got a surprise coming," said Gühler.

"What do you mean?"

"In five minutes you'll have the whole barrage on top of us."

"And what'll you do?"

"Disappear into our hole," said Grundmann.

"Insubordination," said the lieutenant.

Grundmann looked at the lieutenant and said slowly, "We were glad to be having a moment's peace. Now you come along with your mines and give away our position for good."

"No one will spot my men."

"Who're you telling that to?" whispered Grundmann. "We've been lying here in the mud for a week. We know more about it than you do."

"You don't know anything," said the lieutenant.

"We don't want your mines," said Gühler. "We don't need your mines."

Gervin and Schneider came crawling out of their hole. "What's the matter?" said Gervin. "We thought the Amis had come."

"They want to lay mines, the bastards."

"For Christ's sake!"

"*Los!*" said the lieutenant, "get to work." He began detailing his men.

90

"Should have brought us chow instead," said Beijerke, peering out of the hole.

"They're running around with their helmets camouflaged," said Gühler.

"From division?"

"Yes. They'll find out."

"They haven't seen any war yet?"

"Apparently not."

"Come on," said Grundmann, "into the hole. The whole goddam barrage'll be down on us any minute."

"I ordered you to provide cover," said the lieutenant.

"*Scheiss*," said Grundmann, and vanished into the hole.

They heard the sappers moving about in front of their hole. Stones went rolling down the mountain. Snatches of conversation came to them. Picks and shovels clinked against the stones. The voice of the lieutenant giving orders rang through the night.

"*Mensch*, maybe they won't louse things up for us!" whispered Beijerke.

"Sure to," said Gühler.

"All those men out there. It'll look like a prepared position."

They listened to the movements outside. The clinking of picks and shovels increased.

"Absolutely crazy," said Grundmann.

Pöhler sat in the corner without moving. "It was so nice and quiet," he whispered.

The sound of the guns came up from the valley. One of the sappers hurtled through the opening on top of them. Then came a second, then another, and then the lieutenant. They were shouting and panting.

"You bastards," shouted Beijerke. "You dirty bastards."

Another came flying into the hole and still another. He threw himself on top of the lieutenant who was already lying almost directly under the beams.

"Get the hell out of here," Pöhler bellowed. But the roar of the barrage drowned his voice. Outside, the shelling continued. It grew from minute to minute.

Another man tumbled into the hole. They all yelled, but he pushed his way in on top of them. Gühler felt the weight of the bodies slowly crushing him. His arms went stiff. His hands began to go to sleep. His legs were completely dead.

"Now a direct hit," he thought, "and it's all over."

The hole began to stink. They all lay on top of each other. Gühler felt the lieutenant's knee in his belly. The beams above them began to move.

"They're slipping," yelled Gühler.

There was an explosion in front of the hole near the opening.

"Out!" yelled Gühler. "Get out!"

But they crushed him with the weight of their bodies and their fear.

"The rocks!" he shouted. "The rocks!" He tried to push against the heavy bodies but fell back exhausted. "The beams are slipping," he said.

He heard a crash. He pressed his face against the wall and closed his eyes. But the beams above him stayed in place. They suddenly settled firmly and didn't move again.

"It isn't the tenth yet," thought Gühler.

The barrage howled across the mountain. After two hours it was silent again.

"Is it always like that?" asked the lieutenant.

None of them spoke. They pushed their way slowly out of the hole.

"Yes, it's always like that," said Gühler. "Always, *Herr Leutnant*. From morning till evening and from evening till morning."

"Get the hell out of here," yelled Beijerke.

They pushed their way out of the hole one after the other. They moved without making a sound.

"I hope you've had enough," said Grundmann.

The lieutenant said nothing.

"He pushed my whole face in with his elbow," said Beijerke.

The lieutenant crawled out of the hole.

"*Auf Wiedersehen in Kanada*," said Grundmann.

"Good luck," said the lieutenant. That was the last they heard of him. They listened outside but couldn't hear a sound on the slope.

"They learned their lesson," said Beijerke.

They huddled together, laid their steel helmets ready on their knees, and went to sleep.

In the morning the shelling began again at the regular time. At first they could distinguish between the individual guns. "That one's for us," they said, or "That one's not for us."

Toward midday it became quieter. Grundmann crawled to the opening, pushed aside the blanket they had hung up as protection against splinters, and looked out. A thin humming became audible inside the hole.

"Gühler!"

"What?"

"They've left a box of mines directly in front of the hole."

They all stared at him.

"What?" said Gühler. "In front of the hole?"

"By the entrance."

"That's not very funny," whispered Gühler.

The slope lay under the barrage until the evening. During the night Gühler and Grundmann crawled out and dragged the box of mines away. They crawled a yard or two at a time, pulling the box behind them.

"If a shell had slammed into that!" said Grundmann.

They shoved the box under a protruding rock and crawled back.

"They nearly blew us all to hell," said Gühler when they were back in their hole.

"Is it gone?" asked Beijerke.

"Yes," said Grundmann.

They wiped the sweat from their foreheads and listened to Pöhler, who began to talk about cake again.

"A really good chocolate cake with little truffles on top. Can you imagine it?" His voice sounded fat and deep, as if his mouth were watering. "Just one more chocolate cake, and for all I care the whole shooting match can go to blazes."

"Who's going for the rations?" asked Gühler.

Beijerke and Pöhler said nothing.

"Neither of you has gone yet," said Grundmann.

"Since Beijerke caught hell up front," said Gühler, "he hasn't been worth a damn." He took the mess kits and climbed out. "The others over there can go," he said. He made his way over the stones to the other hole. "You go get the rations," he said.

"Who, us?"

"Yes," said Gühler, "you."

Gervin crawled out of the hole.

"Schneider's finished," he said. "Schneider's absolutely finished. He prays all day long, then he howls like a dog and then he begins to pray again."

They took the mess kits and crept up the mountain.

"He was in Russia," began Gervin again when they had reached the rear slope of the mountain. "He froze off his toes but he says this is the real hell."

"A little foretaste," said Gühler.

They slid along to Buschmann's dugout and let themselves into it.

"What is it?" asked an anxious voice. Konz sat at the entrance and wouldn't let them pass.

"Don't come in. Buschmann's worked up. He beat it to the rear today. Simply took off. He couldn't hold out any longer. They've brought him back up again."

"Have you got anything to eat?"

"Yes," said Konz.

They took the rations and stole back again. As they were crossing the mountain the heavy artillery started up. They looked at the burning valley which stretched as far as Cassino. The woods and the houses were on fire. The flames hardly moved in the windless night. The smell of fire covered the valley and moved up the mountains with the smoke. Black fountains of dirt spouted continuously on the road at the bottom as the shells exploded. It was as bright as day down there in the light of the flames.

"Ghastly," whispered Gervin.

"Come on," said Gühler.

They crawled a little way and then rested, putting the canteens beside them on the ground.

"Will we ever get out of here?" said Gervin.

He was still very young. He had the face of a child.

"Maybe," said Gühler. "Maybe we'll get out of here yet."

They crawled over onto the forward slope. In front of their hole they sat and divided up the rations. Suddenly Gervin fell over backward. His head fell forward and his body backward. Gühler took hold of him.

"What's the matter with you?"

Gervin didn't answer.

"Hey, Gervin!" whispered Gühler. He let the body fall slowly back to the ground.

"Gervin," Gühler whispered. "Gervin." But he only heard a long-drawn-out groan. He held the shaking hands.

"What's the matter, Gervin? What is it?"

Grundmann crawled out of the hole.

"What's going on?" he asked.

"There," said Gühler and pointed to Gervin who lay stretched out on the stones.

They knelt beside him and felt over his body.

"Done for," said Grundmann. He moved his hand across Gervin's head and his fingers came away covered with blood. "Through the head," he said.

"How's that possible?" whispered Gühler.

"God knows."

"Maybe a stray splinter."

"Perhaps," said Grundmann.

They dragged Gervin along behind them, a yard or two at a time, just as they had done with the box of mines. They laid him beside the box of mines.

"He'll be all right there," whispered Grundmann.

"Yes," said Gühler.

Beijerke and Pöhler had pulled the rations into the hole. They slid down to join them and began to eat.

"I've got the damndest hunger," said Grundmann.

"Pitch in," said Beijerke. He took a piece of bread and pushed it into Grundmann's mouth.

"Quiet," said Gühler.

"What?" whispered Beijerke.

"It's starting again."

And the barrage began again.

IX

ONE evening they found Hesse of the second platoon sitting in Buschmann's dugout. He said, "It's all over out there. Gortz is dead. The foxholes are all shot to pieces. The Poles have deserted."

Buschmann lay in the corner. "Those goddam Poles," he said.

Grundmann and Gühler sat at the entrance to the dugout.

"What do you expect from the Poles?" said Gühler. "First we keep them in prison camps, then we push them into the army, and finally we send them into action against the Americans. Of course they desert."

Buschmann looked at him and said, "They're just a lot of rabble."

"They're Poles. What have they got to do with us?"

"They were our 'racial comrades' until recently," said Buschmann contemptuously.

"Yes," said Hesse. "It doesn't make sense any more. The Amis have got the ridge over there. We're just candidates for coffins here."

"Well, call it quits then," said Gühler.

"Yes, it doesn't make sense."

Grundmann said nothing. He held his helmet in one hand and stared at the ground.

"I can't take any more," said Hesse. "They've made a shambles of everything out there. Day and night they pound the living guts out of you. The men are all finished. They're just waiting for the Americans to come."

Grundmann still didn't say anything.

"The Amis!" said Gühler. "They won't come. They save every man they can. They'll just keep pounding till there's nothing left alive here."

Buschmann's hands shook. Gühler saw them shaking and looked away.

"Do what you like," shouted Buschmann suddenly. "Do what you like."

"What we like?"

"For all I care you can hang out the white flags. Go ahead, I don't give a damn."

"Surrender?" said Gühler.

"I'm through," yelled Buschmann, "all through, see? I was two years in Russia, but this is hell. It's madness. It isn't war any more."

"War's always madness," said Gühler slowly.

"Yes, you, you bastard, you always were a little rat."

Gühler crawled close up to Buschmann. He looked into the feverish, fear-flickering eyes before him.

"Say that again," he whispered, "say that again."

"Cut out that crap!" said Grundmann. "Cut it out!"

Konz writhed into the hole, pushing the curtain at the entrance to one side so that they saw the brilliant glare of the flaming mountains.

"The mountains are burning," whispered Konz.

"They've set them afire with phosphorus shells."

"Let them burn," said Grundmann.

"And the machine gun's gone."

"Which machine gun?"

"The heavy one," said Konz. "It just flew apart. In a thousand pieces."

"There you are," said Hesse. "It's senseless. Let's go back."

"And who'll take responsibility for it?" shouted Buschmann. "No one's given us any orders."

"Don't hold your breath till they come," said Gühler.

Hesse's long face tightened.

"Let's just get the hell out."

"Desertion," said Buschmann. "Back there they'll hang you from the nearest tree."

"You beat it yourself once," said Gühler.

Buschmann didn't answer.

Konz crawled over to Gühler and said, "Shut up, Gühler, shut up!" There was a sudden silence in the hole. They heard the shell bursts creeping up the mountain.

"Here it comes again," Buschmann whispered.

He gripped Gühler's arm and said, "Put a white flag out! A white flag! It's crazy to stay here, absolutely crazy!"

The light inside the dugout went out. The curtain was blown aside repeatedly by the blasts of exploding shells, and Konz kept pulling it back again. They jammed their faces up against the walls or lay down on the ground, their heads covered with their arms.

"Stop it! For God's sake stop it!" yelled Hesse.

The explosions moved away from the hole again and moved away down into the valley. Grundmann still sat by the entrance. He lifted his head and said, "How do you know that the Amis will come if you surrender?"

"They'll come all right," said Hesse.

"And what if they don't come? What if German reinforcements come instead? You're done for then."

Hesse shrugged his shoulders. "What reinforcements are coming?"

"Paratroops, maybe. They'd put you straight up against a wall."

Buschmann's voice was hoarse. "I don't care. I don't care what you do."

Grundmann stood up. He picked up his canteen and mess kit and turned toward the entrance. "Come on. We've got to go," he said.

"What are we going to do?" asked Gühler.

"Nothing," said Grundmann. "Nothing at all."

Gühler looked at Buschmann and said, "You're a coward."

"He says I'm a coward!" yelled Buschmann. "*He* does!"

"Give the order and we'll surrender."

"Ha!" said Buschmann, "and get me strung up. Just me."

Gühler turned away. Grundmann said, "We've got to get going."

They both crawled out of the hole. Hesse shouted after them, "What about the white flag?"

"No! We'll stay where we are till they come for us."

Konz crawled out after them. The night was bright as midday. They saw gigantic flames on the mountain ridges. "The sky's on fire," thought Gühler.

German rocket guns were firing over in the other valley. The sound echoed around the mountains like groaning. "They scorch the earth and burn the sky," thought Gühler. He lay on his belly and looked up at the burning mountains. "We're still alive," thought Gühler. "We're still alive, anyway." The shells of the heavy artillery chugged over them unceasingly into the burning valley.

They propelled themselves along with their feet and elbows. It seemed to them as if they were caught in the light of some enormous searchlight. The burning sky was dazzling to their eyes. The shell bursts came storming up the mountain. They flattened themselves into the burned grass.

"Go on," shouted Konz behind them, "go on." He came crawling past them. He moved with a sort of rolling motion like a machine. "Keep moving, you bastards, keep going!"

They crawled after him as far as a hole on the rearward slope. He slipped down into it and came out again with some rations.

"Those'll be the last," he said.

"Why?"

"Not a dog's chance of getting through any more."

They stuffed the rations into their mess kits and pockets, and each took a loaf of bread under his arm. They crawled on again. The bushes where they had previously been able to walk upright now lay torn up by the roots. They crawled forward foot by foot.

"I can't go on," said Grundmann.

"My knees," whispered Gühler, "Christ!"

They rolled over on their backs and stared at the sky. The moon floated pale and forlorn across a sea of fire.

"We ought to give up."

"Yes," said Grundmann.

"What, you're for it too?"

"Yes. It's hopeless."

"But how?" said Gühler.

"Yes, how?" whispered Grundmann.

Neither of them spoke. The loaves and the canteens lay beside them.

"I could go to sleep here," said Gühler.

"Here? With all this racket?"

"I don't hear it any more."

Gühler closed his eyes. The stars, the burning mountains, and the pale moon revolved above him like a carousel. Grundmann gave him a push and said, "Gühler. Buck up, man."

They picked up the mess kits and the loaves and crawled on. Whenever the shell bursts began creeping up the mountain they lay still. Then they writhed forward bit by bit down the forward slope.

As they came to their hole they heard someone singing.

"What's that?" whispered Grundmann.

"Schneider," said Gühler. "We left him all alone in his hole."

"Mad?"

"Possibly."

They pushed themselves over the rock until they came to Schneider's hole. They heard him singing in a cracked nasal voice: *"Ein' feste Burg ist unser Gott...."*

"Schneider," they whispered into the hole. "Schneider, can you hear us?"

"Ah, so there you are, my dears. I've been waiting so long for you."

"He's gone crazy," said Grundmann.

"Come closer, my dears. Come into my garden," said the voice from below again.

"Good God, what are we going to do now?" said Grundmann.

"Nothing," said Gühler.

They heard him praying down in the hole. It sounded like a singsong chant.

"Throw him down some bread and leave him there," whispered Gühler.

They threw the bread into the hole. There was silence below them. Then they heard him say, "We must break bread for the five thousand."

They crawled back to their own hole. Pöhler and Beijerke sat huddled in their blankets and stared at them out of glassy eyes.

"What's the matter with you two?"

Beijerke pulled the blanket off his head and said, "I could murder them all, the sons of bitches."

"Who?"

"All of them," said Beijerke, "all of them."

A smile stole over Pöhler's face.

"If I only had a piece of candy," he said, "just a tiny one. Sweet, with brandy inside. Maybe Kirsch, or Hennessy."

"It's my birthday the day after tomorrow," said Gühler.

"Oh, the day after tomorrow we'll all be dead."

"We'll live until my birthday, I guarantee," said Gühler.

"You will, maybe. But what about me?"

Pöhler gathered up his blanket and crawled inside again.

"Stop that nonsense," said Grundmann.

He divided up the rations and pushed a piece of bread and cheese over to each of them.

"My fingers stink as if I'd been out with a tart."

"It stinks worse than that in here," said Gühler. He crawled out of the hole. "I can't take it any more."

Grundmann looked at him anxiously with his big child's eyes. "Don't be foolish. It's dangerous out there."

"Makes no difference. Nothing makes any difference."

Gühler lay on the rock and watched the flames devouring the mountains above him. He listened to the hoarse barking of the artillery down in the valley, the throb and drone of the rocket guns on the other side of the ridge, the shells bursting behind him and the dull crackle of the flames over the rock. He lay there and thought of nothing. Suddenly he opened his eyes wide. It was as if someone were bending over him saying, "Come inside, come into the hole." The voice sounded like his own. "Yes," he said, "I'm coming."

He wriggled slowly into the hole. A thick wave of stinking air came up and hit him. "I'm finished," he thought, "I'm all through." He sank down in a corner and pushed Beijerke's feet aside. "Pull your feet in," he shouted.

"Shut your trap," said Beijerke.

A shell exploded with a crash just in front of the hole. Then another and another. The curtain at the entrance flew across the hole to the wall at the back.

"Take cover," shouted Gühler.

They lay on top of each other against the back wall. Pöhler kept whimpering, "My head, my head." Slowly the artillery began battering their position again. It kept it up all through the night. In the light of the exploding shells Gühler saw the others praying. Once he found Grundmann's face with eyes wide open close against his own. "I can't go on, Gühler, I can't go on."

Gühler had hung the blanket up in front of the opening again. He sat there holding it up. He looked at Grundmann's hands folded in prayer and heard Pöhler whimpering. Then he collapsed, closed his eyes, and let go of the blanket. "The beams," he thought. "The beams will start slipping soon." His head fell forward on his knees. He felt himself drifting back to childhood. Clearly and sharply he could see the days of long ago. Once he woke up and thought, "Where am I?" And then, "I'm tired. My God, I'm tired."

Grundmann crawled over to him and shouted, "Gühler, Gühler, we must hang the blanket up again. We're getting all the filth in our faces."

"Let me alone," he said, "let me alone."

He watched Grundmann trying to hang the blanket up in the opening. He saw him blown head over heels by the blast of an explosion.

"It's over," he thought, "it's all over."

He saw everything. He noticed every movement. But he felt nothing any more.

X

THE barrage kept up all the next day. Toward evening it became quiet. Grundmann went alone over the mountain and came back with a noncom and two men.

"What are they doing here?" said Gühler.

"They're all that's left of the first platoon," said Grundmann.

He crawled a little way up the mountain with the noncom and showed him a hole which the sappers had blown there. He came back again.

"Who's that?" asked Gühler.

"Prohaska," said Grundmann. "Don't you know him? From the first platoon."

"Oh, yes," said Gühler, "Prohaska."

Beijerke's head popped out of the hole.

"Haven't you got anything to eat?"

"No rations," said Grundmann. "Maybe tomorrow morning."

"No rations," moaned Beijerke. "No rations."

Grundmann threw the empty mess kits into the hole.

"We can die like cattle here. Nobody gives a damn about us any more."

"It's all over," said Gühler. "Tomorrow night they'll come. You'll see."

"Let's hope so," answered Grundmann. He slipped wearily into the hole. "I've got to sleep," he said.

Gühler remained sitting in front of the hole. Prohaska came creeping down the mountain toward him.

"They'll begin again in a minute," he said.

"Not tonight," answered Gühler.

"Why not?"

"I don't know. I've just got a feeling."

"Yes, it's like that sometimes."

"They'll come tonight," whispered Gühler.

They listened to the sounds below them on the mountain.

"Quiet!" whispered Prohaska.

"What is it?" asked Gühler.

"Footsteps. Do you hear?"

They both slipped slowly to the ground.

"Footsteps?" whispered Gühler.

"Yes. Can't you hear?"

"Yes, now I hear them too."

They didn't dare move. They lay there staring down the mountain. But they couldn't make out anyone.

"They're coming," whispered Gühler. "I knew they'd come."

"Yes," answered Prohaska.

"Should I wake Grundmann?" said Gühler.

"Let him sleep," said Prohaska.

They heard footsteps everywhere on the mountain.

Stones were dislodged and rolled down the rocks. But they saw no one.

"They're going round the mountain," whispered Gühler.

The footsteps came closer and went away again. Then they saw shadows on the road moving slowly round the bends toward the pass.

"They're breaking through without opposition," said Gühler.

"Who's going to shoot at them?" answered Prohaska. "Everyone's finished up here."

"They'll come round from the rear tomorrow," began Gühler again.

"Tomorrow," said Prohaska, "tomorrow we'll be prisoners." They lay still again and listened to the night. Not a shot sounded.

"They've got rubber soles," said Gühler.

Grundmann came crawling out of the hole. He lay down beside them. "What's up?" he said. "Everything's so quiet."

"Nothing'll happen tonight," said Gühler.

"Why?"

"They're breaking through. Can't you hear them?"

They heard the steps in the night again. Prohaska whispered, "When they come—no shooting. We're throwing in the towel, see?"

Grundmann said nothing. He lay there and stared down the mountain. "It won't do, children, it won't do," he said suddenly.

"I'll wring your neck," whispered Prohaska. "You fire a single shot and I'll wring your neck."

"What about when we come back?"

"From being prisoners?" asked Gühler.

"Yes," said Grundmann.

"The war will be long lost," answered Prohaska.

They lay still again and listened to the footsteps slowly receding.

"*Los!*" said Prohaska, "let's hang some white flags out."

"Flags is good," said Gühler.

"Pull your shirts off and hang them on the end of your rifles. Or stick the machine gun up in the air and hang any old white rag on it."

"No," said Grundmann.

"Why not?"

"We've stuck it out here for fourteen days. We'll manage to hold out till morning."

"They'll throw hand grenades down the hole at you."

"Let them," said Grundmann.

Gühler said nothing but looked at Grundmann. Prohaska twisted his face into a grin.

"You're a regular goddam hero, aren't you?"

"Shut up," said Gühler.

They were all silent again. They heard Schneider singing in the other hole. It sounded soft and devout.

"He'll sing the Amis over to us yet."

"It's hopeless," said Gühler quietly. "Schneider's gone mad. Beijerke and Pöhler are finished. The machine gun's rusted. The Amis are in our rear."

"Yes," said Grundmann. "It's hopeless."

"Well, then!" whispered Prohaska.

"We'll wait until they come, but without a white flag," said Grundmann.

"Have it your way," said Prohaska.

They crawled into their holes.

The guns were silent all night. When the first light of the breaking day seeped into the hole, Gühler nudged Grundmann and said, "Hey. It's my birthday."

Grundmann yawned sleepily.

"*Mensch,*" he said, "we made it after all."

Suddenly there was a shadow at the entrance of the hole.

"There they are," whispered Gühler.

"Grundmann?" said someone outside.

"Yes," answered Grundmann, "what is it?"

"This is Maeder," said the voice outside.

"Maeder!" said Grundmann. "How'd you get here, man?"

"Corporal Maeder from the second platoon?" asked Gühler.

"Yes," said Grundmann.

Maeder slipped into the hole. He had his submachine gun on his arm.

"Where'd you come from?" asked Grundmann.

"From the rear," said Maeder. "They sent me up forward, the supply people, you know. They're living in clover back there. They told me to go up forward. They were tight, the bastards."

"How'd you get through?"

"I came over the mountains. Over the ridges all the way. Didn't see a soul."

"No Amis?" asked Gühler.

"No Amis," answered Maeder. "I was with Buschmann. He sent me to you. Rations came up during the night. Schnapps and beer. Buschmann's half stewed already. He said for you to come get your rations. I brought a few bottles of beer with me."

"Beijerke, *mensch*, Beijerke! Go get the rations," said Grundmann. Beijerke's eyes widened.

"What, me?" he said.

"Yes," said Grundmann sharply, "you. Today's your turn. It's quiet out there today."

"Can't someone else go?"

"No," said Grundmann. "You're going."

Beijerke got ready and crawled out of the hole.

"Get moving," said Grundmann. "Take off before the Amis come, so we'll have something to eat first."

"Right," answered Beijerke.

Maeder pulled three bottles of beer out of his pockets. "My God!" he said. "It's quiet here with you."

"The war's over," answered Gühler.

Maeder stared at him. Gühler picked up a bottle and opened it.

"Sure it is," he said. "For us it's over."

"Say that again," said Maeder.

"In a few hours we'll all be prisoners," answered Gühler.

"Is that what I came up here for?"

"It looks like it, my friend. It looks like it."

He took the bottle and clinked it against Grundmann's.

"*Prosit*," he said.

"To the birthday boy," answered Grundmann.

"This gets crazier all the time," said Maeder.

Pöhler crawled sleepily out of his blankets.

"Hear! Hear!" he said.

Pflup, pflup went something down in the valley.

"Mortars!" shouted Grundmann.

They put on their helmets and huddled together. The shells exploded in front of their hole but lower down.

"Don't let the beer get cold," said Gühler.

112

"*Prosit*," said Grundmann.

Outside all was quiet again. The first rays of sunshine filtered through the slits between the beams.

"Do you think Beijerke'll come back?"

"The Amis have got him by now," answered Gühler.

"Yes," said Maeder, "they're playing at war back there. You ought to see them. When the bombers come over they fill their pants. But they herded all the drivers up into the mountains. No machine guns, no ammunition. The poor bastards died like flies."

"In that fire, no wonder," said Gühler.

"Yes," Maeder began again. "First the Amis knocked out the Ninth. Then Buchwald got into position with his mortars. But he had nothing but duds. One dud after another. They dragged up some new ammunition but they were all duds too. Nothing but duds."

"The whole war's one big dud," said Grundmann.

"*Prosit*," said Gühler.

"Shh," whispered Grundmann suddenly.

There were footsteps outside. They heard stones being dislodged and rolling away. Then a few voices. Then steps again.

"Here they are," said Gühler.

"Yes," whispered Grundmann. "It's over."

"*Mensch!*" whispered Maeder. "Get outside and let them have it!" He reached for his helmet and his submachine gun.

"It's all over here," said Gühler and laid his hand on Maeder's outstretched arm.

"If they hear us they'll throw hand grenades into the hole," said Pöhler, who had suddenly become quite animated.

"Who knows any English?" asked Grundmann.

"We must call to them," said Gühler.

They listened to the sounds outside. There were still footsteps and voices there.

"They're talking English," whispered Grundmann.

"How do you tell them not to shoot?" asked Pöhler.

"No shot," answered Grundmann.

Gühler looked at Grundmann and nudged him.

"*Los*," he said, "call to them."

Grundmann lifted the blanket from the entrance and looked out. Outside everything was quiet. The morning sun shone into the hole.

"No shot!" Grundmann called. It sounded soft and miserable. The voices and footsteps stopped abruptly.

The reply came in German: "*Kameraden?*"

"Yes," they all shouted. "Yes."

"Don't make such a noise, man," said Grundmann.

"Throw your arms away and come out!" said the voice. There was silence in the hole. Gühler took Pöhler by the arm and said, "Come. It's all behind you now."

"Thank God for that," whispered Pöhler. "Thank God for that."

"Who's going first?" said Gühler.

Nobody answered. They sat there and looked at each other.

"If I'd only realized," said Maeder.

"*Los*, Grundmann," said Gühler.

"All right," answered Grundmann, "I'm going."

"*Scheissdreck!*" said Maeder.

One by one they crawled out of the hole and put up their hands. Three Americans were standing in front of them. One of them had his pistol pointed at them, the other two their Tommy guns.

"Look at his pistol shaking, man," whispered Grundmann.

"Shut up," said Gühler.

"If I knocked him down, we could run for it."

"Take a look up there," Gühler whispered back.

American soldiers were standing all around the mountain above them. They had their Tommy guns ready. Here and there a heavy machine gun had been set up, leveled at them.

"Yes," said Grundmann, "it's over."

The American soldiers felt their pockets.

"We probably look like a lot of bandits," said Gühler.

"Worse. You've got a beard like an Italian mule driver."

They clasped their hands on top of their heads. Suddenly they saw a dirty white shirt appear from Prohaska's hole.

"That ninny," said Grundmann.

The three came out of their hole and joined them.

"Any more?" asked one of the American soldiers.

"My God! We almost forgot Schneider," shouted Grundmann.

He went over to the hole with one of the Americans, crawled inside and pulled Schneider out. Schneider, tall and haggard, was muttering continually to himself. His eyes burned crazily in his sunken face. His hair hung all over his forehead.

"Come on, Schneider. Follow us."

"Where to?" whispered Schneider.

"To heaven," said Grundmann. He took Schneider's hand and pulled him along behind.

"*Verrückt!*" said Grundmann to the American soldiers, tapping his forehead.

"Batty," said one of them.

They went down the mountain. They went one behind the other, with their hands atop their heads. The sun burned fiercely on the naked rock. They went deeper and deeper into the valley.

"I wonder where Beijerke is?" said Grundmann once.

"I hope he's all right," answered Gühler.

Grundmann was silent for a moment. Then he said, "I shouldn't have routed him out."

Two of the American soldiers walked behind them. They held their Tommy guns ready on their arms. One went ahead leading the way.

"They're still afraid we'll beat it," said Grundmann.

"They could leave us alone. We'd come anyway."

The farther down they went the more exhausted they became. They stumbled over the stones, their heads drooped forward, and their knees began to give. Their uniforms were torn, their faces smeared with mud. They stank of sweat and filth. Gühler saw Grundmann totter in front of him.

"Pull yourself together," said Gühler.

"Yes," whispered Grundmann.

They went on and came to the road that led down into the plain. Pöhler swayed suddenly and sagged down on one knee. The sweat streamed down his face, which was chalky and feverish.

"Sit down," said one of the soldiers.

They sat on the edge of the road. One of the soldiers offered Pöhler his canteen. Gühler looked up at the mountains. The rocks stood stark and jagged in the blue air.

"That's where we were, up there," he said.

Grundmann wearily raised his head and looked up.

"Get going," said the American soldiers.

XI

THEY came to a small farm in the valley behind which American mortars had taken up positions. American soldiers came up to them and took their watches. Gühler gave his up indifferently. It hadn't gone for the last four weeks.

"What do you think of the war?" asked the soldier, who examined the watch critically, and then put it in his pocket. He spoke German.

"Not much," said Gühler.

"Yeah," said the soldier. "Put Hitler, Mussolini, Stalin, and Roosevelt all together in one big sack, throw 'em in the ocean, and we might have some peace for a change."

"Perhaps," said Gühler.

"Yeah, we've got to settle with the whole bunch of 'em up at the top."

An officer came over and asked about their weapons.

"They're still up there," said Grundmann, pointing up to the rock. The officer spoke to the soldiers for a minute. They pointed up the mountain. One of the soldiers came over to them.

"We've got to go get your weapons. Who's coming with us?"

They stood behind the house in the sun and watched the mortars firing up at the rocks. They saw the little clouds of smoke rising up on the rock-face, which now looked brown and earthy. None of them said a word.

"Two must come with us," said the soldier.

They shrugged their shoulders and looked at each other.

"Up there? Never again."

"One of us must go," said Grundmann.

They all looked at the mortars, watching the soldiers pick up a shell, drop it down the barrel, and then duck down.

"Just like we do it," said Maeder.

The American officer came over and said to Maeder, "Officer?"

"Noncom."

"You go."

"*Los*, Grundmann, you come too. I'm not going alone."

"All right," said Grundmann. He shook hands with Gühler. "I'll never find the hole again."

"You don't need to."

They went off up the road with the Americans. "Poor bastards," said Pöhler. He sat down on the steps of the house, tired and exhausted, and began complaining about his watch.

"Forget about your watch," said Gühler.

The American soldiers stood all around them. One of them told the others how they had been captured. They laughed. One came up and said, "Cigarette?" They each took a cigarette and lit it.

118

"What a wonderful taste," said Pöhler.

"Compensation for your watch," said Gühler.

The mortar went on firing. Over and over again the soldiers dropped the shells down the barrel and ducked. Suddenly a heavy shell burst on the road just in front of them.

"German artillery," said Gühler.

"*Scheiss!*" said Prohaska. "The whole time we're up there they don't fire a single shot for us, and now they start blasting."

The American soldiers ran into the fields and disappeared behind a tall avenue of trees. A second shell fell close beside the house. They saw the soldiers on the mortar jump up.

"*Los,*" said Gühler, "follow the Amis."

They stood there, alone and abandoned, beside the house.

"Look out! The next one'll hit the house," shouted Gühler. He ran down the tall avenue, behind which the Americans had disappeared. A third shell burst with a roar behind him. "There goes the house," thought Gühler. They ran down between the tall trees and saw a deep ditch just in front of them. American soldiers were lying in the bottom of it. "Into it," said Gühler. They crawled down the steep slope of the ditch and threw themselves down among the soldiers. "Afraid?" said one of the soldiers lying beside Gühler. His face was almost chocolate brown. Gühler shrugged. "Were you in Tunis?" Gühler shook his head. The shells were bursting closer and closer to the ditch. They flattened themselves into the ground. Gühler felt the breath from the chocolate-brown face beside him.

"Christ!" said Prohaska. "First they haven't got two

shots to spare for us and now they knock our brains out when we're prisoners." They lay flat on the ground again. Outside there was silence.

"It's over," said Gühler.

The soldier beside him grimaced and said, "Tunis, Sicily, Salerno—always boom-boom!"

"Yes," said Gühler.

"Hitler nix gut," said the soldier again.

They heard a scream outside. It sounded like the crying of a beaten child. "That's Pöhler," Gühler said. They jumped up and crawled up the slope of the ditch. The soldiers followed them. Pöhler lay in front of the house screaming. Prohaska bent over him.

"What is it, Pöhler?"

"The swine," he whined. "The swine."

"In the back," said Prohaska.

"How? Shot?" Gühler asked.

"Shell splinter," said Prohaska.

The Americans brought up a stretcher. They took hold of Pöhler under the arms and laid him on it. He cried out once or twice and closed his eyes.

"How'd it happen?"

"Direct hit on the house," said Prohaska. "He ran into the house."

"What a dope!" said Schneider.

Pöhler opened his eyes and said, "Shut up, Schneider."

The Americans lifted up the stretcher and carried it down the road. Gühler followed a little way behind. Pöhler lay on the stretcher with his eyes shut. He whimpered with pain. The black stubble of his beard stood out on his creased, fleshy face. Dark shadows lay under his eyes.

"I don't want to leave you fellows," he whispered. His

teeth chattered while he spoke as if he were shivering with cold. Gühler bent over him.

"You'll come back to us. You'll come back for sure."

"You're just saying that."

"No," said Gühler, "honest. You'll see. We'll meet again."

"Where?"

"In America. America for sure. There's no war there. They'll give you your watch back. There'll be chocolate and whipped cream and everything just like peacetime."

"Good," whispered Pöhler. Then he opened his eyes. "Do you really think it'll be like that? Like peacetime?"

"Yes," said Gühler, "of course."

One of the American soldiers gave Gühler a push. "Get back," he said.

Gühler took Pöhler's hand. "*Mach's gut,* Pöhler." But Pöhler didn't answer.

Gühler walked slowly back again. American soldiers ran across the road in front of him carrying mortars, and took up their position in a ditch. He watched the clouds of dust appear again up on the rock face. It looked as if plaster were falling from some gigantic wall.

Prohaska and the others were still standing by the house. An American soldier with a Tommy gun ready was standing beside them. Schneider sat on the ground, calm and self-assured, and stared coolly at the soldier.

"Funny kind of machine pistol," he said.

"Is he all right again?"

"He's just putting it on," said Prohaska.

Grundmann and Maeder came back with the American soldiers. They were carrying a stretcher with an American on it. There was a bandage around his head and he was groaning softly. They put the stretcher down on the ground.

"What happened to him?" Gühler asked.

"Had his jaw blown off," said Grundmann. "We didn't get far. We ran into some stuff up the road. It took half his face off."

"Was he the one that wanted to tie the whole lot up in a sack and throw them in the ocean?"

"Yes," said Grundmann. "A decent chap."

"The decent ones always get it first," said Gühler.

The Americans picked up the stretcher and carried it down the road.

"They just carried Pöhler down there, too."

"You're joking!"

"Really," said Gühler. "He got a shell splinter in the back."

"I hope he comes through all right."

They sat down in the shade of the house and waited. A new troop of prisoners came down the road.

"Buchwald, man!" shouted Maeder.

He ran up to a noncom with short black bristly hair whose uniform looked like a muddy sack.

"Well," said Buchwald, "everybody survive all right?"

"Depends how you look at it," said Gühler.

"They made a nice mess of us. We were to the right of you last night. They came round from behind and shot us up with their Tommy guns. The silly bastards with us fired back. Olbrich was the first to get it. Had half his guts shot out. I yelled to the others to give up, but they kept firing. Then Reiter was killed, the one with the beautiful voice, remember? The last was Nowak, our driver, shot in the belly."

122

"Yes," said Grundmann. "Why didn't you quit right away?"

"At least they put up a fight," said Maeder.

Grundmann said nothing. He looked as Maeder picked up a stone and threw it into the field. Then he turned slowly around again.

"You bastard," he said. " 'Put up a fight'! And Olbrich, Reiter, and Nowak had to die for no good reason."

Maeder didn't say anything. He stared at the ground in silence.

"You're right," said Buchwald, "but they were all jittery."

An American truck stopped on the road. Three soldiers with Tommy guns sat inside it.

"Get in," said the soldier who had been guarding them.

They climbed on the truck and drove back through the fields. The sun came streaming slantwise across the mountains and burned into their backs. Italian workmen wearing huge straw hats stood in the fields and shook their fists at them threateningly as they passed. They drove through a small village. The inhabitants came out of the houses and threw stones at them. A half-decayed sucking pig landed in the truck.

"*Tedeschi kaput! Tedeschi kaput!*" came the shouts from doors and windows. The Americans raised their Tommy guns. They drove into an olive grove where artillery was lined up wheel to wheel.

"There they are," said Gühler.

The guns stood silent under their camouflage nets. Mountains of ammunition lay neatly piled up in crates behind them.

123

"Those are the ones that gave us such hell up there," said Grundmann. They climbed down from the truck. American soldiers gathered around them curiously. They sat down under a tree. An American officer came up with an interpreter and began a short interrogation. The prisoners emptied their pockets and threw everything on the ground. The interpreter examined everything. The officer leafed through Gühler's pay book and said, "Your birthday today?"

Gühler nodded. The officer laughed. They went back to the tree and sat down on the grass. They saw American soldiers standing naked under a shower which had been fixed up in the field.

"Brother, that's the way to run a war," said Buchwald.

A few Americans came over and shook hands with Gühler. "Your birthday," they said.

"Yes," said Gühler.

He suddenly had an acute desire to get under the shower and wash off the whole war. The naked bodies of the Americans shone white in the glistening water.

"I wouldn't mind trying a civilized war like that for once."

"And we stink like a lot of pigs," said Grundmann.

Some American soldiers came up with coffee, chocolate, cigarettes, and tins of food. They put it all down on the grass in front of Gühler and said "Happy Birthday!" Gühler looked at them and laughed. He didn't know what to say, but he thought, "If they'd only let me have a shower. If I could only take off these rags and just have a shower." The soldiers showed him how to mix the coffee. They stirred it in cold water in an old tin and held it up to Gühler.

"Come on, you must celebrate too," he said to the others. They came round and helped themselves to a drink from the tin. More and more soldiers came up with cigarettes and tins of food, and chocolate. "Happy birthday," they all said pointing at Gühler and laughing.

Now from all over the valley shots were fired. They saw the half-naked soldiers working at the guns.

"*Nix gut fur Kameraden*," said one of the Americans.

"A little salute for your birthday," said Buchwald.

The flashes from the gun barrels made a thin wall of fire all across the plain.

"Maybe they aren't dishing it out," said Grundmann.

They drank the strong coffee, smoked their cigarettes, and watched the half-naked soldiers who had previously been standing under the showers and were now working the guns. Prohaska blew the smoke from his cigarette in little rings into the air, and said, "If everything with them is as good as their cigarettes, we're going to have a wonderful time."

An army chaplain with a gold cross on his collar came up and asked them how they were.

"The war'll soon be over," he said. "And then you can all go home again."

"Do you hear? Go home, he said," whispered Grundmann.

Gühler said nothing. He lay on his back and listened to the thunder of the guns. An officer came out of a tent and dispersed the soldiers who were loitering around them. The soldiers went away slowly and reluctantly.

"They aren't supposed to talk to us," said Grundmann.

"Did you understand what the officer said?"

"Yes," said Grundmann.

"To them we're all Nazis. Do you realize that?"

Grundmann lay down beside him on the grass.

"What are you thinking about?"

"We're free, do you understand? We're prisoners, and we're free."

"I don't see that."

"We're out of the machine, out of the meat grinder."

"And into a new one."

"No," said Gühler. "Never. Over there we'll have a life of personal freedom even behind the barbed wire."

"You're an optimist," said Grundmann.

Buchwald had gone to sleep. His head drooped on his chest. His face was pressed into his prickly beard. When they shook him he opened his eyes sleepily and said, "I can't go on. I'm finished," and went to sleep again.

Toward evening three American soldiers came up and led them away. They drove off down the road and left the roar of the guns far behind them. They came to a little farm where many prisoners were waiting.

"You'll be interrogated here," the other prisoners told them. "They'll want to know everything about you—whether you're Nazis or not, where your positions were, where the artillery is."

They sat down in the yard and waited. Each of them in turn went up some steps and through a glass door to the interpreter who was conducting the interrogation.

"What will you tell them?" asked Grundmann.

"The truth."

"Everything?"

"No," said Gühler, "not the positions."

They sat there waiting. Twilight came down and made them sleepy. "If we could only get a little sleep," said Prohaska. But they just sat there waiting and asking each one who came out through the glass door what he had said.

"Nothing," they all said. "You've got to play dumb."

Grundmann went in. He walked clumsily up the steps. His overcoat hung torn and muddy almost to the ground. He still carried his helmet in his hand like some empty cooking pot that he had no more use for. But the glass door had hardly shut behind him before it opened again. Grundmann came down the steps, his face flushed.

"Well?" said Gühler. "How is it?"

"I told him I'd been a Hitler Youth leader and he threw me out."

"Why'd you tell him that?"

"Didn't you say to tell the truth?"

"Yes," said Gühler. "Yes, I did."

Then they fell silent again and waited. They watched Buchwald go up. Almost half an hour passed before the glass door opened again.

"He's staying in there forever," said Grundmann.

"He's not being as silly as you."

Buchwald came back. He sat down on the fence beside them.

"Were you in favor of the war?"

"No," said Gühler.

"This son-of-a-bitch Hitler and his war."

"Careful," whispered Grundmann.

"Why?"

"Take a look at the faces all around you. Most of them haven't given up yet."

"Yes," said Buchwald, "I think you're right."

Prohaska came over and nudged Gühler. "Your turn," he said.

Gühler put his haversack down beside Grundmann and went slowly up the steps.

XII

THE interrogator was wearing civilian clothes. He sat behind a neat, smooth-topped writing table. When Gühler came in he got up and sat on the arm of his chair. Gühler stood awkwardly in the middle of the room. He didn't know whether he ought to salute or not.

"You were a National Socialist?" said the interrogator. He looked indifferently up at the ceiling as he said it, as if the question didn't interest him at all.

"No," answered Gühler.

The interrogator looked at him. He stood up and took a few steps across the room.

"You were not a National Socialist?"

"No," said Gühler slowly and awkwardly, "I was not a National Socialist."

"Hm," said the interrogator clearing his throat. "You're the first. Your comrades answered all my questions by saying they had nothing to say. Always the same, as if it had been hammered into them."

"Yes," answered Gühler. "They were threatened that they'd be shot if they said anything."

"Do they still believe that Germany will win the war?"

"Many do."

"Do you?"

"No," said Gühler, "I don't."

The interrogator went back to his table and made a few notes. "Sit down," he said.

Gühler sat down heavily on the chair which stood ready in front of the table. The interrogator continued walking up and down the room. The boards squeaked a little.

"Why do you think that Germany will lose the war?"

"Hitler will lose the war. It's Hitler's war, not Germany's."

The interrogator who had been standing by the window when he asked the question turned around sharply.

"Isn't that the same thing?" he said.

"No," answered Gühler, "it's not the same."

"Perhaps it's not the same to you."

"For me and for many others too."

"Why didn't you emigrate, then?"

"That would have been cowardly."

Gühler heard the boards squeak behind him. He felt the interrogator's excitement as he walked up and down behind him. Then he said, "I spent six months outside Germany, in Paris, because I had to. Then I went back again. If there's an evil to be fought it must be fought in one's own country."

"That's nonsense," said the interrogator.

"Perhaps," answered Gühler, "but we tried it."

"And why did you become a soldier?"

130

"Because I had to become a soldier."

"You didn't resist?"

Gühler said nothing for a moment. He looked at the interrogator who stood with his back to him looking out of the window. Then he said slowly, "A dead man can't resist."

The interrogator came back from the window and sat down in his chair. He crossed his legs, made a few notes, and offered Gühler a cigarette.

"You have a remarkable attitude," he said.

"It's not remarkable for us," answered Gühler.

"And you think that Hitler's finished?"

"Yes," said Gühler. "No supplies, too many enemies, and a wretched policy."

"How much longer do you give him?"

"Not much longer."

"Why did you hold out so long up there? We aren't getting through the pass."

"If you can't go back and can't go forward, you stay in the middle."

"Why couldn't you go back?"

"Behind us were the trees we would have been hanged from, and in front of us was the artillery."

"You could have deserted."

"An individual can desert, but not a whole company. A company must have orders. No one who wants to hold onto his head gives the order."

"What about morale? The morale of your comrades is high."

"That's not morale. They've no judgment of their own and they don't see the general picture. They just wait until something happens to them. They just stay where they're put. Until they get another order. Orders are the only things that count."

Gühler leaned back. He had spoken quickly and animatedly. He felt political passion awakening in him again. The interrogator looked at him and smiled. He opened a packet of cigarettes.

"Take one," he said.

Gühler took a cigarette. The interrogator leaned across the table and gave him a light. He said, "And the morale in Germany?"

"Bad."

"Do you think there'll be a revolt against Hitler?"

"No."

"Why not?"

"The only choice is between a lost war and Hitler. Many people think both are equally fatal. Many want neither the one nor the other. A few want a revolt, but the terror is stronger."

"You think that we'll have to march right into Germany?"

"Yes. The German people are in exactly the same position as we at the front. In a barrage there's always a chance you'll come out of it alive. There's no chance at all before a firing squad."

"But many people still believe in Hitler."

"Many believe in him. Many hate him."

"You hate him?"

Gühler looked at the interrogator and then down at the muddy toes of his boots. "Yes," he said.

The interrogator got up and went over to the window. He looked out into the yard.

"Your comrades down there," he said, "they're prisoners now. What are they thinking now?"

"About what's coming next. Probably about being hungry and when they're going to get something to eat."

"I'm having a longer talk with you than is usual."

Gühler said nothing. He looked down at his filthy hands and thought, "If only it were usual to be allowed to wash in captivity."

The interrogator went back to his writing table. He opened the drawer and pulled out a map. He put the map on the table and said, "Can you tell me where your positions were?"

"No," said Gühler.

"Why not?"

"I'm not an artillery officer."

"But you're an enemy of the Nazis."

"There aren't any Nazis up there, just my comrades."

"You'd be helping to shorten the war."

"No," said Gühler slowly, and stood up. "War has its own rules. Every position that I give away means thirty to forty direct hits for my comrades who still have a chance of getting away with their lives."

The interrogator rolled up the map and pushed it into the drawer.

"I can't force you," he said.

"Thank God," answered Gühler, "you're not a Nazi."

"Don't make remarks like that."

Gühler shrugged his shoulders.

"I don't understand you," began the interrogator again. "If you're against Hitler, then you must fight on our side against Germany."

Gühler took a cigarette. The interrogator again leaned across the table to give him a light. Gühler looked him full in the face as he did so. He said slowly:

133

"I'm a Socialist and a German. For me there is only one possibility. That is to work to put my ideas across in my own country. But not against my country. Not in the interests of foreigners."

The interrogator walked once around the writing table. He turned and said, "That's a hard judgment."

"It's not a judgment at all. It's a political attitude."

"I'm an Austrian. I left when the Nazis came in."

"You had no other choice."

"No, I had no other choice."

He went to the writing table and turned over some papers. He picked up Gühler's pay book and looked inside it.

"You were politically active?"

"Yes."

"Even after you came back from Paris?"

"Always, as long as it was possible."

"And the Gestapo?"

"They didn't spot me, except for one incident just before I was called up."

"You weren't in any Party formation?"

"No."

"And it never occurred to you to leave?"

"There are no lost positions in politics."

"What do you mean by that?"

"I mean that in politics one can't give up, until there is no chance left."

"But there were no chances left."

"Everything was forbidden, certainly. But you can't forbid an attitude of mind and there are many people in Germany who share it."

The interrogator picked up his pay book and leafed

through it. He lit a cigarette and said, "It's your birth-day?"

"Yes."

"Congratulations. A nice birthday present for you, being taken prisoner."

"There could have been worse."

"Such as the barrage?"

"You must have shot away a fortune up there on the mountain."

"We can afford to."

"I know."

"And the effect? What was the effect up there?"

"Not many casualties."

"And the effect on morale?"

"Very considerable."

The interrogator picked up the papers and put them in a large envelope.

"These papers will go with you," he said.

He gave Gühler his hand.

"Thank you. It's been very interesting for me."

Gühler shook hands with him and went to the door.

"You'll have it good with us," said the interrogator.

Gühler turned around. He looked at the interrogator. The dark eyes beneath the high forehead were devoid of sympathy.

"I don't want to have it any better than any of the others," said Gühler slowly and emphatically. He sud-denly felt hot and uncomfortable.

"America is a land of many opportunities," said the interrogator. He smiled noncommitally.

Gühler pulled the door shut behind him. He went slowly down the steps. His legs felt tired and heavy. Grundmann came up to him.

"You look white," he said.

"I don't know," answered Gühler, "I must have something to drink. I'm finished."

"Come on, there are some American soldiers in the yard giving us lemonade."

The soldiers took them into a barn that was spread with straw. They each got a tin of meat, some coffee, chocolate, and cigarettes. Gühler threw himself down on the straw.

"I must close my eyes a moment."

"Go ahead," said Grundmann.

They lay close together, for the night wind blew coldly through the barn, making them shiver. After a while Grundmann said, "I've been thinking it over. You're right. They should stop the whole filthy business."

"And Hitler?" murmured Gühler.

"He should make room for someone else."

"Thank God, you've realized it at last."

"Yes. It wasn't easy."

American soldiers went through the barn flashing a lantern into each of their faces.

"They count us the whole time," said Grundmann.

"That's all part of being a prisoner," answered Gühler.

They were awakened again during the night. Someone was sitting beside Gühler shaking him.

"What's the matter?"

"Get up, Gühler! Get up! We've been looking for you everywhere."

"Beijerke!" said Gühler. He sat up.

It was dark in the barn but he could feel Beijerke standing over him.

"How did you get here?"

"I couldn't find the hole again. I lost my way and they picked me up."

"Thank God," said Gühler.

"The others are all here too," said Beijerke.

"Who?"

"All of them: Buschmann, Konz, and the rest."

"You're joking," said Gühler jumping up.

"Hell, no. I've been creeping from man to man in this stinking barn trying to find you."

The prisoners lay beside each other and on top of each other in the darkness like great dark clods of earth. Grundmann stretched himself in his sleep.

"What is it, Gühler?"

"Get up. They're all here. Buschmann, Konz, Beijerke."

They stood in the doorway in the light of the American lanterns.

"Well," said Buschmann, "so you all made it." He had a tin of food in one hand and looked at Gühler uncertainly. Behind him stood Konz with his greatcoat collar turned up.

"Did you all come through all right?"

Buschmann laughed. He stuffed himself with pieces of meat from the tin and kept chewing as he talked. "They hauled us out of the hole with an Italian mule driver, one of the ones that delivered the mules. He was completely nuts, the bastard. Had some sort of gun and wanted to blow our heads off."

"What happened?" said Grundmann.

"The Amis took his gun away from him."

Buschmann threw the empty tin out the door. "Give me a cigarette," he said.

137

Gühler took an American cigarette out of his pocket and gave it to him.

"The positions had all been betrayed, all of them. We should have put the mule drivers straight up against the wall instead of letting them run around inside our positions."

The American soldiers came and took them off to be interrogated. Buschmann gave the cigarette back to Gühler and went out. In the doorway he turned around and said, "I hope you all kept your mouths shut."

"Certainly," said Gühler. "That's one thing we know how to do."

They stayed behind with Konz and Beijerke.

"He's sounding off again in fine style already," said Grundmann.

"The same thing all over again," said Gühler. "It'll all come back."

Beijerke and Konz stayed by the door, waiting to be called for their interrogation.

"Come on, let's lie down again," said Grundmann.

They stretched themselves out on the straw. Buchwald, Maeder, and Schneider lay beside them. They snored deeply and made gargling noises in their throats.

"I'm glad they all came through all right," said Grundmann.

"Seems crazy, in that barrage," said Gühler.

"They only used high explosives all the time. That's why."

"Where'd you hear that?"

"There's an artillery spotter over there who says that was the mistake they made."

"Oh," said Gühler, "so that's why they keep asking about the effect on morale."

"Yes, they ask everyone that."

"What do you really think of Buschmann?" whispered Gühler.

"Just putting it on."

"Not a Nazi?"

"No, just going through the motions, like most of them."

It grew quiet inside the barn. An American soldier stood at the door with a Tommy gun ready on his arm. He had directed his flashlight toward the ground. The shadows of Konz and Beijerke could be seen in the flickering light. An earthy, sweaty smell lay sour and heavy over the sleeping prisoners.

"My birthday's over," whispered Gühler.

"Yes," said Grundmann. "Nice birthday!"

XIII

THE next morning was fresh and clear. They crawled sleepily out of the straw and went out into the yard. The rumbling of the front came from the north. They tried to wash their hands under the pump in the yard but they had no soap.

"If a man could only get the filth off!" said Grundmann. He held his head under the pump and let the water run over his hair.

An American captain stood in the yard talking to two German officers. German prisoners stood around listening.

"Germany can never win the war," said the captain. "We've got far too much equipment and we have plenty of time."

"Certainly," said one of the officers. "But equipment isn't decisive in this war."

"What is decisive then?" asked the captain.

The two officers looked at each other but didn't answer.

"They're stumped," said Buchwald. "We'll be getting the fairy tale about the secret weapon next."

"Come on," said Gühler, "let's get something to eat." They went back into the barn and were each given a can of rations. Then they sat down in the sun and began to eat. Grundmann came over and said, "Can't we promote ourselves a couple of those tins?"

"I have already," said Buchwald. He opened his haversack in which three tins were tucked away.

"Where did you get them?" asked Gühler.

"From your birthday yesterday," said Buchwald. Two Negro soldiers came into the yard and reported to the captain.

"There's a couple of fine soldiers for you!" said Grundmann. "They talk to their officer as if he were dirt."

"Lucky them," said Gühler.

Three trucks drove into the yard. The Negroes let down the tailboards.

"Everybody in!" Buschmann bellowed.

"Listen to him," said Buchwald. "Is he back in charge already?"

They climbed into the trucks.

"We're off to America," said Grundmann. One of the Negro soldiers sat down beside him.

"Nix America," he said.

They drove farther south. Enormous ammunition dumps lined the road. "Did you ever see anything like that with us?" Grundmann asked. They drove over blown up bridges and through devastated towns. In the olive groves by the side of the road they saw innumerable tanks.

"Hopeless," said Buchwald, "absolutely hopeless."

"We might as well call the undertaker," answered Grundmann.

Gühler sat on the floor of the truck beside the Negro. The Negro pointed to Gühler's ring. "Ring *gut*."

Gühler nodded but said nothing. He looked out at the tanks which stood by the side of the road with their gun nozzles depressed.

"In prison camp," said the Negro, "finger off, ring gone." He laughed showing his white teeth and went through the movements of cutting off a finger. "Give me ring," he said.

Gühler shook his head: "Nix ring."

"Not good man," said the Negro. "Finger off in prison camp with big knife."

The muffled quaking of the front receded farther and farther behind them.

"We're all through with that, anyway," said Buchwald.

"For good, let's hope," answered Gühler.

The sun burned hotly down onto the truck. They were overcome by drowsiness again. They let their heads droop, and slept with open mouths. Toward midday the trucks stopped at a group of barracks surrounded by a high barbed-wire fence.

"Barbed wire," said Gühler.

They climbed stiffly out of the truck and followed the Negro soldiers through the main gateway. American soldiers stood by the gate counting them.

"All Jews," said Grundmann.

"Americans," said Gühler.

The search began. All sharp and pointed objects were taken away from them. They let everything happen to

142

them, dully and apathetically. Grundmann said, "Are they still afraid of us?"

"Regulations," said Gühler.

They were taken to a great shower room where they had to wait. An American soldier came over and told them to get ready for a shower. They threw off their filthy clothes and stood naked in the sun. Beijerke came over and felt Gühler's arm muscles.

"Boy, have you gotten thin!"

They were taken under the showers where they let the hot water run over their bodies. Huge pieces of soap lay beside the showers.

"Not bad at all, these Amis," said someone standing beside Gühler.

Two doctors went through the room making a routine inspection.

"That's the same everywhere," said Grundmann.

They stood lined up as if for a roll call. Then they got their clothes back and were taken to the main street of the camp.

"A *Feldwebel!*" said the American soldier. Buschmann stepped forward. "You're a *Feldwebel?*"

"Yes, sir."

"Take command of these men."

Buschmann put himself at the head of the group. The soldier disappeared and came back with a piece of paper. "Gühler!" he said. "Which is Gühler?"

"Here!" said Gühler.

"You're not going with them."

They all looked at Gühler. He stepped slowly out of the ranks and stood beside the column.

"What's the matter?" said Grundmann, excitedly.

"Don't know," said Gühler.

"But you must stay with us, man."

"Buchwald," said the soldier. Buchwald stepped forward. "*Unteroffizier* Buchwald?"

"You're staying here too."

The soldier gave Buschmann a sign and went off down the road through the camp. "March!" said Buschmann.

"Like old times," muttered Grundmann.

"Exactly," said Beijerke.

They followed behind Buschmann but without keeping in step, like a lot of ragged tramps. Their haversacks, which were the only things they had been allowed to keep, hung over their greatcoats. Their beards bristled on their sunken faces.

Grundmann turned around. "*Mach's gut*, Gühler," he said.

Gühler watched them disappear through a second gate behind another barbed-wire fence. Then he turned to Buchwald. "What's the matter with us?" he said.

"Who knows? Maybe we're in a special detail."

"Did you say anything at the interrogation?"

"That I wasn't a Nazi."

"Aha," said Gühler. "So that's the way the wind blows."

Buchwald took off his haversack and sat down on the stones in front of the administration hut. "What can they want with us?"

Gühler said nothing for a while. He looked over to the gate behind which the others had disappeared.

"So we two were the only ones," he said slowly. "Is it possible?"

A soldier came out of the hut. "Come with me!" They got up and followed him. The soldier opened the door of a barracks in a side street off the main road. "You stay here for the time being until you're called."

The barrack was almost empty. A noncom was sitting in one corner. He came over to them. "Well, what are you doing here?"

"We don't know," said Gühler.

"Ah," said the noncom. "Here's where you wait to be interrogated."

"But we've been interrogated."

"Some are pulled out and interrogated again here."

"What a lot of crap," said Buchwald and threw his haversack on one of the mattresses which lay on the floor. They took off their greatcoats and lay down on the mattresses.

"Them and their lousy interrogations," said Gühler.

"That's how it is, though," said the tall noncom. He stooped slightly when he walked. "Especially artillery men. Everybody from the artillery gets specially interrogated."

Gühler stretched himself out on the mattress and said, "Were you with the artillery?"

"Not exactly," said the noncom.

"I see," said Gühler. He rolled up his greatcoat and made it into a pillow.

"Have you got a looking glass and a razor?" he asked the noncom.

"I smuggled one through."

"Great!" cried Gühler. "Off with this beard."

The tall noncom pulled the mirror out of his haversack. Gühler jumped up and went over to the window with it.

"So that's me," he thought. He saw two eyes burning feverishly out of deep hollows, and a black, bristly beard.

"Is that really me?" he said. Buchwald laughed.

"Perhaps it isn't," he said. "Perhaps it's somebody else."

"Yes," said Gühler. "Perhaps I've become someone else."

The American soldier threw open the door. "Santo!" he shouted.

"Here," said the tall noncom.

Santo followed the soldier out. Some new prisoners came in and threw themselves down on the mattresses. One of them said, "They're just playing with us, man."

Santo came back and sat down beside Gühler. "The things they want to know," he said.

The door kept opening during the night. New prisoners came in. The stabbing light of the American flashlights leaped over the sleeping bodies. Gühler slept fitfully. Once he heard Buchwald whispering beside him, "If we hadn't said anything, we'd be with the others."

"Yes," said Gühler.

All through the next day the soldier kept on flinging open the door.

"Buchwald!" he roared once.

Buchwald came back after an hour, collected his things, and got ready to go.

"What's the matter?" asked Gühler.

Buchwald didn't say anything. He rolled up his blankets and his greatcoat.

"Just a lot of crap."

It was only Gühler who wasn't called. He lay on his mattress all day, talking to Santo, sleeping or staring at the ceiling. A little noncom kept telling everyone about the effect of the American artillery on the mountains at Cassino.

146

"How many times have you been interrogated already?" Gühler asked him.

"Oh, several times. They're very polite, because they know well enough that I'm a specialist."

"Do you tell them about the doubtful effect of high explosive shells?"

"They don't agree of course, but I know better."

"So you do tell them that then."

"Why not?" said the little noncom.

Gühler turned away. His feelings became more and more confused. Pictures of the front crowded his sleeping hours. He saw the gigantic walls of fire on the burning mountains. The prisoners came and went. Slowly the hut emptied. Days passed without Gühler being called. "They've forgotten about me," he thought.

One evening Santo packed up his things and shook hands with him. "Don't get too bored," he said.

"I must get out of here," said Gühler.

He was left alone. All day long he walked up and down the hut. Once he saw the interrogator sitting in front of him at his writing table. "You'll have it good with us," he said.

One afternoon the soldier came in and said, "This way." Gühler followed him across the camp road.

As he went into the little room where the American captain sat, he raised his hand to his cap and clicked his heels. Santo had told him that he had to give a smart military salute. The captain saluted back without smiling or altering the expression on his face. He riffled through some papers on the table. Gühler remained standing in the middle of the room.

"Third Division," said the captain.

"Yes," answered Gühler.

"Third battalion, twelfth company."

"Yes," said Gühler.

The captain spoke sharply, as if giving orders.

"You were not a National Socialist."

"No."

"You're against Hitler?"

"Yes."

"How many vehicles were there in your company?"

Gühler said nothing for a moment. He looked at the captain, whose eyes were lowered on the papers in front of him. There was something severe and sarcastic about the corners of his mouth.

"I don't know that," said Gühler.

"Were they new trucks?"

"Yes."

"French?"

"Yes."

"Did each section have a truck?"

"Yes."

"How many machine guns were there to each section?"

Gühler looked at the captain again. He sat upright, playing with a letter opener on the table. His eyes were gray and hard on Gühler. There was a trace of contempt in them. Gühler said nothing. He thought, "So that's it. An enemy of the Nazis is automatically degraded into a traitor."

He saw the sneer in the eyes of the man opposite him.

"Now then, come on," said the captain.

Gühler was silent.

"I asked you how many machine guns there were in each section."

"Three machine guns."

"And how many submachine guns?"

"Four submachine guns."

"And how many automatic rifles?"

"Seven automatic rifles."

The captain stood up and cleared his throat.

"Seven automatic rifles," he said slowly. "That can't be right."

Gühler said nothing. He looked the captain full in the face.

"How many heavy machine guns did you have in the company?"

"Ten heavy machine guns."

"Impossible," said the captain. "Impossible."

"Yes," said Gühler. "We'd just been re-equipped."

The captain sat down again. He looked at the papers on the table and said, "Are you speaking the truth?"

"The whole truth."

"Here's the map," said the captain, pulling it out of a drawer. "Where were your positions?"

Gühler bent over the map. He saw San Pietro on it and, in front of it, the mountain where they had lain.

"Point to the mountain," said the captain.

Gühler's finger traveled slowly over the map. It moved away to the right of San Pietro.

"Is that where the twelfth company was?" asked the captain.

"Yes," said Gühler. "There."

"And where was the tenth?"

Gühler's hand traveled over the map again. It stopped at a height far to the left of San Pietro. "There," he said.

"That's impossible. There was another division over there."

149

"No."

"Show me where you were again."

Gühler pointed to a height far to the right of Cassino.

"No," said the captain, pointing to the mountain on the left of the pass road. "That's where you were." He looked hard at Gühler.

"There was another company there," said Gühler.

The captain took a step back, looked sharply at Gühler, and said, "Why don't you tell the truth?"

Gühler shrugged his shoulders. "If you know better, sir, why do you ask me?"

"I thought you were interested in us winning."

Gühler didn't answer. He stood in the middle of the room with his heels together as if in a German company orderly room. He saw tiny furrows on the captain's otherwise smooth forehead, and said, "I want Hitler to be defeated."

"Yes," asked the captain. "Go on."

"That's an internal political matter."

"Sure," said the captain, "sure. But America's victory is your victory too."

"Perhaps. Perhaps it will be victory and defeat at the same time."

"For you?"

"For all enemies of National Socialism in Germany."

"And why don't you tell me the truth?"

"Because I'm an enemy of the Nazis, but not a traitor in the sense you think."

"In the sense I think?"

"In a military sense, as opposed to a political one."

The captain folded the map and threw it on the table.

"You can go," he said.

He rapped on the table. The American soldier who

had brought Gühler in came into the room. "Come on," he said.

Gühler saluted. The captain turned his back without returning the salute.

XIV

DURING the night Gühler was taken across to the main camp. The vast gate creaked closed behind him. He walked alone across the camp road looking for the number of the barrack he'd been told to go to. It was raining and the ground was soft and muddy. There were no lights in the huts. They lay in the darkness like animals stretched out beside the road. He went into a hut and asked where his own was. The rain ran down his greatcoat and into his boots.

He found his hut. The sour atmosphere hit him in the face as he went in. He remained sitting by the door and stared into the dark room. He heard them laughing and whispering. "It's as if I didn't belong to them any more," he thought. He saw them sitting and lying there in the darkness, like dark black lumps of earth.

"Yes," one of them was saying. "And then he asked me the name of the battalion commander and I said, 'Don't know,' and then he said, 'What, you don't know the name of your captain?' 'I don't know anything at all,' I said. And then he got furious and shouted, 'You're a real Nazi,' and I said, 'Right, I am!' "

"Are you one?" asked another voice.

"Well not actually, not directly," said the first voice. The others laughed.

"Do I really belong with them?" thought Gühler.

Someone flung open the door of the hut. For a moment the cold draught of air cut through the thick sticky atmosphere above the sleeping forms.

"Shut the door, goddammit!" shouted someone. Gühler saw two shadows standing in the doorway. They shut the door behind them and he heard them shake themselves. "Damn this rain!" one of them said.

Gühler sat up. It was Santo's voice. It sounded cool and relaxed with its slight trace of a Swabian accent. He got up and went over to them. "Santo!"

"Yes, what is it?"

"Don't you recognize me?"

"Gühler, *mensch!* Gühler! Well, are you with me?"

"What do you mean, with you?"

"Ah," said Santo, "of course you don't know. I'm in charge of this hut."

"Where's Buchwald?"

"They're all in a special hut—corporals and sergeants."

"Why is that?"

"Everything's run on strictly Prussian lines here. Noncoms together. Rank and file together."

"I see," said Gühler.

They walked along the row of sleeping forms. Santo went first. "Here's a free mattress," he said. "You can bed down there."

"Thank God!" said Gühler. "I'm dog tired." He took

153

off his greatcoat, rolled it up into a pillow, and threw himself down on the mattress.

"Did you just come in?" asked a voice next to him.

"Yes."

"Today?"

"Yes."

"What's it look like at the front?"

"Bad. We're going back all the time."

Gühler didn't say more. He was very tired. Everything seemed suddenly to become heavy and oppressive.

"Isn't that Gühler?" said someone. It was Konz. He crept over to Gühler's mattress and said, "Where have you been all this time?"

"Outside."

"What do you mean, outside?"

"They wanted to find out everything they could from me."

"Did you tell them anything?"

"No."

"Good. They're already keeping track of what you say around here."

"Who is?"

"A few crazy Nazis."

"Are there some of those kind here too?"

"They're all throwing their weight around again, now that they're here where it's safe."

"And you?"

"I've had a bellyfull."

"Where's Grundmann?"

"In the noncoms' hut."

"Prohaska and Maeder too?"

"Maeder's deputy camp leader. He's showing his muscle again."

154

Konz crawled back to his mattress. Gühler pulled off his boots and heaved over on his side. He felt the tension in his nerves gradually relaxing. But when he closed his eyes, the burning mountains closed in on him again.

"Hey, you," said the man next to him, "I thought you said you only came in today."

"No, four days ago."

"Then why did you say you only came in today?"

"I don't know."

"Are you afraid of the Nazis?"

"Perhaps," said Gühler.

The hut was quiet again. He heard Santo whispering to someone. Someone else was tossing about in his sleep shouting "Fire! Why don't you shoot? Fire!" Gühler closed his eyes.

"You can catch T.B. here," said the man next to him.

"T.B.?"

"They feed you twice a day and each time only enough to keep a cat alive."

"It'll be better in America."

"America?" said the other man. "That's just the hell of it. The transports are going to Africa and America. It's just a matter of luck whether you get on the right one."

"Africa?" asked Gühler.

"To the de Gaullists in the Sahara. They're building a railway there with prisoners of war."

"How do you know?"

"The first topic of conversation here from morning till night is food. The second is whether we leave to-morrow or the day after or God knows when, and whether we go to America or Africa."

155

"How long have you been here?"

"Two months."

"Oh, well," said Gühler slowly. "Then there's plenty of time." He drew up his knees and turned over on the other side.

Gühler awoke the next morning with a start. It was as if he were in a Prussian barrack room again.

"Out of bed!" someone was bellowing. "*Los!* Out of bed."

It was still only half light inside the hut. Dawn seeped in through the windows. Santo came across to Gühler and said, "Get up, Gühler, we've got to be counted."

"Counted?" asked Gühler.

He pulled on his boots, rolled up his greatcoat, and stood his mattress up on end as he saw the others doing. He went out with Santo. They fell in in front of the barrack ready to march off in fives. Under their arms they carried American mess kits.

"Quick march!" said Santo.

They marched across to the wide road running through the middle of the camp and there formed up according to huts. A noncom stood in front of each group as hut commander. A *Feldwebel* stepped out in front and shouted: "Attention!" Maeder was standing behind the *Feldwebel*. He looked washed and fresh, and the ribbon of the Iron Cross shone on his chest. An American soldier walked down the ranks counting the occupants in each hut. When the soldier had passed, the rear ranks began to fall out. "Stay where you are!" shouted Maeder.

No one paid any attention to him. They walked slowly off down the side streets of the camp, talking as they went. Konz who was standing beside Gühler said, "Come on, we've got to duck. This is when they assign the working parties."

Konz took a step backward into one of the rear ranks and disappeared. The *Feldwebel* came along with Maeder. Each had a notebook in his hand and made work assignments as they went.

"What about this one?" asked Maeder. He behaved as if he didn't see Gühler at all. He looked past him into the rear ranks and called out a few names. Santo went up to the *Feldwebel* and said, "This man's ill."

"He doesn't look it."

The *Feldwebel* looked up from his notebook and passed on.

"What does he mean, I'm ill?" Gühler wondered.

Maeder followed behind the *Feldwebel*, holding himself erect, his back rigid. Gühler stood motionless looking after him. Then Santo, who had been standing out in front all this time, turned around and said, "Let's go and have some coffee."

"Yes."

"Have you got a canteen?"

"No."

"We'll take both of mine."

Maeder stepped out in front again. He threw back his shoulders and shouted: "Attention!"

No one took any notice. They fell out and trotted across to the kitchen, where there already was an enormous line.

"Silly bastard," said someone behind Gühler.

In the kitchen they were given their rations and took them into the hut.

"Why did you say that I was ill?" said Gühler.

Santo looked at him and laughed. There was a glimmer of warmth in the dark eyes set deep under the low forehead.

"It's always good to have something wrong with you here. Have a good rest first."

Gühler spent all day lying on his mattress. He slept the whole time. In his few wakeful moments he saw the face of Santo, beside him, bending over him. Then came the fever. He felt it gradually getting control of him. The darkness gathered around him remorselessly. He was overcome by the darkness of forgetting. The experiences of the last few weeks sank below the surface of his consciousness. The war sank back into the night from which it had come.

Once when he woke up he found Grundmann sitting on his mattress.

"You must go to the hospital," he said.

Gühler sat up. He pushed back the blankets which Santo had got for him. He looked into Grundmann's calm face and said, "Thank God you're here."

"You've got a fever. Lie down. You must go to the hospital." And then, "The transports are leaving every day. We must try and stick together."

"To America?"

"Yes, we must go to America. I've made so many plans. Perhaps we'll be able to study over there. They say we can live quite freely there."

"What's the feeling in your hut?"

"Some of them are feeling their oats again. They're winning the war again now that they're safely out of the whole mess. But Buchwald and I return their fire whenever we can."

158

"What's Buschmann doing?"

"Telling heroic stories of the fighting on the mountain. But he shuts up pretty quick when I'm around. He doesn't feel any too chipper."

"Are there many Nazis with you?"

"Not many. Everybody talks pretty freely among us. All over the camp, too."

"Thank God," said Gühler, "we're free of it at last."

Grundmann went out. Gühler looked after his broad back with his head set almost directly on top of his body and thought, "He's made it." He pulled the blankets up over his head. He felt at peace.

He fell asleep.

XV

EVERY day they waited to be taken to America. Three times a day they fell in on the camp road and were counted. But as the weeks passed, the remnants of discipline collapsed. They sold their decorations, their antitank badges, their close-combat insignia, and their Iron Crosses to the Italian children who stood behind the fence offering fruit. The children snatched greedily at the Crosses, pushing apples through the wire in return. The children sold the badges to the American soldiers as souvenirs. Transports left every day. Every morning they ran to the board on which were posted the names of those due to leave that day. Sometimes they watched the air battles being fought over Naples. In the evenings they stood for hours in front of the kitchen, hoping for tidbits. They were patient as animals. They cursed Maeder who had become mess officer. They cursed the noncoms who brought the food to them. They cursed the war. But they waited patiently hour after hour, with their mess kits under their arms.

One evening Grundmann came over to Gühler, who

160

was standing in the line, and said, "We're off tomorrow."

"Are you sure?"

"Yes, and we're together. I've fixed it all with Maeder."

"Who else is coming?"

"Everyone: Buschmann, Buchwald, Konz, Beijerke—the whole bunch."

A shrill whistle came from the guard towers all around the camp.

"Air raid," said Grundmann.

Maeder came rushing out of the kitchen. He ran down the waiting line shouting, "*Los, los!* Off the road, off camp road!"

The long line slowly broke up. They made their way over to the huts and stayed there with their mess kits under cover of the eaves. They heard the barking of the antiaircraft guns all around Naples. Thousands of antiaircraft shells crossed the dark sky like red rain. Then the real rain began. It came down in thin streaks which beat against the walls of the huts. They put their mess kits under their coats and slipped inside the huts, hungry and tired.

"Tomorrow," said Grundmann. "Till tomorrow."

"Certain it'll be America?"

"You can bet on it."

Gühler went back into his hut. Santo sat on a table distributing two cigarettes to each man. The others sat there pulling contentedly on their cigarettes.

"We're off tomorrow," said Gühler to Santo.

"I know. I'm going too. It'll be better in America."

"No more Nazis, and freedom to do as you like."

"And to be able to read anything you want to again!" said Santo. "Anything. And say anything. Can you imagine it?"

"No," answered Gühler, "I can't imagine it any more."

"Neither can I," replied Santo.

One of the men sitting nearby, who still wore a beard and looked like a pirate, said, "You think America's a sort of never-never land?"

"Of course not," Santo answered. "But it's a democracy."

"You and your democracy. They'll have your ass in a sling in short order over there. Nothing but Jews and racketeers. They're practically done for, anyway. I give them two months—no longer."

Gühler looked into the speaker's bearded face and felt the fanatical eyes glaring at him. He nudged Santo who sat there without speaking. Then he said, "And why should they collapse?"

"So you really think they'll win the war? You're probably a traitor like those filthy Poles over there, who all deserted and now are having such a good time."

"I don't think so," said Gühler sitting down beside Santo. "It's just that I don't see why you think the Americans will collapse."

"Naturally, if we had nobody but people like you we'd lose the war tomorrow. But the rest of us have something to say about it too."

"Sure you have. But that's got nothing to do with the Americans collapsing."

"We'll finish them off with our U-boats. Their fleet is gone already. All they've got is a few old scows that they'll lose any day. And what about the strikes? Haven't you heard about the strikes?"

"That sounds a little far fetched to me."

"All right," said the bearded man. "You're just one of those. But we'll remember your names. You'll be coming home again."

"I hope you'll be coming home too," said Gühler. He stood up and nudged Santo. "Good night," he said. "There's no point in arguing with him."

"No," said Santo. "Good night."

The others sat there like lumps of soggy dough, without any will of their own. They stared ahead into the darkness, breathing heavily, saying nothing. Santo got up and said, "Well, haven't any of you got an opinion?"

No one answered him. They had pulled their caps down over their foreheads and planted their elbows on the table.

"I'm an Austrian," said one of them. "All that crap means nothing to me anymore."

"Go and join the Poles, then!" said the bearded man. "If you consider yourself an Austrian, then you belong with them."

Gühler made his way through the rows of sleeping men to his mattress. Behind him he heard someone say, "It's all a lot of shit. The Amis ought to give us more to eat and more cigarettes."

Gühler lay down on his mattress. Konz, who had changed mattresses and was now beside him, whispered, half in his sleep, "Tomorrow we're taking off for America."

"I know. Grundmann told me."

"I just can't imagine America. I only know it from

Indian stories. You know, prairies and cowboys and all that crap."

"It'll be different from that," whispered Gühler. "Very different. But it's rich and we'll have it good."

"Do you think so? I'm skeptical about everything."

"Why about everything?"

"One disappointment's enough to stop believing anything."

"What was your disappointment?"

"The war, the Nazis, Hitler, the whole lousy mess we went through. At first I thought one ought to enter into it all, be tough, endure, and all the rest of it. But now after that filthy time we had up there on the mountain, and all the equipment the Amis have got, those silly speeches they fed us—hell, it's all nothing but a big gyp."

"And what do you expect from America?"

"Nothing. Absolutely nothing. A bit more freedom than here. More to eat and more to smoke. Otherwise nothing."

"That's not bad considering we're prisoners."

"Oh, sure. But all I care about is to get home again, see?"

"Have you heard anything more of Filusch?"

"He was here, but he went off on one of the transports before we got here."

"To Africa and the de Gaullists?"

"Yes, they say that one went to Africa."

"Tough luck."

"That's what you get for deserting. One shouldn't be in too much of a hurry."

"So you know about it too?"

164

"Beijerke spends all his time blabbing about the way Filusch ran over to the Amis."

Gühler heard Santo going softly through the hut. He came past his mattress and said, "Till tomorrow."

The next morning Gühler got up before the barracks was awakened. The excitement of the coming journey had gripped him. He went into the washhouse and let cold water run over his head and body. The morning grew in a shimmering haze of red. The sky became clear and glassy. Gühler was standing on the camp road when suddenly the sound of approaching aircraft came from behind the railway embankment. He saw three fighters swoop across the embankment and fly low over the barrack roofs. They fired their machine guns at the road and into the huts. Gühler could see the black crosses under their wings. He threw himself to the ground beside the hut. Behind him some prisoners were cursing and swearing.

"The bastards," they shouted, "why don't they go and unload their shit somewhere else?"

Gühler's soap had fallen into the sand. He picked it up and went into the hut, which was humming with excitement.

"Were they really German?" asked Santo.

"Yes."

"They fired into the hut through the roof."

"A last farewell from home," said Gühler.

They were all talking at once. They cursed out loud and shouted at each other. Only the bearded man found an excuse for the planes.

"You're a fine lot of Germans," he said. "After all, they couldn't possibly know that we were down here."

"What about the red crosses on the roofs? I suppose they can't be seen from up there, for Christ's sake!" shouted Konz.

"You'd be smarter to keep your mouth shut," said the bearded man.

"We've kept our mouths shut long enough, you ugly bastard," said a fat little prisoner who, red and indignant, was rolling up his blankets.

Santo pushed his way into the quarrel and nudged the bearded man. "Next time keep your trap shut, see?"

Konz had the pale, cheesy look that he had had at the front. He stood beside the bearded man who was staring furiously at Santo.

"The swine," said Konz. "We never saw a sign of them at the front and now they come shooting us up here."

The hut quieted down again. They folded up their blankets and got ready to leave. They gave up their mess kits to Santo. Except for their haversacks they had no other baggage to take across the sea. They fell in on the camp road and waited for their names to be called out. They received a card with their transport number and hung these around their necks on bits of string. The labels made them look like cattle about to be shipped off. They stood patiently in the sun waiting for their names. Then they stepped forward and took their places in the order they were told. Maeder stood on a little dais, calling out the names.

"Grundmann," shouted Maeder.

"Here," shouted Grundmann.

He saw Grundmann step forward. He still had his helmet with him because he had left his cap behind at the front. Then Gühler heard his own name called and followed Grundmann.

"There you are," said Grundmann. "I didn't fix it badly, did I?"

"Very well," said Gühler.

"Maeder's a crackpot of course, but otherwise quite useful," said Grundmann.

The dividing up of the various transports lasted until the afternoon. Then the trucks drove into the camp. They picked up their things and climbed up. They drove off through the streets of Naples. The Italians came out of their houses or stopped in the streets as the trucks drove past. "*Tedeschi kaput!*" they shouted. "*Tedeschi kaput!*"

They threw rotten tomatoes at them. A young boy came running out of a house and threw a stone. A priest in a black soutane rushed out of the gate behind him and gave him a box on the ear. A woman lifted up her skirts. "Swine! Swine!" came the shouts from all sides.

Gühler who stood beside Grundmann behind the driver's cab watched the excited crowd in silence. A flying tomato hit Grundmann on the head. He wiped off the juice which had splashed onto his arm.

"No bricks yet, anyway," he said.

A group of young men threw some stones at the truck.

"We'll give you something to remember," one of them shouted.

"Got him in the back!" shouted another.

The American guards picked up their Tommy guns and pointed them threateningly at the excited mob.

There were shouts of "Swine! Swine!" and then again: "*Tedeschi kaput! Tedeschi kaput!*"

167

One of the Negro soldiers showed his white teeth and laughed. "Prisoners nix gut," he said.

The trucks drove slowly through the streets of the city toward the harbor. The crowd was full of hate and cursed them from the sidewalks. A powerful wave of revulsion and disgust came over Gühler. The trucks drove through a barrier into the harbor area. They stopped in front of a ship. Its dirty gray superstructure rose high above the quay.

An officer walked past their truck and spat at it. He did it slowly and carefully and there was a boundless contempt in his gesture. One after the other they climbed clumsily up to the deck of the ship. They still looked desolate and filthy in their ragged tunics and torn great-coats. Their faces were sunken and miserable. Two Negro cooks stood by the rail in white caps and white jackets laughing at their heavy-footed clumsiness. In contrast with the dazzling whiteness of the cooks' clothes, they looked like creatures from the jungle. One after the other they climbed into the open hatches and went down the steep ladder into the hold. American soldiers stood by the hatches with their Tommy guns leveled at them.

They found hammocks ready for them and fastened them to iron poles. Grundmann came up with two hammocks and said, "*Los!* We've got to get into a corner together."

They hooked their hammocks up side by side. Grundmann hung his steel helmet above him, rolled his great-coat up into a pillow, and threw himself into his hammock. "*Auf wiedersehen, Europa!*" he said.

Konz and Santo came and slung their hammocks on the tier above.

168

"If we get some decent chow here," said Konz, "they can keep sailing for four weeks for all I care."

"It won't be much longer than that," said Gühler.

Buchwald came along. He smiled at them with his bright little eyes. "Got your lifebelts yet?"

"Lifebelts?" asked Grundmann.

"In case of U-boats. Supposing we get torpedoed. At least they're thinking of our safety."

They lay on their hammocks and waited for the ship to move. The first meal was served in the evening.

"Thin," said Konz.

Santo, who had just come from the kitchen, clapped Konz on the shoulder.

"And you only get that twice a day."

"We'll starve," said Konz. They lay there waiting for the ship to sail. It became suffocating in the hold. The hatches were closed. Only some of the prisoners had got hammocks. The others lay on the floor, under the stairs, jammed up against each other all over the narrow hold.

Toward evening they heard shouts of command on deck. Then the gurgling of the water against the sides and the laboring of the engines.

"We're off," said Grundmann nudging Gühler who was lying on his back with his eyes open. "Do you feel kind of solemn, too?"

Gühler said nothing. He felt the ship heaving with the rhythm of the engines. It seemed to him like the deep breathing of some great beast just before it springs into the unknown.

XVI

THEY sailed through the Mediterranean. The hatches were opened only a few hours each day. When this happened they crowded onto the stairs and gulped in the fresh air. American soldiers stood by both hatches with Tommy guns trained on them. One morning they saw the coast of North Africa in the distant mists, but they were not allowed on deck. Day after day they sat in the stifling atmosphere of the hold. The rations got smaller and smaller. They lay on their hammocks, doubled up with hunger, hardly moving. Only when the hatches were opened did they stagger over to the stairs and push and shove against each other to try and get a glimpse of the sea. One night they sailed past Gibraltar. Grundmann had exchanged his steel helmet for cigarettes. They lay in their hammocks smoking.

"Why don't they let us on deck?" said Grundmann. "Are they still afraid of us?"

"They say a lot of people on earlier transports jumped overboard round here and tried to swim to the Spanish coast."

"Crazy," muttered Grundmann. "I wouldn't mind being that crazy once."

Searching his pocket for odds and ends of tobacco, Gühler found the little card with the Madonna on it that the woman had given him at the station before they left for the front. He looked curiously at the slanting handwriting.

"Do you know Italian?" he asked Grundmann.

"Not a word," said Grundmann.

"What do you know? Your English isn't much good either."

"What's the card?"

"A woman gave it to me when we left Terracina. But I can't read it."

"I'm not interested in women. I'm only interested in food. Just imagine a really delicious cutlet, about the size of a plate. . . ."

"Does Santo know Italian?"

"Ask him. I think so."

Santo leaned down from his hammock. "What do you want?" he said.

"Do you know Italian?"

"Yes, give it here."

Gühler handed up the card. He heard Santo murmuring above him. "Well?" said Gühler.

"Where'd you get this?"

"From Terracina. A little souvenir."

Santo jumped down from his hammock. By standing upright he was able to lay his arms on Gühler's hammock.

"I'll have to whisper it to you."

"Is it as important as all that?"

Gühler turned to him curiously and said, "She was

wonderful. She hated war and she hated us, but she made a distinction between the war and our country and the human beings in it. She had a thin face, quite thin."

"Oh, I know those Italian women," Santo laughed.

"No, you don't know any women like her. You don't find many like her in any nationality."

He saw her running through the fields again in front of him, running in the milky white light of the flares beneath the dark open sky.

"She hated us?"

"Yes, perhaps because she loved us. She hated our brutality and our megalomania. She knew that we'd lose the war and she hoped we would."

"The Nazis, you mean?"

"No, all of us stomping around her country in jack boots."

"But aren't we just as much opposed to the whole filthy business?"

"For her we were defending something that was a crime, even though we rejected that crime. Even though we fought against it."

Santo didn't answer. He turned over the little card with the picture of the Madonna on it.

"Anyway, she liked you."

"Why, what's on it?"

"It says, 'May Our Lady protect you in battle.'"

Gühler said nothing. He looked at Santo, took the card out of his hand, and stared at the slanted handwriting in wonder.

"Do you think, perhaps . . . no, it's ridiculous."

"A talisman?" said Santo. "A talisman works some-times."

Santo walked across the swaying room. He held onto

the hammocks for support and climbed over the bodies lying on the floor. Gühler held the card in his hands. He saw before him the dark eyes he had last seen in the station as he was leaving Terracina. No, he hadn't behaved well then. He should have said something kind and comforting to her, but he had done nothing except stammer.

"May Our Lady protect you," he thought. "Our Lady."

He took the little card and put it into his breast pocket. He heard Grundmann murmuring through some English words beside him. He had collected a whole list of English words and written them out. Grundmann had got the idea into his head that he was going to study at an engineering college when they got to America. He had forgotten that they were prisoners.

At nights they sat for hours in the latrine talking about America. The war receded further and further into the background. Sometimes they argued about politics. It wasn't often that a voice was raised in favor of Hitler.

"Hitler isn't worth the powder to blow him up," said a little Berliner once after a heated discussion. He ran around the hold in a long *Luftwaffe* coat arguing wherever he went. A few paratroopers who were in the latrine protested. But the protest in favor of Hitler was hesitant and half hearted.

"He's all washed up, anyway," said Buchwald, whose hate grew more and more explicit every day.

One of the paratroopers came over and said, "You ought to be ashamed of yourselves."

Buchwald let out a great snort of laughter. But the noise around him almost drowned his laughter. The ship

173

rolled heavily and the sea water splashed up in the latrines.

"Ashamed!" shouted Buchwald. "It's about time the others were ashamed, the one's who've made such a rotten mess of everything."

"Pay no attention to them. They're batty," said the little Berliner who was called Pips.

Gühler didn't often take part in the discussions. He had long conversations with Grundmann and Santo on their hammocks. But he noticed the thawing out of political apathy which gradually took place on the whole ship.

It was two weeks before they were allowed on deck. They climbed out of the hold carrying their blue life-belts. Foaming white crests stretched to the horizon. The ship rolled heavily in the troughs. Torpedo boats chased in and out among the ships. They could see the sailors standing on the decks laughing as they dashed past.

"Heil Hitler!" the sailors shouted and thrust their arms up in salute, laughing.

The prisoners looked down at them in silence. No one returned the laugh.

"Balls!" Grundmann shouted back once, unable to contain himself any longer.

"For them we're all Nazis," said Gühler. "No use getting excited."

There were many submarine alarms. They put on their lifebelts and, cursing and swearing, staggered up on deck into the night.

"They surely wouldn't torpedo ships carrying prisoners," said Grundmann.

"You can't tell the difference in a convoy," answered Gühler.

174

The rations became more and more meager. They sold everything they still possessed to the American crew—watches, decorations. The *Feldwebels* and other non-coms sold their silver epaulets and many of them tore off the eagle-and-swastika insignia from their tunics and bartered them as souvenirs. They were hungry.

When Christmas Eve came they had been at sea almost four weeks.

"What'll happen this evening?" they said during the afternoon. "Will the Amis give us any sort of treat?"

When evening came they lay in their hammocks or sat on the floor waiting for the miracle. They had no tree, no candles, nothing to remind them of Christmas. Just as on every other day they stood in long lines in front of the kitchen. The rations were the same as always. They lay hungry in their hammocks. A diffused, murky light filled the room. Two Skat players sat on the floor, knocking on it sharply from time to time.

"What a Christmas!" Grundmann whispered.

Gühler clasped his hands behind his head and thought of past Christmases. One he had spent in Poland, another in a cattle car on a troop train. They had sung in the cattle car and looked up at the stars above the rattling train. He lifted his foot and gently prodded the hammock above him.

"What are you thinking about, Santo?"

"About my little daughter," said Santo, leaning out of his hammock. "She'll be standing under the Christmas tree now. She was eight yesterday."

"What does she look like?"

Santo smiled to himself.

"Oh, quite cute, curly brown hair. She's got my eyes,

you know. And she wrinkles up her nose when she laughs. But she's pretty smart, my little girl—you've got to watch yourself with her."

"How long since you saw her?"

"Oh, a good two years," said Santo. "I don't like to think about it. Say two years a prisoner—that makes four years."

"Perhaps you'll get home quicker than that. The Americans will soon release us."

"Let's hope they finish the whole thing off soon."

Suddenly there was a *Feldwebel* standing in the middle of the room. A couple of noncoms stood behind him.

"Quiet!" they roared.

There was absolute quiet in the suffocating room. The Skat players, still holding their cards, turned toward the *Feldwebel*.

"Here it comes," whispered Gühler. "The Christmas miracle." In a corner a mess kit rattled. A metallic, grinding voice filled the room. The *Feldwebel* was speaking.

"Comrades, it is Christmas Eve—the fourth war Christmas. At this great hour when danger threatens the Fatherland . . ."

A restless wave of protest ran through the hammocks.

"Who the hell is this?" said a high, clear voice.

". . . let us remember our dear ones at home, but remember also him who is leading Germany to victory . . ."

"Balls," said one of the Skat players. "Come on, let's play." They turned around and slapped their cards on the floor.

"Quiet!" yelled one of the noncoms.

"Shut up, we don't want to listen to that crap,"

shouted someone from the corner where Grundmann lay.

"This could get lively," whispered Grundmann.

". . . our *Führer* Adolf Hitler . . ."

A chorus of whistles started up in one corner.

"Shut up!" they shouted. "Shut up!"

The *Feldwebel* looked around furiously. A fat cook came running out of the kitchen, waving a soup spoon.

"We don't want to hear any more of that shit!" he shouted. "We don't want to hear it, see?"

A roar of applause broke out in one corner.

"*Heil!*" someone shouted, and laughed. In another corner someone in a hammock kept banging a spoon against a mess kit. The Skat players shouted "Grand slam, down with their pants!"

"Yes, down with their pants, down with them!" shouted Buchwald, almost beside himself with rage. Gühler and Grundmann looked down at the uproar. The *Feldwebel's* mouth was opening and shutting:

". . . to our leader Adolf Hitler a threefold victory . . ."

"*Heil!*" answered one quavering voice. Even the noncoms were silent.

"*Sieg heil!*" shouted the *Feldwebel*.

"Throw 'im out! Throw 'im out!" shouted Pips, who was standing behind the *Feldwebel* in his long *Luftwaffe* greatcoat. The paratroopers slowly pushed their way through to the *Feldwebel*. They looked threateningly around the room. The *Feldwebel* started up the *Horst Wessel* song. He had a high, shaky voice. The paratroopers joined in, then the noncoms.

On all sides there were shouts of "Shut up! Shut up!"

The Poles, whose hammocks were close to Gühler's,

began to sing a Polish Christmas carol. Their voices rose deep and melodious above the harsh rhythm of the *Horst Wessel*.

"There'll be a brawl in a minute," said Grundmann. "Some merry Christmas!"

They heard Santo singing above them. "*Stille Nacht, heilige Nacht ...*" he sang.

"*Los!*" said Grundmann. "Everyone join in. We'll sing them out of the room."

They joined in *Stille Nacht*. The Poles beside them stopped their own carol and added their voices. Slowly the song grew. More and more voices joined in. Their singing swelled up loud and full throated. Grundmann and Gühler nearly sang themselves hoarse: "*Stille Nacht, heilige Nacht ...*" Then the whole ship was singing. The *Horst Wessel* stopped abruptly. They saw the *Feldwebel* walk away with a furious shrug of the shoulders. No one bothered about him any more. Even the paratroopers and the noncoms were singing along now.

Gühler stretched himself out on his hammock and was silent. He listened to the carol which was now being sung devoutly, with feeling. He found himself thinking again about the woman in the little hut at Terracina.

"The Madonna," he thought. "Perhaps it was the Madonna after all."

He saw the woman sitting alone in the little hut, her arms across her knees, one of the millions of women who waited in vain with empty hearts.

He heard Grundmann singing beside him. He sang with a deep, inner fervor. He took the picture out of his pocket and looked at it again.

The carol ended, but in the murky light the melody still seemed to be there, inaudible in the room. The Skat players had put their cards away and were lying on the floor. No one spoke. Gühler heard Grundmann gulping beside him. He sat up a little and looked at him.

"What's the matter? Homesick?" he whispered.

Grundmann didn't answer. He pulled the blanket over him without speaking. Then the Poles began singing. They sang softly, almost humming, only for themselves, as if they were alone on the ship. No one said anything.

Gühler lay there musing about the songs that the Poles continued to sing from their hammocks. He heard Santo whisper above him, "If they only knew at home that we were prisoners. That would be the best Christmas for them."

"They'll know by now."

"If they could see us here in our hammocks."

"Can't you just picture your Christmas tree and all the things round it?"

"Yes," said Santo. "If I close my eyes I can see everything: the little girl with her things—she'd be in bed by now I suppose—"

"They'll see us like that too," said Gühler.

Beside him Grundmann whispered, "God, this war! This lousy, rotten war."

"Forget it," said Gühler. "There's still plenty ahead of you, a whole lifetime."

"You're right," he whispered and pulled his blanket over him again.

There was silence. Gühler pulled his blanket over his head. He felt the hunger in his stomach, a hollow biting pain. But he thought, "The carol was stronger than hunger." He heard the melody echoing inside him, crude, rough, sung by five hundred hungry prisoners.

Then the candles started moving toward him, thousands of candles which slowly engulfed the ship. He saw the faded Madonna picture above him and behind it the face of the lonely woman at Terracina. The faces merged into one another, altered, and were suddenly the face of his mother. He fell asleep.

XVII

THEY awoke the next morning out of the deep stillness that filled the whole ship. Nothing moved. The rhythmic pulsing of the engines had stopped. The eternal slapping of the waves against the sides of the ship had ceased. The German in charge of the transport stood on the stairway and shouted, "Ready to move!"

They jumped out of their hammocks, put on their greatcoats, and folded up their blankets. The hatches above both stairways were open. The dirty gray of a dawning winter's day poured in through the hatchways. Gühler scoured the last remnants of tobacco out of his pockets and stuffed them into his pipe.

"Where do you think we are?" said Grundmann, who was still lying in his hammock.

"In America," said Santo.

"Don't be silly. I mean, whereabouts in America?"

The commands of the German officer came down the stairs.

"Fall in on deck, by units!"

They followed each other up the stairs onto the deck. A cold, overcast December morning awaited them. They saw the flat wooden sheds on land, and the cranes, and behind them the white smoke of a locomotive. A few ships were lying in the river mouth, gray and motionless.

"America," whispered Grundmann.

Gühler said nothing. He looked at the country that stretched before him into the distance, empty and monotonous and dotted with hills. The trees on the hills stood bare beneath the heavy, leaden sky. The wide, dirty river wound off into the landscape. They crowded on deck and arranged themselves according to the numbers on the white transport cards which they still carried on their chests. The morning wind blew cold across the sea, making them shiver. But they only stared out into the wide, flat country that seemed to them endless and full of mystery.

A river steamer set out toward them from the shore. Thick black smoke from its funnel streamed low over the flat surface of the water. Amid the wooden barracks by the side of the road they saw a tall Christmas tree with huge green, red, and yellow glass balls on it.

"Christmas morning," said Gühler to Buchwald who stood behind him looking uneasily at the ship's whistle, which was letting out a thin white cloud of steam. Buchwald bent toward him and said, "Now we're finished with the Nazis."

The dark, humming sound of the whistle gushed across the water and disappeared among the hills. The river steamer came alongside. They heard the calls of the sailors and the officers shouting commands. Then the first of them began to file off. They watched the boat steam across to the harbor. They stood jammed close

182

against each other, freezing and waiting. A thin, drizzling rain fell from the leaden sky. They watched the steamer come back again and heard the same shouts and words of command as before.

The wooden ladder by which they climbed down to the steamer was wet and slippery. A couple of civilians stood on deck looking at them curiously.

"Where have you come from?" asked one of them.

"Italy," answered Gühler.

He was given a cigarette, which he put in his pocket. The shameful feeling of being a beggar, of entering this country as a beggar, grew in him as they stood among the red armchairs in the cabin, forbidden to sit down.

When they reached the harbor they were taken into a barrack. They marched across the street in their filthy boots and torn greatcoats with the old haversacks slung around them. Civilians stood in the street laughing at them. But the prisoners stared at the ground in front and didn't look at them.

In the barrack an American soldier made a short speech in German. He said that they were prisoners in a free country, that nothing would happen to them here, that they would get everything they needed, but that they had to conduct themselves according to the customs of this country. Then they had to undress, give up their clothes, and walk naked through a room where they were deloused. The steam of the delousing spray was hot against their bodies. They waited in the next room for their clothes, naked and wedged up against each other on narrow benches. In the late afternoon they were taken to the station. The light of the tall arc lamps seeped down through the misty rain. They went past tall Pullman cars which seemed to them the very symbol of peace.

"Don't tell me we're going in one of those!" said Grundmann.

They were all together again: Buchwald, Santo, Grundmann, and Gühler. They stood beside the train looking into the brightly lit cars.

"Those aren't for us," said Buchwald. "There'll be a couple of cattle cars waiting for us somewhere."

They heard someone shout the order: "Entrain!"

They tore open the doors and plunged into the cars which were high and narrow, with upholstered seats. There were three tins of food on every seat. They fell back against the upholstery and laughed aloud. The warmth of the seats came pleasantly through their clothes. Huge raindrops ran down the windowpanes. Grundmann said, "It's beginning well."

They opened the tins. An officer came down the aisle and asked if they had anything to smoke. They didn't answer at first. Then Santo said, "No, we haven't had anything to smoke for weeks."

The officer shook his head in puzzlement and disappeared. A soldier came along with a large cardboard carton and threw each man a packet of cigarettes.

Slowly the train steamed out of the station into the night. At both exits to the car an American soldier stood by the open lavatory door, swinging a wooden truncheon. Buchwald came back from the lavatory and said, "I just can't shit with someone watching like that." They all laughed and smoked their cigarettes and lay back lazily in their seats.

During the night they pulled out their seats and lay down to sleep. Only Gühler stayed sitting up. He looked out at the dark night flying past the window and found it impossible to sleep. He saw the gay illuminated advertisements in the streets, the brightly lit windows of the houses, and behind every one of them the Christmas trees with their great, colored ornaments. Pips sat asleep opposite him. He had discarded the long *Luftwaffe* coat and looked like a boy of seventeen. His head drooped on his chest. His mouth hung open. His hair had begun to fall over his forehead, and two glowing spots of red had formed on his cheeks.

An officer came through the car, stopped in front of the sleeping figure, and shook his head. He looked at Pips for a moment and then passed on. Gühler stared out of the window again. A small blockhouse flew past. It lay in a sort of rainbow light with numerous automobiles standing in front of it. Then he saw the officer coming back with some slabs of chocolate in his hand. He stopped in front of Pips and stuffed them carefully into his pockets. Pips didn't move. The officer went softly away. The next morning when Pips discovered the chocolate he jumped up and danced around the train.

"Didn't I always say that we'd get everything we wanted in America?" he shouted.

They journeyed farther and farther into America. All day they looked out of the window at the little wooden houses flying past, with elegant automobiles parked in front of them. They saw the tractors at work in the fields, crossed the hills of Virginia, passed through Chicago and St. Louis. They saw the dilapidated Negroes' huts in St. Louis with dirty washing hanging out on the verandas, and stared in amazement at the big cars that stood in front of some of the huts.

They got out of the train that evening. In front of

them they saw the barracks town lit by searchlights, bright with the light of a thousand arc lamps. They fell in beside the train. American soldiers took charge of them. One of the soldiers stood in front of Buchwald and said, "You'll do all right over there. A regular sanitarium for you."

"Well," said Buchwald, "I don't quite believe that."

"Cheeks like this in four weeks," the soldier said, puffing out his cheeks.

"That'd be nice," answered Buchwald.

"You'll be home for next Christmas."

"An optimist," said Buchwald.

Gühler looked at the soldier and then over at the brightness of the camp. He had the feeling that a whole new life, full of untold possibilities, lay before him.

Words of command came out of the night. They turned around and marched toward the bright camp. They marched in fives, with tired dragging steps. The hunger of recent months had worn them down. The fever of the front still burned in their sunken faces.

American officers stood by the barbed-wire gate counting them. One column after another marched past them into the camp. A Christmas tree reared high into the darkness behind the gate, gleaming with a thousand lights. They marched past the Christmas tree down the main road of the camp.

Prisoners from the camp, packed shoulder to shoulder, lined the sides of the road. They all wore the same blue coats and blue caps, which looked like sou'westers in the darkness. They stood there in silence, like a wall. Not a word of welcome, not a sign of greeting, not a shout escaped their ranks.

"Deserters!" Gühler heard someone whisper beside him. He looked at the hostile faces in astonishment but said nothing. He sensed the threat that emanated from the silent wall. They marched faster and faster down the long road.

"Traitors!" came the whisper from the dark ranks all around them. "Deserters! Cowards!"

"They must be crazy," said Buchwald, who was marching beside Gühler.

"They're *Afrika Korps*," said Pips behind him.

"Where are you from?" one of them asked Pips.

"Italy," Pips replied.

"Deserted, eh? Deserted. Well, we'll soon put you straight again!"

"Shut up," he heard Pips say.

The dark wall pressed in on them, cold and hostile and full of hate.

"What's it all about?" said Grundmann.

"They think we're deserters," answered Gühler.

They marched past the sou'westers, still bent, tired, hungry, and apathetic. Beside the broad, solid figures in the blue coats they looked like starved and hapless outcasts.

"Deserters! Cowards! Traitors!" came the mutters all about them.

"A nice reception," said Buchwald. "They all seem to be Nazis."

"The reward of the front-line soldier," said Santo.

They marched on in silence. They felt as if they were running the gauntlet. The thick-packed wall of blue-clad prisoners stretched out before them as far as they could see.

"The dirty bastards," whispered Pips behind Gühler. Gühler turned round and nudged him. "Be quiet," he said.

None of them said a word. They walked gloomily through the narrow lane of silence from which they heard only the words: "Traitors! Deserters! Cowards!"

At the end of the road they were taken into a barrack. They took off their clothes and threw them into a pile. An American soldier said, "Throw it all away. Everything's new here."

They walked naked into the shower room. Grundmann and Gühler stood under a shower and let the hot water pour over their bodies. The porcelain basins gleamed white all the way down the long washroom. The mirrors shone on the walls.

"Life'll be all right here," said Grundmann. Gühler said nothing for a moment. He looked at Grundmann's squat body beside him and felt the optimism that it gave off almost physically. He said, "I didn't like the reception."

"Oh, they're crazy."

"Maybe they're not crazy—just goaded into it."

"Nazis, you mean?"

"Not all of them of course. But a lot of them, and probably the ones who set the tone here."

"But they should be cured by now, man!"

"Perhaps it's broken out again here. Maybe they became Nazis here for the first time."

"They're all *Afrika Korps*, they say."

"*Afrika Korps* or not, I don't like those fanatical faces."

They went out of the washroom into one of the bar-

188

racks. They put on clean underclothes and looked like newly dressed children to each other. They were given the same blue uniform that the others had been wearing. Buchwald came up to them and said, "We must see that we stick together when they divide us into barracks."

They went down the camp road in their new clothes and were taken to their barracks. The beds stood one above the other in the huts—steel frames with soft mattresses.

"We'll sleep all right here, man," said Grundmann.

They tried out the mattresses and bounced happily up and down on them. Then they formed up in front of the barrack again and marched over to the kitchen. As they entered they stopped for a moment in astonishment. Tables covered with white cloths stood before them. Behind the tables sparkled a Christmas tree. Mountains of cakes, fruit, vegetables, eggs, and butter—everything for which they had been yearning for so long was waiting for them on the tables.

"Didn't I tell you—America!" said Grundmann.

They stood there for a moment and then fell upon the tables and began to eat.

"Look," said Buchwald after a while, "I've talked to one of them. He said a lot of us didn't have the eagle and swastika on our tunics, and besides we were taken prisoner in Italy. Only deserters could be taken prisoner there."

"How so?"

"Well, in Tunis they didn't have any ammunition left and they surrendered on orders, because they couldn't be evacuated across the sea. But there was no such order in Italy and anyway it would have been easy to avoid being taken."

"Idiocy," said Grundmann. "Pure idiocy."

Santo just looked at Gühler with his warm bright eyes and smiled.

"Let's concentrate on the sausages," he said. He picked up his plate, went over to the serving counter, and came back with three sausages. Then he said slowly, "I'd advise you to be more careful here. There's no point in riling them. Apparently they all think Hitler's winning the war."

"Idiots," said Buchwald.

Santo laughed good-naturedly. He picked up a sausage, leaned across the table, and stuffed it into Gühler's mouth.

"What do you think?" he said.

"I don't like it at all," said Gühler. "There's the atmosphere of a concentration camp about it. Don't you know those faces? That's how they looked in 1933. Fanatical and capable of anything."

"You gloomy old bastard," said Grundmann.

Pips came over to their table. He looked almost like a child.

"What do you think of the chow, eh?"

Santo stood up and whispered something into his ear.

"Why?" Pips answered aloud.

"Better for you and better for all of us," said Santo.

Santo sat down again. Pips patted Santo confidentially on the back and went over to the counter.

"What did you say to him?" asked Gühler.

"Nothing," said Santo. "Only that he ought to keep his mouth shut."

They ate cutlets, pineapple, and oranges, and smeared the butter thickly on slices of white bread.

190

"Where are Beijerke, Konz, and the others?" asked Gühler.

"Over with the first battalion," said Grundmann. "Most of our people are with the first battalion. We're almost the only ones in this barrack."

They went back to their barrack. Searchlights played on the roofs from the guard towers stationed all round the camp. It was dark on the camp road, which was frozen hard and smooth. Their barrack lay some distance away, by the great barbed-wire gate near the American headquarters.

"That's where the Poles are," said Grundmann pointing to the first three barracks on the other side of the road.

"Separated again?"

"Yes, in so far as they've said they're Poles."

As they went into the barrack they met Prohaska.

"Well, well," said Gühler. "What are you doing here?"

"Barrack commander," he said, "for the time being. Then you're getting a *Feldwebel*."

"It wouldn't work without a *Feldwebel*, I suppose."

"No," said Prohaska. "Everything's nicely arranged according to rank again, here."

They undressed and lay down on their beds. Prohaska came through, seeing that everyone was in bed.

"The Amis will be coming in to count in a minute," he said.

At ten o'clock the lights went out. Grundmann lay in the bed above Gühler. "*Mensch*, am I glad to be able to rest at last!"

"What about the studying?"

"That'll come yet. You'll see."

An American soldier came through the barrack. He walked quickly, lighting up each face with his flashlight as he passed. He counted out loud to himself.

"O.K.," he said to Prohaska, who walked along behind him.

XVIII

THE next day Gühler and Grundmann walked across the camp to the soccer field. They walked slowly through the various streets of the camp, looking at the barracks, which were of one story only, built flat on the ground. There were fifty men to each hut. From the soccer field they could see the whole camp. There were over a hundred barracks standing behind a double row of barbed wire. The prisoners loitered on the field in their blue coats, watching a game of soccer.

They walked slowly along the line. They felt the same hostile glances following them again. "There go two of them," they heard someone say behind them. It sounded contemptuous and scornful. They stopped a moment behind the lines to watch the soccer game. Someone turned around in front of them and said, "Two of the new ones." Again the same scorn and contempt.

"I'm not staying here," said Gühler.

"Come on," answered Grundmann, "let's go back."

The gray sky hung low over the open plain. Thin black smoke came from the barracks' chimneys and moved away flatly across the roof-tops. A few snow-flakes danced in the air.

"Winter's coming," said Grundmann.

They went up the camp road. Buschmann came down it toward them. "Well," he said, "settled in all right?" He fixed them sharply with his bright little eyes.

"Not quite yet," said Gühler. "Everything's still too new."

"What, you don't like it here? But it's wonderful. The food! And the morale here! They've got the Amis just where they want them, I can tell you!"

Gühler didn't say anything. He looked at Buschmann's bowlegs. He was wearing an enormous pair of rubber boots.

"Nice pair of boots you've got," he said slowly and emphatically.

Grundmann looked at Gühler and laughed ironically.

"What's the dirty laugh for?" asked Buschmann.

"Your boots are a bit too big," said Grundmann.

"Mm, yes. I'll have to get them changed."

They said no more. They shook hands with Buschmann and watched him hurry away on his bowlegs toward the soccer field. "We'll have to be careful with that one," said Gühler. Grundmann nodded. They walked slowly across to their barrack. As they went through the door they were met by the sounds of excited conversation. They heard Buchwald's voice. He was telling jokes. "The secret weapon!" he said. "The white flag is the secret weapon!"

One of the old prisoners was standing beside Buchwald. He was broadly built and wore his coat collar turned up.

"Why didn't you chase the Amis out of Italy? If we'd

194

been there they would have got what was coming to them."

Gühler went up to them. He nudged Buchwald before he could answer and said, "Well, about chasing people out—it's not so easy without artillery or planes."

"Don't try to tell us you didn't have any artillery."

"Just as little as you had in Tunis."

"But you had ammunition. Your supplies at least were functioning."

"No, we didn't have ammunition."

Gühler felt the gray eyes stabbing at him out of the blurred face.

"And how did you get taken prisoner?"

"The way prisoners are usually taken."

"Don't give me that stuff, man. You simply don't get taken prisoner fighting on a land front unless you desert or throw in the towel."

"Perhaps you can't go on."

" 'Can't go on'! There's no such thing with us."

Gühler turned around. Pips was standing beside him, very excited and red in the face.

"Come off it," he said. "You don't know what the hell you're talking about."

"Shut up, Pips," said Gühler.

The other man went slowly out of the barracks. At the door he turned calmly and deliberately around and said, "We'll talk more about this." He shut the door behind him.

"Any more of them in the hut?" asked Gühler.

Buchwald got up from his bed. "What do they want with us?"

"Don't you see?" answered Gühler. "They want to cross-examine us."

Gühler went over to Pips and sat down on his bed. He had bought himself some English language books from the canteen, and was copying out some of the words.

"I'm going to a class tomorrow," he said. "I want to learn English quickly, you know. Maybe you can study for a school certificate here."

"Sure, but it takes time."

"Oh, I can stick it out. I've got a lot to catch up on. I went to a National Socialist leaders' school but we didn't learn a thing there except how to stand at attention."

"An NS leaders' school?" said Gühler.

"My old man wanted me to go, you know. But I got fed up. The old man was too cowardly. He used to curse them all at home, but me—I had to go to the leaders' school."

"What are you going to do when you get back?"

"Oh, it'll all be different then. The Nazis'll lose the war. That's sure."

"Are you certain?"

"Sure. I'm not goofy."

He looked at Gühler and laughed. His full rosy upper lip was set very close under his little snub nose.

Gühler said, "There are plenty of Nazis in the camp."

"So I've noticed."

"I wouldn't go around telling everybody that we're losing the war."

"Hitler's losing the war. We aren't."

"Exactly. But I wouldn't say that so openly."

"That's what Santo said."

"Don't you think he's right?"

"We're in America, after all, we can speak freely

again. To hell with these idiots running around here. The Amis will help us if they try any tricks."

"Just the same," said Gühler, "be careful who you talk to."

He left Pips alone and went over to his bed. During the afternoon they were counted again. Then they were summoned to the battalion orderly room, had their names entered on the list, and received an invitation for a performance in the camp theater.

They went to the theater that evening. It was a long narrow room with a large stage. Everything was very smart and well looked after, rather like a cinema in a small German town. The first three rows consisted of red leather armchairs. This was where the important people in the camp sat: the battalion commanders, the company commanders, the *Feldwebel*, and *Oberfeldwebel*. They wore full uniform, and their medals shone on their chests.

"They're putting on the dog again," said Buchwald, who was sitting beside Gühler in one of the rows at the back. Gühler said nothing. The atmosphere, which was strange and cold and very military, depressed him. Pips sat on the other side of him. He sat there silently, lost in thought, staring in front of him. Gühler leaned over to him and said, "What's wrong?"

"They've squealed on me."

"Who?"

"The paratroopers on the ship."

"How do you know?"

"Shh," whispered Pips.

The show was beginning on the stage. Gühler hardly

paid any attention to it. He leaned over to Pips again in the darkness and said, "Who told you that?"

"Shh, they're right behind us."

Gühler turned around unobtrusively. The prisoners were standing two rows behind them. He looked at their faces in the half light. They were the brutal faces of thugs. He knew those cold cruel eyes, those foreheads with nothing but hate behind them. He knew those faces. They were the same everywhere. He could have detected them however dark it was and from any crowd however large.

"What do they want with you?"

"I don't know," answered Pips.

"Why won't you tell me anything?"

"Be quiet, they can hear us."

"Are you afraid?"

"They're watching me all the time, can't you see?"

Gühler looked at the stage on which three tap dancers were performing. He had the feeling of being under observation himself. He could not forget the faces in back of him. During the intermission one of them came through the rows of chairs to Pips and said, "You. Come outside."

Pips got up and followed them out. Gühler didn't turn around. He stayed quietly where he was as if he hadn't noticed anything.

"What do they want with him?" asked Buchwald.

"I don't know," said Gühler. "Perhaps he's wanted at the orderly room."

Ten minutes later Pips came back. He made his way along the row looking very pale and small and sat down in his place in silence. He said nothing. Gühler nudged him. "What is it?" he whispered.

Pips answered very quietly. He hung his head as if he were whispering to his knees.

"Don't ask me. They're watching to see if I say anything."

The curtain rose on the stage. The lights went out. Gühler leaned forward a little and said, "What did they want with you?"

"They want me to tell them which of us are not Nazis. They know that I said on the ship that Hitler wasn't worth the powder to blow him up. They say they'll beat me to death if I don't give them the names."

"Did you tell them?"

"No."

"Will you tell?"

"No."

"You must get out of the camp and go to the Americans."

"They said if I went to the Americans they'd hang me at once. Besides, they said they've got their friends over in headquarters and they hear everything that goes on."

"I see," whispered Gühler. "Terror. Naked terror."

He was seized by a helpless rage. He felt his hands shaking. He didn't hear a word that was said on the stage, but he sat quiet and motionless looking at the stage.

"I'm scared," whispered Pips.

Gühler felt the faces staring at his back again. He knew what was going on inside those heads. He knew their eternally unsatisfied sadism. But he said, "They wouldn't dare lay hands on you."

"Don't let them see that you know me," whispered

Pips again. "I've told them I only know you slightly. They want to know who you are."

"You didn't tell them?"

"No, I said I only got to know you two days ago."

They were silent again. Pips had put his hands between his knees and was staring at the floor. On the stage someone was singing to a guitar. It was an American song, sung in a nasal voice. He heard the prisoners clapping. The lights went on.

"Wonderful," said Buchwald beside him.

The whole audience stood up and applauded loudly.

"Come on," said Gühler to Pips. "We'll beat it before they notice."

They pushed their way quickly out of the hall. Behind them the prisoners were still applauding loudly. "More! Encore! More!" they shouted.

A dark icy night was waiting for them outside. They went up the main road of the camp. Gühler had taken Pips' arm. Pips' figure was small and bent beside him.

"Are you cold?"

"Yes, I'm cold."

They went into their barrack, which was brightly lit but completely empty. Pips sat down on his bed and said, "What should I do?"

Gühler didn't know what to say. He walked up and down in front of Pips with his hands in his pockets. Suddenly it struck him for the first time that the hut was empty. The feeling of being completely alone overwhelmed him.

"Where are they all?"

"In the theater, of course."

"All of them?"

Pips didn't answer.

"What'll I do when they come?"

"Aw, they won't come. It's all bluff."

"Yes, they will. I know they'll come."

"How do you know?"

"They came for my brother once. He had always been against them and said something he shouldn't. They looked exactly like that then. They beat him and I was still young and screamed with fright. Then they dragged him away. They were just the same. They had exactly the same eyes. They'll come. I know they will."

Slowly the door began to open. Gühler whipped his head around and looked at the door. Suddenly it flew open. He saw Pips shrink into himself. He saw his eyes open wide with fear.

"Help me!" he whispered.

They came in—broad-shouldered, bull-necked with cold, fanatical eyes. They came with heavy steps one behind the other. Gühler sensed the atmosphere of terror. He felt the fear constricting his breath. But then he went suddenly cold inside, like ice. He watched their movements as if he were watching them on a screen. His thoughts were clear and calm and he noticed every gesture. He counted them. There were twenty of them.

Pips still sat on his bed, pale, his eyes full of dread. He stared at them. They arranged themselves around him.

"This has nothing to do with you, understand?" one of them said to Gühler. They pushed him aside.

"What do you want with him?" said Gühler.

"You'll soon see," answered one of the two who stood in front of him.

"Did you say that Hitler wasn't worth the powder to

blow him to hell?" shouted one of them, standing directly in front of Pips.

Pips didn't answer. He kept his head down and said nothing.

"I asked you if you said that Hitler wasn't worth the powder to blow him to hell?"

"No," whispered Pips. "No, I didn't say it."

"We'll make you tell the truth quick enough." He raised his fist and hit Pips in the face. Pips swayed a little and remained sitting where he was.

"All right. Speak up!"

"No," said Pips. "No."

The speaker raised his fist again and hit him on the nose and then under the chin. Pips began to whimper.

"The swine," said another. "Kill him!"

He raised his fist and hit Pips on the head from the side. Pips flew back onto the bed.

"Did you say that Hitler wasn't worth the powder to blow him to hell?" roared the man who had spoken first.

Pips said nothing. Blood ran out of his nose and over his mouth.

"What the hell's the point of all this?" said Gühler.

The two men in front of him turned around and pushed him onto the bed opposite.

"One move out of you, boy, and you'll get the same."

Then they all began beating Pips. Gühler heard him scream.

"Let me have a crack at him," said one of them. "I haven't had a crack in a long time."

He was wearing knuckle dusters. The others stood aside. The man with the knuckle dusters raised his fist and hit Pips with them. Pips collapsed on the bed. But they dragged him up again and continued beating him.

The blood streamed over his face. His head drooped lifelessly on his chest. As the blows rained down on his head it flew this way and that as if it no longer belonged to his body. They all took turns slugging him. Then they lifted him high and hurled him to the floor.

"Kill him! Beat him to death!" shouted one of them, kicking the unconscious body with his boot.

"He's had enough," said the spokesman.

They took hold of Pips by the legs and dragged him out of the barrack. The bloody head bumped hard against the floor as they went.

"Are you one too?" said one of the men who were holding Gühler. He had a broad, flat face into which the eyes were set like two senseless buttons. Gühler looked at him and said nothing.

"Well, you'll all have your turn. We're going to clean up the lot of you."

Gühler said nothing. There was no use in saying anything. He was afraid. Fear congealed his rage and hate. The others came back into the barrack. They slammed the door behind them. "What about him?" said one of them, pointing to Gühler. "We can take care of him now too."

"Leave him. It'll be his turn tomorrow," said the spokesman. He looked contemptuously at Gühler.

"If I only had something to defend myself with," thought Gühler. "Something I could kill them with, a hand grenade, a machine gun." He felt an agonizing hate pouring into him. His gums were dry. The mob went noisily out of the barrack.

"Where'd you leave the other one?" someone asked.

"Under the shower. Let him soak up water till he busts," said the leader.

203

They slammed the door behind them. Gühler sat on his bed, looking straight ahead of him. He was very cold. He felt the barrack like a prison all around him. The air seemed heavy with terror, with hate and blood and fear. He saw the great smears of blood on the floor opposite him. He didn't move. "Concentration camp," he thought. "Like being in a concentration camp." He saw the interrogator from back there in Italy standing before him. He saw him standing by the desk saying, "You'll have it good with us." Suddenly he laughed to himself, a tormented laugh.

"It could drive you crazy," he thought, "but they don't understand. They'll never understand."

The door of the barrack opened softly. Buchwald came in, then Grundmann and Santo and the others. "What's been going on here?" said Buchwald.

"They've beaten up Pips," whispered Gühler. He suddenly found it difficult to speak, as if it was an eternity since he had spoken last. He said, "Why didn't you come? Where were you all this time?"

"They barred the way outside. No one could get in," said Grundmann.

"The swine!" whispered Buchwald. "The filthy swine."

"Where's Pips now?" asked Santo.

"Under the shower. They practically murdered him and threw him under the shower."

"We must get him at once."

But none of them went out, none of them. They stood there and looked at Gühler. They were terrorized, gripped by panic. Gühler felt how fear reduced them to cravens.

"And that can happen here in America?" said Santo.

Gühler didn't answer. He kept staring in front of him. He saw how the fear gripped them, how it rose inside the hut and crept into them.

"But what can we do?" began Santo again.

"Nothing," whispered Gühler.

Prohaska came into the hut.

"*Los!*" he said. "On your beds. Put the lights out. The Ami is coming."

They lay down on their beds, still fully dressed, and pulled the blankets over them. The light went out. No one spoke. The glare of the searchlights on the guard towers came in through the windows. They heard the door open and saw the gleam of the flashlight run along the beds.

The American soldier stopped in front of Pips' bed. "Where is he?" he said.

"Sick," answered Prohaska.

There was silence in the barrack again. Grundmann jumped out of bed and went over to Gühler.

"We must defend ourselves," he said.

"How?"

"We must go to the Americans and lodge a complaint."

"And when we come back they'll break every bone in our bodies."

"We must do it anyway."

"It won't do any good. We're only prisoners. We're just German soldiers."

"All the same, I believe in America. America is the land of freedom. They'll help us."

"You believed once before. It's better not to believe in anything any more."

"You shouldn't say that."

"Yes, we'd already forgotten what it meant to have to keep your mouth shut. Now we've got to learn it all over again."

Buchwald came over to them. "We must go and look after Pips," whispered Grundmann.

"Come on, then," said Buchwald.

They slipped out. Gühler heard the door shut softly behind them. He still lay there, staring out of the window through which he could see the searchlight of one of the guard towers playing over the camp.

"They're protecting the terror with their machine guns," he thought. "They're guarding the Nazi terror."

He heard the click of the door again. A soft groaning noise came toward him. In the half darkness he saw them carry Pips in. They laid him on his bed. No one helped them, although everyone in the barrack lay on his bed holding his breath with fear and listening to every sound.

"He's been rejected," he thought. "Fear has made him an outcast."

He got up quietly and went over to them. Buchwald and Grundmann were sitting on the bed, bending over Pips.

"Is he still alive?" whispered Gühler. He tried to look into Pips' face. But he could only see a swollen, pulpy mass. He bent close over him and heard the faint, rattling breathing. "Thank God," he whispered.

They stole back to their beds. Pips started groaning behind them. No one in the barrack moved. No one spoke.

"They're all afraid of doing anything for him," thought Gühler. "One word of pity and tomorrow they're all traitors themselves."

He lay down on his bed. Buchwald and Grundmann

stayed with him. They sat there in silence staring ahead of them into the half darkness of the barrack. They heard Pips begin to whimper.

"It'll be the turn of one of us tomorrow," whispered Gühler. Neither of the others spoke. Pips suddenly let out a scream. He began to cry. Grundmann said, "We must go to the Americans."

"Yes," said Buchwald. "They must help us."

But there was fear in Grundmann's voice, too, the sneaking, creeping fear of the terror.

"They weren't afraid at the front," thought Gühler.

"It's still Christmas," said Buchwald. They heard Pips cry out in pain.

"For God's sake, shut up!" shouted someone farther up the barrack. No one answered him. They sat there in silence. Then they got up and lay down on their beds. Pips groaned all night long. Sometimes he just wept quietly to himself, but now and again his voice rose suddenly to a piercing scream.

Gühler lay awake on his bed.

"Christmas," he thought. "Love and forgiveness. Hate is stronger than all of them."

XIX

WHAT'LL I do about him?" said Prohaska the next morning. They fell in before the barrack to be counted. It was still dark and the cold sat in frosty patterns on the windows of the barrack.

"Report him sick," said Gühler.

They stood in the camp road in fours. When the American sergeant arrived, Prohaska roared: "Attention!"

They stood stiff and upright, with knees pressed close together, while they were being counted.

"Just like with the Prussians," said Buchwald.

Inside the barrack the stove was glowing. They threw more and more wood in and stood around it shivering. None of them spoke of what had happened the night before. They smoked American cigarettes and then threw them away half smoked into the fire. Three of the men who had beaten Pips came into the barrack. Their greatcoat collars were turned up and their caps pulled down over their ears as they pushed their way in.

"Camp Gestapo," whispered someone beside Gühler.

The three of them walked through the barrack and stopped in front of Pips' bed. Everyone round the glowing stove stopped talking. Gühler watched the three of them. He saw them talking to Pips. Then they went out again. They didn't say a word. Gühler walked casually over to Pips.

"What did they want?" he whispered.

Pips opened his swollen lips. They were like two thick boils beneath his swollen nose. His eyes were almost completely closed.

"I can't speak very well," he said slowly. "My teeth— all my teeth are loose."

"I must know what they said to you."

"No, it's better for you not to know."

"Did they want to know the names again?"

"Yes, that too."

"What else?"

Pips groaned. He put a hand to his side and his thick lips twisted painfully.

"What's the matter?" whispered Gühler.

"Everything's broken," he said laboriously. "My ribs, everything."

"I must know what they wanted from you."

"I can't say. They'll kill me."

"You can tell me."

"No, better not. No," whispered Pips. "They said they'd kill me if I talked."

"Talked about what?"

"About beating me up."

"Who are you not to talk to?"

"The Americans."

"The Americans?"

Gühler looked into Pips' face. Congealed blood was still caked beneath his eyes and around his mouth.

"I'm to go to the camp doctor and say that it happened playing soccer. The doctor knows all about it already. He'll transfer me to the hospital. I'm to say the same thing to the Americans."

"And what are you going to do?"

"I don't know," whispered Pips, "I don't know."

Two medical orderlies came into the hut. They wore white arm bands with red crosses. Gühler got up and went over to the table.

"Morning," said the orderlies.

Gühler sat on the table but didn't answer. The orderlies were wearing German uniforms. They carried themselves in stiff military fashion and their faces were red and fresh from the cold.

"What's with him?" said one of them, jerking his thumb over his shoulder at Pips.

"Sick," said Gühler.

"Soccer accident, eh?"

The orderly grinned. He had ugly, decaying teeth, which looked like gray stumps inside the narrow lips. Gühler looked at the teeth and said nothing.

"Slipped on the ice," said the other orderly with a laugh.

Pips lay there staring at the orderlies.

"What do you want with me?" he whispered.

"*Los*, get up!"

Pips tried to pull himself up but fell back groaning on the bed.

"Come on, don't fool around. Get up!"

"I can't," whispered Pips.

"The doctor's waiting for you. You're to go straight to the doctor. *Los*, stand up!"

Pips again tried to get to his feet. He twisted his face and groaned softly. But he managed to get the top part of his body upright and propped himself up on his hands.

"So you fell down and someone accidentally kicked you in the puss, eh?"

"Yes," whispered Pips.

"Silly, to be playing with all this ice around," said the orderly with the bad teeth.

They took Pips under the arms, lifted him off the bed, and set him on his feet.

"There you are. All set."

Pips groaned and put a hand to his side.

"Broke a few ribs, eh?"

They led him out of the barrack. They held him so that he had to walk upright. But his head drooped on his chest and his legs shuffled slowly over the floor. Gühler sat on the table and watched them go. There was silence in the barrack. They sat on their beds or stood around the stove. Grundmann came over and said, "What should we do?"

"I don't know," whispered Gühler. "How do the others feel?"

"They're all scared to death. Everybody's afraid to open his mouth."

"Terror," whispered Gühler. "We'll soon be all alone."

"What did they want with Pips this morning?"

"To keep it from the Americans. He's to say he fell on the soccer field."

"Will he?"

"I don't know, but he won't have any courage left."

"We must go to the Americans. We must tell them what's happening."

"This evening," whispered Gühler.

Buchwald came through the door of the hut, shaking the snow from the collar of his greatcoat.

"It's snowing," said Gühler.

They watched the snowflakes through the ice patterns on the window. They went over to Buchwald and sat down on his bed.

"They've put a watch on the gate so they'll know if anyone goes to the Americans," said Buchwald. He leaned toward Grundmann and spoke more softly than he had done before. "They're interrogating everyone and if they find out you said anything they'll come and let you have it."

"Christ!" said Grundmann. "What a rotten filthy business."

Prohaska came through the barrack. He put pots of white paint and stencils with PW cut in them on the table. "*Los,*" he said, "get to work. Paint your coats and pants."

They took off their trousers, put them on the table, and painted a huge PW in white oil paint on each leg. Then they put their trousers on their beds to dry and began to paint their coats. They squeezed the brush on the stencil and smeared the whole thing with paint. There was a smell of turpentine and oil.

Pips came back, propped up by the orderlies. His head was bandaged and one arm hung in a sling.

"Where are your things?" said one of the orderlies.

Pips didn't answer. He let himself fall back on the bed and just lay there.

"Do you know where his things are?"

"Yes," said Gühler. "What's going to happen to him?"

"He's going to the hospital."

Gühler collected Pips' things and stuffed them into a barracks bag. The orderlies watched the others as they stood around the table painting their clothes.

"Do it right," they said. "The Amis are very strict about it."

Gühler bent over Pips. He held the English books in his hand. "What shall I do with the books?"

"Pack them," whispered Pips.

"What did the doctor say?"

"He said I should be more careful next time. There's ice all over the camp."

"Nazi?"

"With him you still have to say 'Heil Hitler!' "

"What's the matter with your arm?"

"Broken."

The orderly with the bad teeth turned around and said, "Come on, not so much talking there."

Gühler packed everything up very slowly. He took each piece of clothing, unfolded it, then folded it up carefully again and pushed it down into the bag.

"What are you going to say to the Amis?"

"They know already," whispered Pips. "The doctor talked with them on the phone. A heavy fall, he said, a heavy fall on the soccer field. Arm broken, ribs crushed, nose broken by kick from a soccer boot."

"Well, ready?" said the orderly turning around again. They took hold of Pips under the arms and lifted him up. "Bring the bag," said the man with the bad teeth.

Gühler picked up the bag and swung it to his shoulder. Pips tottered in front of him between the two orderlies. No one took any notice of him. No one said a word to him. They bent over their clothes, pretending to be very busy.

When they went out of the door, Gühler saw someone standing on the other side of the road. As they appeared he turned around and began pacing slowly up and down.

"The swine!" he thought. "The dirty swine!"

But directly he felt the pressure of fear rising inside him again. He breathed in fear at every breath. An ambulance was standing in front of the door. They lifted Pips up and shoved him in like a piece of meat. He let out a scream and whimpered softly.

"Makes a hell of a row, doesn't he?" said the orderly with the bad teeth, grinning at Gühler.

"Take it a little easy," said Gühler.

"He had it coming, the bastard."

Gühler didn't answer. He picked up the bag and pushed it in beside Pips.

"Look after your things."

"Yes," whispered Pips.

The two medical orderlies stood beside him. They wouldn't leave him alone with Pips. Gühler said, "*Wiedersehen*, Pips." But the orderlies slammed the ambulance doors in his face.

"Get your puss out of the way," said the one with bad teeth. Gühler took a step back and said, "Shut your trap."

The orderly laughed. The half-decayed teeth distorted his round face. "A bit jumpy, eh?"

"Beat it," said Gühler coldly, but his hands were shaking inside his pockets.

The orderlies climbed on to the ambulance and drove

off up the camp road to the main gate. Gühler stood there for a moment looking after it. Soft light snow-flakes fell from the iron-gray sky. He turned around and went into the barrack. He felt in his back the eyes of the man on the other side of the road.

In the afternoon they paraded for the lowering of the American colors. The *Feldwebel* walked up and down in front of them, seeing to the dressing of the ranks.

"A pack of Italian swine," the *Feldwebel* shouted in front of Gühler as he looked down the line.

An American captain came down the ranks. The German *Feldwebel* came out of his barrack and yelled: "Attention!" They threw their shoulders back. They stretched in ranks of fours all the way down the camp road. "Eyes right!" yelled the sergeant-major. He took a few paces over to the American captain and snapped his hand to his hat. "Third battalion on parade!" The American captain returned the salute. From the American army camp on the other side of the barbed wire came the strains of the American national anthem. They stood stiffly at attention until the last strains had died away in the falling snow. The battalion sergeant-major stood rigidly in front, still saluting, staring fixedly out to where, invisible to the rest, the American flag was being lowered. Then they were counted again.

Noisily they ran back to their barrack, took off their greatcoats, and flung themselves on their beds.

"Dismiss!" yelled the sergeant-major.

"Good Christ!" said Buchwald. "Everywhere the same old crap. Fall in, dismiss, fall in, dismiss."

"Education for democracy," said Grundmann.

They both sat down beside Gühler on his bed. Gühler stared straight ahead of him. He was thinking of the coming evening and the threats the thugs had made the day before. Buchwald nudged him.

"What do you think?"

"Soldiers are soldiers. It's the same everywhere."

He saw them coming down through the hut. An *Oberfeldwebel* and three noncoms. The *Oberfeldwebel* wore three white stripes on his arm; the noncoms one. They came up to them with serious faces.

"They've got exactly the same eyes," thought Gühler.

"Corporal Buchwald," said the *Oberfeldwebel*.

Buchwald got slowly to his feet. He stood up slowly but Gühler noticed how his face changed color.

"I'm Buchwald."

"Be a little more military," said the *Oberfeldwebel*, quietly but sharply.

Buchwald looked at him and said nothing. His lively little eyes stared at the *Feldwebel*.

"A word with you alone."

They surrounded him and took him over to the door. There they stopped.

"You're a traitor to your country."

"Me?" said Buchwald.

"Yes. You're undermining the morale of the armed forces."

"Who told you that, *Herr Feldwebel?*"

"Don't be so insolent. You'll be tried by camp court-martial. Then you'll be ready for hanging."

"You've got to prove something against me first."

"We can prove it against you."

"What?"

"You said that the white flag was Germany's secret weapon."

"I didn't say that."

"We've got witnesses."

"No," said Buchwald, "I only said that as a joke."

"You don't expect us to believe that."

"It's the truth."

"Since you're a noncommissioned officer we can't just have you beaten up. The honor of the corps of non-commissioned officers is at stake. That's why you'll appear before a court-martial."

"But I haven't said anything."

"Leave that for us to judge."

The *Feldwebel* and the three noncoms looked at Buchwald contemptuously.

"Pull yourself together, man. You're still a soldier under oath of allegiance to the *Führer*."

"*Jawohl, Herr Oberfeldwebel*."

"You'll be hearing from us."

They looked at Buchwald again as if he were a louse to be squashed, and went out.

"The swine!" whispered Buchwald. "The dirty swine!"

His face was pale with fear and anger. He took hold of Gühler by the shoulder and shook him.

"What shall I do? If one of them lays a hand on me I'll cut his throat."

"What with? One of those butter knives?"

Buchwald flung himself down on his bed.

"I must get out of here. I'm going to the Americans at once."

"We'll go this evening."

"Someone told me today," said Grundmann, "that a few weeks ago they forced a man to commit suicide. They sentenced him to death and then locked him in a room and gave him a piece of rope. In the morning he'd hung himself."

"What did the Amis say about it?"

"Prison psychosis. Suicide. Quite simple."

That evening they put on their greatcoats and went out. The light from the searchlights seeped through the thickly falling snow.

"A good thing it's snowing," said Gühler.

The others didn't speak. They had put up their greatcoat collars and pulled their caps down over their ears. The Christmas tree still stood in front of the gate. They walked along the road which ran around the camp inside the barbed wire. Buchwald said, "We must look out for their sentries. If they see us we're done for."

They stopped in the cover of one of the barracks. They looked over toward the gate, behind which stood the brightly lit barracks of the Americans. There were five prisoners by the gate. They walked slowly up and down in front of it. Their coat collars were turned up and they wore fur-lined caps which made them look like Roman legionaries.

"Camp Gestapo," whispered Buchwald.

A figure loomed up out of the driving snow. He moved quickly toward the camp gate.

"Wait a minute," whispered Gühler. They stopped.

"Where are you going?" they heard a voice shout.

"Medical orderly," said the figure.

"All right," said the first voice.

The medical orderly went up to the gate and shouted something in the direction of the guard huts which lay beyond. An American soldier came and opened the gate. The orderly disappeared with the soldier. The five men loomed up out of the darkness again and walked slowly up and down in front of the gate.

"It's no use," said Gühler. "We'll never get past them."

"Goddam them," muttered Buchwald.

They walked around inside the barbed wire. There were American soldiers in the guard towers on the other side of the double fence. They stood forlornly in the driving snow and stared into the night.

"We're guarded twice over," said Gühler. "The camp Gestapo inside the camp, and outside the Americans with their machine guns."

"Like being in a cage," said Buchwald.

They walked on in silence through the night.

"Whose turn will it be this evening?" began Buchwald again.

"Who knows?" said Gühler. "Mine perhaps."

"Are you afraid?"

"Yes."

"We won't go back into the barrack. We'll wait until we've been counted."

They entered the main road running through the camp where the barracks of the second battalion were. Suddenly a couple of prisoners loomed up in front of them.

"You can't pass here," they said threateningly.

They heard yells coming from one of the barracks. It was the wild screaming of someone in terror.

"Help! Help me!"

The door of the hut flew open. A man came staggering out. He was a tall gaunt man. He stumbled down the steps and collapsed in the snow. The snow beneath his face turned slowly red. Three men came out of the barrack after him. They pulled him up and hit him in the face.

"Get back, you swine," one of them shouted.

They pushed him back into the barrack.

"Come on," muttered Grundmann. "Let's go."

They went back in silence. None of them said a word. The snow fell soft and white and lay in thick layers on the roof-tops. They came to a barrack which lay in the southernmost part of the camp.

"This is where Konz and Beijerke live," said Gühler. "Let's go in a minute."

They shook the snow from their greatcoats and went inside. Buschmann was standing in the middle of the room.

"We're winning," he was saying. "We're winning the war."

"Certainly. What else? We'll beat hell out of them."

"That's Konz," Gühler whispered.

The prisoners stood leaning against their beds listening to Buschmann.

"Everything in the American papers is a lie."

Gühler sat down on Beijerke's bed. Beijerke sat there squat and thickset. "It's all a swindle," he said.

"What's a swindle?"

"All of it. Everything they try to pull on us here. This business with the army communiqué in the shithouse and the daily papers and all the rest of that crap."

"How do you know?"

Beijerke looked at him and twisted his broad face into a grimace.

"*Mensch*," he said, "and all this food. They only give us that because they're afraid of us."

Gühler said nothing. He stared at the floor and

thought, "Fear is stronger than reason. Fear is stronger."

Grundmann came over and said, "Let's go. It's too hot for me in here." They went out into the night. "We've got another half hour," he said.

They walked slowly around the camp. Behind the double row of barbed wire lay the plain and freedom, and the night which obscured both. Grundmann said, "They're all heroes again now."

"Yes. The louder you talk the less danger of being called a traitor," said Gühler.

Buchwald laughed to himself. "Court-martial," he muttered, "court-martial. I'll cut their goddam throats—the lot of them."

They walked on in silence. The terror made them afraid to go back to the barrack. Sometimes they looked around thinking they heard steps behind them. But the deep-lying snow muffled every sound. Then they heard a bugle blowing taps from one of the guard towers.

"Come on, it's time."

They ran into the barrack. Prohaska came over to them. "Where have you been hiding?" he said.

"Did anything happen here?"

"No, they let the second battalion have it this evening."

XX

THE major's gray hair was slicked down and carefully parted. He sat very stiff and upright behind his desk. The lines in his face were strictly under control. He looked at them mistrustfully. They had stolen out of the camp during the morning with the working parties. No one had noticed them.

"I can't do anything for you," said the major. "You're subject to the rules of the Geneva convention."

Gühler looked at the major. It was said in the camp that he had once served in the German army.

"But Major, it's a reign of terror. It's murder."

"There's no reign of terror in my camp."

"But they beat him to a pulp. I saw it with my own eyes."

"Is he in the hospital?"

"Yes, Major."

The major picked up the telephone. They heard him talking. He shrugged his shoulders and shouted something into the telephone. Then he put the receiver back.

"At the hospital they say he was hurt playing soccer."

"That's not true."

"But it's your own doctor who says so."

"Ask him yourself, Major."

The major picked up the receiver again. They stood there watching him. He held the receiver in one hand and waited.

"It's pointless," muttered Grundmann behind Gühler. "We'll only get the same old stuff again."

The major put back the receiver angrily.

"The man himself says he was hurt playing soccer. What more do you want?"

"It's not true," muttered Gühler. "If he says that he says it because he's afraid."

"You can't prove anything against what the man says himself."

Gühler didn't answer. He watched the major get up behind his desk, and said nothing.

"You are soldiers," said the major. "You must submit to the order and discipline in the camp."

"I've been threatened with a court-martial," said Buchwald.

"What kind of court-martial?"

"A camp court-martial. The camp Gestapo have threatened me with hanging. As soon as one's hung one-self they report a suicide."

The major paced up and down the room with his hands behind his back. A map of Europe hung on the wall behind the desk dotted with red and white flags to denote the positions at the front. Gühler strained his eyes toward the flags to see the latest position.

"I can put you under protective arrest," said the major.

"Where?"

"In the guardhouse."

"No," said Buchwald. "That's inside the camp and they'd get me there too."

The major was still pacing up and down. They stood depressed and embarrassed near the door watching him.

"Come on," whispered Gühler. "It's no use."

"You're prisoners," said the major. "Behave yourselves properly and nothing can happen to you. But report to me any case that comes to your attention."

They turned around and went to the door. There they stopped, saluted smartly according to regulations, and went out. The major saluted back and smiled.

A soldier unbarred the gate and let them into the camp. A prisoner came toward them from behind the Christmas tree. He looked at them suspiciously.

"Where have you been?"

"Working party from headquarters," said Gühler.

"Finished already?"

"We only did a bit of sweeping up."

Gühler laughed. The other man turned away. "All right," he said.

They went down to their barrack. The snow crunched under their boots. A few crows hopped along the path in front of them.

"They don't understand us," said Gühler. "They'll never understand us. For them we're German soldiers and all the same. They can't grasp the whole system, because they don't know what terror is. Because they don't know what fear means."

"And Pips—why didn't he tell the truth?"

"Would you have?"

"No," said Grundmann. "No, I wouldn't have said anything. The hospital is swarming with stool pigeons."

"What are we going to do now?"

"I'm not going to the Amis again," said Buchwald. "They can keep their democracy."

"It's got nothing to do with democracy. It's the army."

"We're all tarred with the same brush," said Grundmann.

They went into the barrack. The prisoners were standing around the stove listening to a fat, squat man who was making a speech.

"There's still one more of you guys," he said menacingly. "We'll take care of him this evening."

They lay down on their beds. "Who's the one he means?" Buchwald whispered. The speaker at the stove began spitting out his threats again. His voice rose almost to a scream, "You can be damned sure their turn'll come, all of them, these traitors! We'll beat their brains out, one after the other."

None of those around the stove said a word. The speaker's eyes darted erratically around the hut, fanatical and full of hate.

"There's still one more in here. It's his turn tonight."

Santo was rolling up his blankets and stuffing them into his barracks bag.

"What are you up to?" asked Gühler.

"Transferred to the first battalion."

Buchwald said, "Whose turn is it this evening?"

"One of us for certain. You or I," whispered Gühler.

Santo sat down on the bed with them. He stood his barracks bag up in front of him and tied up the string.

"No, neither of you. I heard over there, it's one of the Austrians who sleep down by the door."

"Which one?"

"The fat one there, with the slick black hair."

Buchwald leaned back on his bed.

"Don't know him," he said. There was a tone of relief in his voice.

"It's not me. It's not me," thought Gühler but fear of the evening didn't leave him.

"What can we do? We must do something," said Grundmann. The others said nothing. Santo tied up his barracks bag and left.

"Don't let 'em get you, and keep your mouths shut," he said.

It had begun to snow again outside. The wind howled around the barracks and blew the snow in great drifts in front of the doors and windows. Gühler lay on his bed all afternoon. Whenever he closed his eyes he saw Pips' smashed head in front of him.

"Nobody can do anything for us," he thought. "Nobody can help us. We're too few. We're powerless."

Suspicion had grown up between them again. No one spoke of politics and no one mentioned the war. In a few days terror had paralyzed all feeling of freedom. Fear crouched in the barracks, beside the beds, everywhere. The faces again became dull, apathetic, listless.

Buchwald came up to him after supper.

"Here," he whispered. "I've got something to show you."

They sat down on his bed and Buchwald lifted the blanket a little.

"The first man who lays hands on me is going to get this on his head."

A heavy club made of beechwood lay underneath the blanket.

"Have any of the others got them?" whispered Gühler.

"Grundmann, the Austrians, and a few others."

"Are you going to defend yourselves?"

"Yes," said Buchwald. "They're not going to get me as easily as that."

"But it's no use. There are too many of them."

"I don't care. I'll get one of them first."

Then they came in. They pushed their way in through the door in single file, broad, thickset, with their hands in their pockets.

"There's going to be a whole bunch of football injuries tomorrow," whispered Buchwald. "The Amis will be surprised."

He leaned backward and put his hand under the blanket. His face was white with fear, but hate burned in his eyes.

The gang followed one another through the barrack.

"What about these people?" said one of them.

Inside the hut it was deathly still. They sat or lay on their beds and no one spoke.

"The Poles come first," said the ringleader.

They went out of the barrack again by the door at the other end.

"They're going to beat up the Poles," whispered Buchwald. They sat still and listened.

Grundmann said, "I'm going out onto the road."

"Stay here," whispered Gühler.

Grundmann put on his greatcoat and went out. When he opened the door they could hear the screams coming from the other side of the road. It was quiet again inside the barrack. Grundmann came back.

"They've beaten up Sokronnek. He's lying outside in the snow bleeding like a pig."

"He was a good guy," whispered Gühler. "He used to sleep near us on the ship."

"But they're still in the barrack."

The door suddenly flew open as if blown open by a gale. They came rushing in and ran through the barrack. "The Amis, *Mensch!* The swine!" one of them shouted.

"*Los*, run!"

They ran out of the other end of the barrack.

American soldiers came in. They went along the rows of beds, swinging their brown wooden clubs and looking at each man in turn.

"Thank God!" whispered Buchwald.

The soldiers struck at the beds with their clubs. One of them stopped in front of Buchwald. With his pale face still convulsed with hatred, Buchwald looked like one of the thugs. The soldier struck at the bed with his club. The bed made a wooden sound.

"What's that?" said the soldier, looking at Buchwald.

He pulled back the blanket and found the beechwood cudgel. Two officers came into the room. Holsters swung down from their waists. The soldier beckoned to them. The officers looked at Buchwald's club.

"What were you going to do with that?" one of them said.

"Defend myself," muttered Buchwald.

"Against who?"

"Against the—"

"To use it on the Poles, huh?"

"Against the camp Gestapo," muttered Buchwald.

"Camp Gestapo?" said the officer. "What's that?"

Buchwald didn't answer. He looked around at Gühler for help.

228

The officer beckoned some soldiers over and said a few words to them in English. The soldiers surrounded Buchwald and led him out of the hut.

"He wanted to defend himself against the Nazis," said Gühler.

The officer looked at him contemptuously and left in silence. Gühler sank back on his bed.

"It's not possible," he whispered. "It's just not possible."

"That's why the bastards came running through the hut," said Grundmann.

"Come on, we must go and help him."

They put on their greatcoats and went to the door. American soldiers were standing in front of it. They pushed them back again into the room. The barrack was surrounded by guards.

"Do you want to piss?" asked one of the soldiers.

"Yes."

The soldier walked along beside them and led them to the washhouse. He stood just behind them and wouldn't let them out of his sight. They returned to the barrack in silence. "Nazi bastards," said the soldier behind them.

They said nothing. The wind came blowing out of the wide plain that lay beyond the thick wall of night and swept the snow across the rooftops.

Inside, two American soldiers were leaning against the beds. Wooden clubs hung from their arms. Prohaska came over to Gühler and Grundmann.

"*Los*," he said. "Into bed. Orders."

They undressed and crawled under their blankets. The lights in the barrack stayed on all that night. Once they heard the guards being changed and Gühler said, "What are we going to do about Buchwald?"

229

"He'll know how to look after himself," said Grund-mann.

"Quiet," roared Prohaska.

Gühler said nothing. He lay on his back and stared into the darkness.

"For them," he thought, "we're all Nazis. All of us. There are no distinctions."

Prohaska came by during the night and stopped by his bed. He leaned over him and muttered, "The place is surrounded. We're suspected of attacking the Poles."

"My God," said Grundmann. "They didn't care a damn about us. We could all have been beaten to a pulp, for all they cared. But now, with the Poles, they inter-vene."

"We're only Germans," whispered Gühler. "So it doesn't matter."

"*Alles scheiss.* That's all I can say." Grundmann turned onto his side. The bed creaked under him.

"No talking," said one of the soldiers.

Prohaska went back to his bed. The long drawn-out notes of the bugle came across to them from the guard tower by the gate. Gühler closed his eyes and listened to the bugle tones. They rose higher and higher and died away on the wind, which blew howling around the barracks.

XXI

THE barracks were under close guard for three days. The American soldiers stood at the doors and let no one out. The prisoners were taken to eat under guard and one soldier stood in the washhouse and watched everything they did. Once when they were being taken to the kitchen they saw the Poles formed up on the road.

"Look, they're clearing out," said Grundmann.

They watched the Poles march out of the camp. American sentries stood all along the road.

On the third day Buchwald came back. He was led into the barrack by two soldiers. Grundmann said, "Well, have they let you go?"

"It wasn't easy," said Buchwald.

"What did they want?"

"Interrogations. One interrogation after the other. But the major recognized me and they let me go."

"And the others?"

"They've caught twelve of them, but they all insist they're innocent. The *Oberfeldwebel* is one of them. He begged me not to say he'd threatened me with a court-martial."

"And you didn't say anything?"

"No," said Buchwald, "I didn't say anything."

He lay back on his bed and closed his eyes. His face looked lax and weary.

"Why didn't you say anything?" asked Gühler.

"I thought it all over," said Buchwald. "I decided we have to settle the whole thing among ourselves. Since I've got to know the Amis I've realized we must settle with the Nazis by ourselves."

"Maybe you're right," said Grundmann.

"For most of the Amis, you're either a Nazi or a traitor. They're a race apart from us. They judge everything from their own point of view, so that what previously was right for us, is suddenly all wrong."

"What do you want to do?"

"Nothing. Say nothing. Keep my mouth shut and wait."

"Yes," said Grundmann, "that's probably best."

"They locked me up together with them," began Buchwald again. "For two days and nights I sat with them and argued. They said we must win the war, or we'd have no chance of survival. I told them we couldn't win the war anymore. And they grew quieter and quieter and one of them said, 'Maybe you're right.' But as soon as they went out and faced the Amis they played the fanatical Nazi again."

"Criminals," muttered Grundmann.

"Not criminals," said Buchwald. "Fanatics. They must either be destroyed or convinced that they're wrong. I'm for convincing them."

"What about your club?" asked Gühler.

"The Amis have got it."

"Yes," said Gühler, "you're right. We must act as if we belonged with them and then try and win them over one by one."

"An underground movement," whispered Grundmann softly.

"Just like in Germany, only even more dangerous," said Gühler. "For I never met such concentrated Nazism as here in America."

Three days later the guards were withdrawn. It was the afternoon of New Year's Eve. The snowstorm had stopped, and a clear frost came out of the plain from the northeast.

In the evening they went to the mess hall to a New Year's celebration. They drank beer and smoked American cigarettes. The American major came in with a captain and walked between the tables. The German battalion sergeant-major followed along behind.

"Happy New Year, and may you all get home this year!" said the major.

"Happy New Year, *Herr Major*," cried the prisoners.

"A song!" shouted the sergeant-major.

The prisoners sang: "Once more against France, England, and the U.S.A. and it'll all be over. . . ."

"Last verse again," said the sergeant-major.

The prisoners sang the last verse again. They thumped their fists on the table and roared out the words crisply, in march rhythm.

The major looked at the captain and laughed. The captain laughed back rather uneasily.

"Captain Smith," said Buchwald. "Formerly Schmidt.

233

Said to have been in the German army until 1935. Active list. Then ran off to the Amis. The Nazis hate him."

The major saluted and went out.

"On your feet!" roared the sergeant-major. The prisoners rose from the tables and went on singing where they stood.

"Once more against France, England, and the U.S.A...."

"It's ridiculous," muttered Gühler.

They were half drunk as they went back through the night to their barrack. They staggered across the roadway. They fell into the snow and had difficulty in getting up again.

"*Alles scheiss*," said Buchwald thickly.

Grundmann was singing to himself, "The Nazis are criminals, they've nothing in their heads...."

"Shut up," said Gühler.

"Balls," Grundmann babbled, "We'll knock their blocks off."

"Nazi bastards," said Buchwald and fell into the snow.

"Shut up, both of you," said Gühler.

"Shut up," giggled Buchwald, "always shutting up. Hell of a note."

They marched into the barrack singing: "Once more against France, England, and the U.S.A...."

They marched all along the row of beds and around the barrack. The others jumped out of bed and marched along behind them. "Once more against the U.S.A. Ha, ha, ha!"

Buchwald jumped onto the table and shouted, "Ha-ha!"

One of them took the fire extinguisher off the wall and squirted a jet of water straight into his face. Buchwald fell off the table. The others lifted up their shirttails and leaped about on the beds with bare buttocks.

"Down with the Nazis!" babbled Buchwald. Gühler held his hand over his mouth and pushed him onto his bed.

"Shut up!" he whispered, "for God's sake, shut up!"

"Where's my club? I'll cut their throats for them," Buchwald mumbled.

The uproar suddenly quieted down. The lights went out.

"Go to sleep!" roared Prohaska.

"Now we're all on the same level," said Grundmann.

Next day they were transferred to the first battalion. They packed their barracks bags, rolled up their blankets, and marched over together in ranks.

Buschmann received them there. He stood very rigid and military on his bowlegs in front of one of the barracks and said, "We're now the eighth company. I'm the company commander. I demand order, cleanliness, and proper bearing. Show that you are German soldiers."

"O.K.," said Grundmann in English.

"And your hair, now. I insist on decent haircuts. Two millimeters off the scalp. As in the army at home. No one goes around looking like a shaggy dog in my company. It's an American order."

"O.K.," said Grundmann.

"What's that, Grundmann?"

"All in order, *Herr Feldwebel.*"

"Good," said Buschmann. "Now we'll get on with dividing you up."

"We'd like to stay together, *Herr Feldwebel*."

"Who'd like to stay together?"

"Gühler, Buchwald, and I," roared Grundmann.

"Like three kids pissing against a wall," said Busch-mann. "Three little piss kids."

"May we stay together please, we three little piss kids?"

"Barrack 133, get going," said Buschmann.

They picked up their bags and went into the barrack. Konz came over to them.

"So you managed it all right."

"Thank God," said Gühler. "And behave yourselves or we'll sic the camp Gestapo on you."

"Hush, man, you must be careful here," whispered Konz.

Gühler threw his bag onto his bed.

"Oh, they're safe behind lock and key."

"No," said Konz. "Everyone's saying that the Amis caught the wrong ones."

"Fall in outside," someone shouted.

"What's going on?" said Gühler.

"Formation."

They fell in on the camp road. Buschmann stood at the end of the front rank shouting: "Front rank, dress!"

They shuffled backward and forward and measured off the distances between each other.

"Stomach in, that fourth man!" roared Buschmann.

They shuffled back and forth again.

"You're still standing there like a goat shitting on a drum!"

"Exactly," muttered Gühler.

Buschmann hurried over to the battalion sergeant-major and reported: "Eighth company paraded for lowering of the colors." The battalion sergeant-major saluted.

Over on the other side of the camp a cannon was fired. They stood stiffly to attention. The *Feldwebels* put their hands to their caps and saluted the American flag, which was being lowered in the military camp. Then came the national anthem. They stood waiting with their hands down the seams of their trousers.

Day after day exactly the same routine took place. They were awakened by a shrill whistle at six. Five minutes later they fell in in the darkness in front of the barracks to be counted. At seven they had breakfast. At eight they marched out of the camp to work. At twelve they came back to eat. At one they marched out to work again. At five they paraded for the lowering of the colors. Then came their free time. At ten o'clock they were counted inside the barracks. Then every man had to be in bed. That was the pattern of their day, day after day.

A few days after their move they were taken to American headquarters in a group.

"We're going to be interrogated again," said Grundmann.

They stood in an anteroom waiting. They went in through the door one after the other. Buchwald whispered, "Are you going to say anything?"

"No, nothing."

"Why not?"

"I don't trust anyone any more," said Gühler.

Captain Smith was sitting behind the desk. Gühler knew that he was expected to carry himself like a soldier.

He clicked his heels and whipped his hand up to his cap. "Private First Class Gühler," he said.

The captain raised his eyes from the desk and looked at him. "Gühler," he murmured. "Yes, Gühler."

He searched around among some papers on his desk, and pulled out an envelope.

"Were you in the Party?"

"No," said Gühler.

"So you weren't in the Party?"

"No."

"Were you in any sort of Party organization?"

"No."

"Are you a National Socialist?"

"I'm a soldier and do my duty."

"Duty to whom?"

"Everyone."

"That's no answer to my question. I asked you if you were a National Socialist."

"I'm a soldier," said Gühler slowly, "as demanded by the state."

"What does that mean?"

"It means order and discipline, decent behavior, keeping your mouth shut, and not being a troublemaker."

"You refuse to answer my question?"

"Yes," said Gühler.

"You can go."

Gühler went to the door, clicked his heels again, saluted, and went out.

"What did you say?" whispered Buchwald.

"Nothing."

"Good, I won't say anything, either. God knows what other boners they'd pull if you told them anything."

They fell in in fours by the gate and marched back.

238

"A song!" shouted Buschmann.

They sang: *"Panzer rollen in Afrika vor...!"*

"Slightly out of date," Gühler whispered.

But they sang the song at the top of their voices and marched in strict order through the center of the camp.

XXII

THE clay ground was thawing. Great gobs of mud clung to their rubber boots. Heavy rain clouds moved across the sky.

"It'll be spring soon," said Grundmann.

They were standing in front of one of the administration barracks in the American camp, working on the drains.

"The hole's got to be deeper," said the overseer.

They jumped into the hole by turns and threw out the earth.

"You should have stayed in the camp in filthy weather like this," said Gühler. "You don't need to work if you're a noncom."

"It gets me down, man, lying on my bed from morning till evening. And besides, Beijerke got wet through to the skin yesterday. I'm taking his place today."

"Next," shouted Konz, who was standing in the bottom of the hole. Grundmann picked up his spade and jumped in. Spadeful after spadeful of wet earth came flying out.

"Take it easy," said Konz in English.

The others stood against the wall of the administration barrack talking among themselves.

"Did you see, there's some women in there?" one of them said. He jerked his thumb toward the windows of the barrack.

"Women?" said Konz. "Where?"

They all tried to look in through the windows.

"Quiet," said one of them.

They kept quiet and pressed their faces against the windows halfway up the wall. They heard a woman laughing.

"Good God," said Konz, "if a man could only get inside!"

They listened. Grundmann came crawling out of the hole and brushed the dirt off his legs.

"*Los*, Gühler," he said.

Gühler took the spade and climbed into the hole. The overseer went across the road to the other side of the barrack.

"Take your time," said Grundmann.

The soldier who was guarding them stood a little way off in the shelter of the barrack, whistling to himself. They heard the sound of a toilet flushing.

"There are women in there," one of them said.

The lavatory window was close to where they were working. Konz stole up to the window. They all kept quiet and watched him.

"You can't see anything through the frosted glass," whispered Grundmann.

Konz turned around and grinned. The window was unfastened and he pushed it gently open with his spade. A narrow slit appeared. They all looked across at Konz.

He stood on tiptoes looking through the opening. He stole back to them.

"You can see her from here now," he said. He placed himself near the hole in which Gühler was standing and looked over at the window.

"There," he said.

A woman came through the door into the lavatory. She stood in front of the looking glass, pulled out a lipstick, and began to paint her lips. She was wearing a red pullover and a gray skirt.

"Nice," said one of them.

The woman pulled her pullover up a bit higher and straightened her skirt.

"Holy Christ!" said Konz.

The overseer came back. They looked innocently around and shifted their feet unconcernedly. Gühler crawled out of the hole. The overseer picked up a spade and measured the hole. A girl came into the lavatory.

"Another one," whispered someone.

The overseer jumped down into the hole. They all looked greedily and excitedly through the window opening. The girl stood in front of the looking glass combing her hair. One of them stole up to the window, stretched up a little, and looked through. He wedged his face against the window frame.

"Get away," whispered one of the others, trying to push him to one side.

The girl at the mirror threw her head back and drew the comb through her hair.

"Get away from there, you pigs," said Gühler. But he, too, looked through the opening in the window at the girl's green dress.

"It's been so long," he thought.

He saw the girl lift up her skirt and turn away. Grundmann gave him a nudge.

"Damn pretty girl, eh?"

"Quit it. What good does it do you?" said Gühler.

The overseer looked up. He saw the prisoners' faces all turned toward the window. "Guard!" he shouted and jumped out of the hole. The soldier came slowly toward them. He was whistling to himself, and then laughed.

"You bastards," he said.

The overseer ran into the barrack. They heard the women squeal and then a peal of laughter. A woman rushed to the window and slammed it.

"All over," said Konz.

The others laughed, embarrassed. They picked up their spades and all began digging at the same time. They shoveled up the dirt and threw it on the grass.

"We're like animals," said Gühler.

Grundmann looked at him. He leaned on his spade.

"Well," he said, "we're only men, after all."

The overseer came back cursing to himself.

"Get to work," he said. "Faster."

He sketched out the ditch they were to dig. They could all see that it was a completely pointless piece of work.

"Always the same occupational therapy," said Grundmann.

The others said nothing but began to dig. The clouds hung low over the rooftops. They shoveled up the earth and threw it away behind them. They worked in silence.

"It's so long since I saw my old woman," said one of them, "it seems like an eternity."

None of them answered. He picked up his spade and

looked up at the clouds. "I wonder what she's doing," he said.

"Fooling around with someone else. What do you expect?" said Konz.

The overseer came and urged them on. "*Los, los,*" he said.

"That slob," said Grundmann.

"Rest," shouted the soldier, suddenly.

The overseer looked around embarrassed. The soldier laughed. They stuck their spades into the earth and collected around the sentry. He counted them.

"Come on," he said.

They followed behind him. It began to rain. The rain came down in great gusts from the low scudding clouds. The soldier ran into a latrine. They ran in after him. "Thank God!" said Konz as soon as they were inside. "It'll rain all day."

American soldiers were standing in front of the washhouse. They laughed as the prisoners came in.

"They can laugh," said Grundmann.

"What do you mean? They've got the whole dirty mess before them. At least it's behind us," said Konz.

They sat down on the benches in the washhouse.

"Have you heard?" one of them said. "Nettuno has fallen."

"Yes, and Berlin's been heavily bombed again."

"All exaggerated! All nonsense," said a man with a hooked nose called Gerlich. "And even if it is true, they'll get the same thing back."

Gühler raised his head and looked at Gerlich. This was the first time he had seen him. His gray eyes were sunk deep under his forehead and he had a large nose.

"I'm scared about my wife," one of them said. "She's in Berlin. I'm really scared about her."

"Yesterday two more people in the camp heard that their wives had been killed. Killed in action, it's called nowadays."

"It's crazy," said the other man. "We sit here while the women get killed."

"We must hold out," said Gerlich. The lines around his nostrils drew together sullenly. "If we want to win this war, we've got to hold out."

Gühler looked at the lines and then at the gray eyes. "We've had all that once already," he said slowly. "Holding out! We held out once before and we lost. The people at home ought to call it quits, and the sooner the better."

There was suddenly complete silence in the narrow washhouse. Everyone looked at Gühler.

"Well, Gerlich, what have you got to say to that?" one of them muttered.

Gerlich turned his attention to Gühler.

"We will win the war. There's no doubt about that," he said.

"How do you imagine that's going to happen?"

"The *Führer* will win it. Or do you doubt the *Führer?*"

Gühler said nothing. They all looked at him. He felt Gerlich's gray eyes on him. Grundmann nudged him.

"Sure," said Grundmann suddenly. "Of course the *Führer* will do it yet."

"Yes," said Konz, "of course. They've got a nasty surprise coming to them."

Gühler still didn't say anything. He sat with his legs drawn up, looking at the ground.

245

"I don't believe it," he said. "I can't believe it."

"I'd advise you not to spread your views around in the camp," said Gerlich.

"Why not? It's better for them to know the truth."

"We need a camp that presents an iron front to the Americans. National Socialist from top to bottom. Understand?"

"No," said Gühler. "Why?"

"To win the war."

"But nobody's going to win the war here."

"Oh, yes. The Americans must not be in any doubt about the morale of the German people."

"That's why we have to have a reign of terror?"

"Do you call it terror to maintain order and the right attitude?"

"Yes," said Gühler, "I call it terror against all of us. It's destroying the comradeship we built up at the front."

"Perhaps it's terror against you and people like you," said Gerlich, "but not against those who are for us."

"There are many against you. Many more than you imagine."

"Why don't they say anything, then?"

"Because they're afraid of you. Afraid of the concentration camp at home. Afraid of the gallows, of your stool pigeons and your strong-arm methods."

"That'll be enough out of you," said Gerlich.

The American soldier came into the washhouse. He beckoned to them and they followed him out. The rain had stopped. They went to the administration barrack, pulled their spades out of the earth, and cleaned them. The overseer collected all the spades together and threw them onto the truck that was standing ready. They formed into fours and marched across to the road. On the road they halted. Company after company of American soldiers was marching along it. Between the companies marched the officers.

"They're being shipped off," said Grundmann.

They stood and watched the marching soldiers.

"For Europe," said the sentry.

"Sheep for the slaughter," said someone. "Just the same as with us."

Gühler suddenly found Gerlich standing beside him. He had pushed his way up to him and was now watching the feet of the marching soldiers.

"I'd advise you not to make speeches like that here," he muttered.

"Why?" said Gühler.

"Because we don't want it."

"And why don't you want it?"

"You know perfectly well."

"And what if I go on?"

"Then we'll have to retaliate, as before. It's the peace of the camp that's at stake."

"Yes," said Gühler. "Of course the peace of the camp is sacred."

He hated Gerlich and at the same time felt a certain sympathy for him that he found difficult to understand.

The last columns of marching soldiers went past them almost at a run.

They formed into fours again and followed the sentry. They were tired and marched with dragging steps.

"When will the whole lousy mess be over?" said Konz.

"Soon," said Gühler. "You can bet on it."

They looked at the cars which were driving past them. Whenever there was a woman at the wheel they all turned around and stared after the car.

"A lot of whores," said Konz.

"Why whores?"

"They're all painted from top to bottom."

"But not whores."

"All the same," said Konz. "They ought to send some of them in to us in the camp. It's enough to drive a man nuts—all this food and never a piece."

Gühler laughed. He slapped Konz on the back and said, "There's nothing about it in the Geneva Convention."

"And that's what's called humane treatment?" said Konz. They went on in silence. American soldiers stood by the gate of the camp and searched them. They stood with their arms up while they were patted all over. Then they marched through the gate into the camp.

The prisoners were standing in the camp roadway. American soldiers were running through the empty barracks, turning the beds upside down, rummaging around in cupboards, and searching through everything.

"What's going on?" said Grundmann.

"Somebody got away again," said Buchwald.

"Who?"

"Don't know. Some idiot."

"What foolishness," said Grundmann. "They'll catch him in three days and then he'll spend thirty more in the cooler."

"For thirty days they'll all try it once."

"What the hell are they thinking of?" said Gühler. "Do they really imagine they could get home from here?"

"This idiotic Nazi propaganda makes them all loony," said Grundmann.

They stood around waiting in the roadway. No one was allowed into the huts. They kept falling in for re-counting. American soldiers ran excitedly in and out of the ranks. The officers swore.

"Just a man missing. Nothing to be done about it," said Buchwald.

"They raise all this row for one lousy prisoner," said Grundmann.

Evening came. They stood and waited. They were very cold. It began to rain again.

"They ought to tan his ass off," said Konz. They ran up and down trying to get warm. Slowly they became resigned to it all. Their legs grew tired. They sat down on the wet grass by the side of the road and stared ahead of them.

"I'm dying of hunger," someone said.

"All because of one bastard who wants to go home."

"Home," said Konz. "Who doesn't want to go home?"

They had to fall in again. They stood at attention. The rain drizzled down into their faces. The *Feldwebel* and the battalion commander counted with the American soldiers.

"Correct," shouted one of the *Feldwebel*.

"Impossible," said the battalion commander.

They counted again. The long rows of prisoners stretched all the way to the gate of the camp and hardly moved.

"Yes, correct," shouted the battalion commander. "God damn it."

The American soldiers laughed. The battalion commander reported to the American captain who stood motionless in front of his quarters. The captain waved his hand.

"Dismiss," shouted the battalion commander.

They rushed into the barracks and threw themselves on their beds.

"What a farce," said Konz.

XXIII

DAY after day they went out into the American camp to clean roads, sweep out barracks, shovel snow, wash cars, or dig ditches. In the evenings they attended lectures. In "History of Literature" they heard Hebbel's *Nibelungen* read aloud by the staff *Feldwebel* taking the different parts, or Kleist's *The Prince of Homburg*. In "History" they heard anecdotes of the lives of the medieval German emperors and the *Feldwebel* made endless notes of dates to prepare for examinations in the German army when they got back. An American soldier sat in on all the sessions to see that the lecturers never used the words "Hitler" and "National Socialist."

So the winter passed. The spring storms came and chased the last snow off the rooftops. The camp road became a muddy morass. It rained for weeks on end. Then came the heat. Day after day the sky made an inescapable glassy blue vault above the camp.

One morning they drove out with the coal party. Buchwald was in charge. They were given their shovels and driven out to the coal train, where they climbed up onto the cars. The coal dust rose into their eyes. "Filthy stuff," said Gühler.

Buchwald stood there laughing with his hands in his pockets. "Stop that silly laughing," said Konz. "You lie around all day on your bed playing skat, and when you do occasionally come out it's only to be in charge of a working party."

"You should have been a noncom yourself," said Buchwald.

The American soldier came over and waved a newspaper at them. "Invasion!" he said.

"Rest," shouted Buchwald.

They threw down their shovels.

"What's up? What did he say?" shouted someone from one of the other cars.

"Invasion!" roared Buchwald. "Come on, rest time."

They jumped down and gathered around the American soldier.

"Thank God," said Gühler, "it's started at last."

The soldier turned around and laughed. Each of them lit a cigarette and looked at the newspaper. Buchwald said, "This is the end."

They picked up their shovels and climbed up onto the cars again. They shoveled out all the coal which the crane couldn't get hold of. Gühler stood alone with Buchwald on one of the cars.

"How long do you give them?"

Buchwald looked at the paper which the American soldier had loaned him.

"Two months and we're finished," he said.

In the evening they marched back into the camp. They returned to their barracks tired and black with coal dust. The unnatural peace of the camp seemed suddenly shattered. There were excited discussions going on everywhere. Someone got up in their barrack and said, "They'll get it in the neck, and then we'll be rid of them for good."

"The propaganda machine's functioning again," whispered Gühler.

"We're letting them in first, ten, twenty kilometers or so, and then we'll ram their invasion up their ass," began the other man again.

"We don't want to listen to that crap," said Grundmann.

"So you're one of them, are you? You want us to lose the war, eh? It's a long time since anybody heard a peep out of you around the camp."

"Shut your filthy trap," said Grundmann.

The other man went up to Grundmann threateningly. "You want your face smashed in?"

Grundmann leaned against his bed.

"The war's lost," he said calmly. "We can't win it now."

"Traitor! Coward!" shouted the other.

"You can come around this evening with your Gestapo," said Grundmann.

The other went out of the barrack. "We'll take care of him, all right," he said as he left.

They all stood around Grundmann. No one spoke. He leaned against his bed, looking pale, and stared at them. Then he shrugged his shoulders and sat down on the bed.

"Why did you provoke them?" said Gühler.

"Because he made me mad."

"Why?"

"We're clearing out."

"Who is?"

"All noncoms and *Feldwebel* who don't want to work. They're being collected over in the second battalion and then being moved to another camp."

"And why aren't you going to work?"

"You know what it's like—pressure from all sides. Over in the American headquarters today they asked us if we wanted to go to work or not. And they all said no. They stood around me and said anyone who went to work was a traitor to his country. He was helping the others win the war. So when the Amis asked me I said no."

"How ridiculous," said Gühler.

"Yes, ridiculous," muttered Grundmann. "But what else could I do? They denounce everyone who reports for work. They declare him a traitor so that no one dares speak to him."

"What if you went secretly and told the Amis?"

"I'm not going to the Amis again. Besides it wouldn't help. The Amis are collecting them all into special barracks, and if I were still here tomorrow morning everyone would know I'd said yes."

"Why not do it and see what happens?"

"No," said Grundmann, "I can't stand this public humiliation, I can't stand it. And I've already said no now anyway."

"All outside for dinner," someone shouted.

They went into the mess hall. Buchwald whispered, "*Mensch*, what am I going to do?"

"Come with me," said Grundmann. "That's all you can do. There are two hundred *Feldwebel* from other camps over there already, and they're going with us."

254

Suddenly a noncom was standing in front of the table where the food was being served. "Everyone listen!" he said.

The clatter of knives and forks died down.

"One of the new ones," said Grundmann.

The noncom jumped up on to the table.

"They say he's a Gau propaganda speaker," whispered Konz.

The noncom raised his hands like an agitator. He almost shouted himself hoarse. "Victory will be ours," he said. "There's no doubt about it. The Jews will lose this war."

A storm of applause burst out through the hall. He spoke of the iron will of the *Führer*, of the *Festung Europa*, and of the necessity of rooting out all Jewish influences.

"Idiot," whispered Gühler.

"But we must also bring about order in our own ranks," said the orator. "Right here in camp discipline seems to be slack. There are defeatists and weaklings even here, sinister elements of whom we must be rid. Any methods are justified to do this. Comrades, don't let your faith in final victory be shaken by such elements. Destroy them wherever you find them."

A storm of applause broke out in the hall again. Some started stamping their feet. "Bravo!" they shouted. Grundmann and Gühler looked at each other but said nothing. They stared at their plates in silence.

"There are noncoms and *Feldwebel* here in camp who want to work for the Amis. That is aiding the enemy's war effort. That is open betrayal of our country. But we'll name them all individually and they'll be spared nothing."

255

"There you are. What did I tell you?" Grundmann whispered.

Buchwald sat in his place looking pale and pushing his blunt kitchen knife through a slit in the table.

The noncom yelled: "To our *Führer* and Supreme Commander, Adolf Hitler, a threefold *Sieg Heil!*"

They jumped up from their tables and shouted *"Heil!"* Then they began singing the *Horst Wessel*. They sang with their arms raised in the Nazi salute.

Gühler kept his lips tightly shut, but he stood there with his arm raised like the rest of them. They went back into their barrack. Gühler found the camp education officer on his bed, a small fat man who had once been a teacher in Germany.

"I've been waiting for you," he said.

"For me?" said Gühler.

"Yes," he said. "The literature and history instructor is being transferred to another camp. I wanted to ask you if you'd take on the teaching of both subjects."

"Me?"

"Yes. Literature first of all. I have found out which of you is capable. You must be equipped for it. I know what you were doing before. I've heard a lot about you on the other side."

Gühler looked at the fat little man, whose misty blue eyes stared out from behind his glasses. Then he said slowly, "But I'm not a National Socialist."

"I know," he said, "I know. You're National German, I've heard about it."

"National German?" said Gühler laughing.

The little man bent toward him and whispered into his ear, "Between ourselves, confidentially, so am I."

"Really," said Gühler. "Really."

"But please," whispered the little man again, "very much between ourselves. Very confidential."

"But I certainly wouldn't let the *Nibelungen* be read. Or the Battle of Arminius."

"Thank God! Thank God! Something new at last."

Two days later Gühler gave his first literature lecture. A dozen staff *Feldwebel* sat in the front row and looked at him curiously. Gühler spoke of the links between the literatures of various nations. Behind the staff *Feldwebel* sat Buchwald and Grundmann. They sat there smiling at him. Every now and again they shouted "Bravo!" or stamped their feet. The *Feldwebel* looked at him in bewilderment. They didn't understand a word. In the intermission they all went out and did not come back.

"They've had enough," said Grundmann.

But there were only four of them left all together and Gühler spoke to empty benches.

The next morning Grundmann and Buchwald left the barrack. They swung their bags onto their shoulders, put their blankets under their arms, and marched off to the second battalion.

The camp was swept by the excitement of victory. More and more rumors of the use of secret weapons ran through the barracks. The rumors became more fantastic every day.

"It'll all be over in a few weeks," they said. "German troops will be marching into New York."

The weeks passed. Day after day the camp was spanned by the glassy blue sky. In the evenings they sat in front of the canteen drinking Coca-cola. From across the plain they heard the muffled howl of the great locomotives on the Pacific railway. Gühler continued to give lectures. The staff *Feldwebel* had deserted him, but he

257

won new pupils and new friends. He allowed Heine to be read and received threatening letters from the camp. "We'll hang you when we get back to Germany."

One evening Böhmer came into the barrack. He was a tall, emaciated man who used his hands when he spoke. Gühler had seen him sitting silently at his classes. He sat down beside him on the bed.

"They say in the camp," he began, "that everyone who goes to your classes has their name taken by the camp Gestapo and will be reported when we get back to Germany."

"I heard something of the sort," said Gühler.

"Are you going to do anything about it?"

"No. What is there to do?"

"I know a lot of people here in camp who aren't National Socialists," he said. "They are all known to each other. You ought to become one of them."

"Yes," said Gühler.

"We must try and win the camp over, gradually and systematically."

"That's my idea too," said Gühler.

"There are Austrians here in the camp you should get to know. They try to counteract the Gestapo's rumors."

"Where can I get to know them?"

"I'll take you along," said Böhmer, "in a few days."

They left the barrack. The broad path that ran all the way around the camp by the barbed-wire fence was dry and dusty. Böhmer and Gühler spoke in low tones. When they sensed someone just behind them they stopped talking.

The next day several barracks were emptied. Buschmann said, "Some new people are coming in this evening."

258

"Where from?" asked Gühler.

"From other camps," said Buschmann.

That evening a thousand new prisoners stood in front of the gate. They stood in fours stretching halfway round the camp. Grundmann came running into the barrack.

"Hey, Gühler! They've come from Normandy."

"From Normandy?" said Gühler.

"All of them captured just recently, three or four weeks ago."

They went to the gate. Prisoners were running toward the gate from all over the camp. They pressed close to the barbed wire.

"Where've you come from?" they shouted.

"Normandy."

"Impossible. Don't be silly. From which camp?"

"You heard me. We're from Normandy."

"Don't try and be funny."

"Just another Ami trick," said someone near Gühler. "They've got a thousand or so riffraff together and told them to say they're from Normandy. Do you believe it?"

Gühler didn't say anything. The thousand men from Normandy marched into the camp. Gühler felt a hand on his shoulder. It was Böhmer. "We must warn them," he said.

"They are either very young or very old," said Gühler.

"Poor bastards," said Böhmer.

"They're just a bunch of tramps," said someone near Gühler. "They're not soldiers."

"Traitors!" said someone else.

"Are you really from Normandy?"

"Yes, straight from there."

"How's the war going?"

"It's lost."

"*Alles scheiss*. You never saw anything like what they're doing to us."

"Much equipment?"

"Nothing but. Thousands of planes. Naval guns. And there we were with our lousy machine guns!"

They had all collected in the camp roadway. The battalion sergeant-major ran up and down in front of them shouting: "Attention!" But nobody moved.

"Bunch of tramps!" shouted Buschmann who stood at the far end of the long line.

Gühler walked along behind the rear rank with Grundmann and Böhmer. Buchwald came toward them. "They're all right," he said.

One of them turned round. "Hey, you. What's going on here? Are there still Nazis about?"

"Plenty," said Grundmann.

"For Christ sake!" said the other. He was large and broad shouldered. They stopped beside him.

"You fellows better be careful here."

"Why?"

"Nazis. The camp's crawling with them," said Gühler.

"Here, in America?"

"More than in Germany. If you open your mouth here there's hell to pay."

"I'll be damned!" said the other.

"We'll take him in our barrack," whispered Buchwald.

The prisoners were divided up among the barracks. They went to Buschmann and Gühler said, "We've got a man over there I'd like to have in my barrack."

"What's his name?"

"Schmidt," said Buchwald.

Buschmann took out his book and wrote down Schmidt in it.

"Seeing it's you," he said.

They went back to Schmidt and took him with them.

"I must bring a few pals along," he said.

They went through the ranks.

"Wilhelm," said Schmidt, "come with me. We'll be all right over here."

By the time they had got into the barrack they had collected five men. Buschmann came up to them swearing.

"What's going on here?"

"They all stay here," said Gühler.

"God dammit!" shouted Buschmann and tore out of the barrack.

They took over the empty beds. They threw their barracks bags onto the beds and sat down.

"Tell us what's going on over there," said Buchwald.

They all stood round Schmidt who sat on his bed very calm and sure of himself.

"It's a hell of a mess."

Two noncoms came in.

"Look out," whispered Gühler. "These are two of them."

The noncoms came up to them.

"No one really believes they've come from Normandy," one of them was saying.

They all stopped talking. Schmidt raised his head and said, "Where did we come from, then?"

"Are you one of the new ones?"

"Yes," said Schmidt, "and I've come direct from Normandy."

"Stop that nonsense."

"It's no nonsense. I ought to know where I've come from."

"He's asking for it," said the other noncom. They looked at each other and grinned.

"They caught hell over there," said Grundmann.

"Nobody asked you."

Schmidt stood up. He was a big man and towered over the noncoms. He tapped one of them on the shoulder and said, "So, my boy, you're still winning the war, eh?"

The noncom took a step back. He turned pale. They all looked at him.

"The war's lost," said Schmidt. "You better get used to that idea."

"We have discipline here in this camp. We don't want traitors."

"Traitors?" laughed Schmidt. "Who's talking about traitors? I say we're losing the war. We're finished. That's all there is to it. If you'd seen all their equipment you'd save your breath."

"What about the secret weapon?"

"All propaganda!" said Schmidt and laughed again. "Just a swindle!"

The two noncoms looked helplessly around them. No one put in a word for them. They all stood around the bed looking at Schmidt.

"Well," he said, "don't look so miserable about it. Life goes on just the same."

The noncoms turned and went out. Schmidt laughed. "Never heard anything so crazy," he said.

262

"Still, you ought to be a bit more careful," said Böhmer.

That evening the Americans barred the gate into the second battalion where the *Feldwebel* and noncoms were. Gühler lay on his bed waiting. "I wonder if they'll come," he thought, "I wonder if they'll come."

But all remained quiet in the barrack. Konz lay in bed next to him. He tossed about restlessly.

"*Mensch*, to have a real woman again!"

"Don't hold your breath that long."

"I can't stand it any longer," he said. "Yesterday someone in the first battalion cut his wrists. Barbed-wire fever."

"Yes," said Gühler, "I know."

"How do you manage?"

"I don't think about it, that's all."

Sounds of life from the outside world came in through the open door. The sounds came to them from the plain out of the night. Gühler heard the shrill laughter of a woman from the other side of the road behind the wire, then the dull roar of a railway engine. One of the soldiers in the guard towers was singing.

"When will we ever get out of here?" said Konz.

XXIV

THEY were awakened in the middle of the night by shouts of *"Sieg Heil!"* and the sound of the *Horst Wessel* coming from the second battalion. "They're celebrating their departure," said Konz.

Gühler jumped out of bed and went to the door. The swastika was flying above one of the barracks on the end of a long pole. The searchlights in the guard towers swept over the rooftops continuously. The swastika stood out in bold relief in the glare of the searchlights.

Schmidt came out of the barrack. He was pulling up his underpants and said, "They must be crazy over there."

Gühler said nothing. Schmidt sat down beside him on the bench.

"If they only knew what was really happening," he said. "If they had the faintest idea."

American soldiers suddenly appeared between the barracks.

"Quick, inside," whispered Gühler. "If they catch us here they'll pick us up."

264

They stole into the barrack. Some cars drove past outside. They heard officers giving commands. The uproar in the second battalion increased.

"Pull the swine off the trucks," they heard someone shout.

Gühler stood behind the door. He saw men running about between the barracks of the second battalion. Stones were flying over the fence. Buschmann came running into the hut shouting: "Everyone in bed? *Los*, the Amis are coming!"

They heard scattered shots.

"Hell!" said Konz. "Now they're shooting inside the camp."

American soldiers came through the barracks. Suddenly everything was quiet on the other side of the camp.

"What was all that about?" said Schmidt.

The next morning Gühler went over to the second battalion. The gates were barred and chained. Noncoms and *Feldwebel* were falling in on the road between the barracks preparatory to leaving. Gühler stood by the gate. He looked down the ranks again and again trying to see Buchwald and Grundmann. Then Grundmann came across to him.

"Are you really going?" asked Gühler.

"Yes," said Grundmann.

"You should have reported for work. You should have stayed here."

"*Verdammte scheiss!*" said Grundmann. "But how?"

"You should've simply reported, whatever the danger."

"If I could get out now, I wouldn't give a damn for

them. My God, they made a fine mess around here last night!"

"What was going on?"

"They threw stones at the Amis, tried to upset the trucks, raised the swastika. They wanted to start a mutiny in the camp."

"A mutiny?"

"Yes," said Grundmann, "and now they're cursing all of you for not joining in."

Gühler laughed. "For not joining in?" he said. "Us? They must really be nuts."

He looked at Grundmann's gloomy face behind the barbed-wire gate.

"You've got to stay here, man. You can't just go with that bunch."

"If I'd reported for work, they would have beaten me. There are so many who would rather have stayed here and worked. But no one had the courage to report. No one. I haven't slept for nights. I've thought about how to do it over and over, but I couldn't think of anything."

"Go say you want to stay here now."

"I tried this morning. I spoke to the American battalion officer but he said I was a Nazi and a troublemaker and it was too late."

"Then there's nothing more to be done."

"No," said Grundmann. "We're going to a punishment camp."

"Crazy," muttered Gühler, "sheer craziness."

Buchwald came across to the gate and pushed his hand through the barbed wire.

"Well, you troublemaker," said Gühler.

Buchwald looked at him. His eyes, which were usually lively, looked tired and glazed.

"I'm a Nazi now. A real Nazi, do you realize that?"

"No," said Gühler, "I don't realize that."

"They can't tell the difference. They don't recognize us. They don't realize the pressure we're under."

"They'll never realize it."

"Last night they finally took action. But it was only the swastika that annoyed them."

"They haven't had any experience with Nazis," said Gühler.

"That's it," said Buchwald. "No experience. We've a whole bunch of Gestapo men among us keeping everything in check and the Amis don't even notice it."

A German command echoed across the camp: "Fall in!"

"We must go," said Grundmann. He had put his hands in his pockets and was staring at the ground.

"The swine," said Buchwald. "The dirty swine!"

"All the best, and don't let 'em get you down!"

"They've got us down already," said Grundmann. He was still staring at the ground as if he had lost something. Gühler pushed his hand through the barbed wire. Buchwald said, "Don't let the bastards get you."

"What about you?"

"We'll come through somehow."

They shook hands. The barbed wire stood between them.

"Keep up your lectures, and keep your chin up," said Grundmann.

"Yes," said Gühler. "Yes, I will."

"*Mach's gut,*" said Buchwald.

They turned and went away up the road. Gühler stayed close by the wire and watched them go. "I'll never see them again," he thought.

"Pick up your barracks bags," roared a *Feldwebel*.

Over on the other side of the soccer field an American military band began playing on the station, where American soldiers were being entrained for overseas. "Food for the fishes," said someone beside Gühler. "More food for the fishes."

Gühler ran down between the battalion barracks to the main gate. He watched them marching through the gate, with their barracks bags on their shoulders. They marched around the camp outside the barbed wire to the station. They marched in fours, their feet rising and falling with such precision that they might have been on a parade ground. "Tanks are rolling forward in Africa . . ." they sang. The song had a tough military ring, as if they were German troops advancing in battle. "Show," muttered Gühler. "Nothing but empty show."

He kept pace with the marching columns, following them on his side of the wire. On the other side Buchwald and Grundmann were panting under the weight of their barracks bags. Drops of sweat stood out on their foreheads.

"*Auf wiedersehen*," shouted Buchwald.

A new song started up at the head of the column: "Once more against the U.S.A. . . ."

Buchwald and Grundmann did not sing along. They trotted under their barracks bags in silence. The dust of the dry sandy road blew up beneath their feet. Then they sang: "The little bird in the wood," and "In the homeland, in the homeland, there we'll meet again."

Gühler saw that both Grundmann and Buchwald

268

were now singing too. The song swelled up louder, far louder than the marching songs, in the shimmering summer air. "Now they're all singing," thought Gühler. "They're all singing now."

The quick rhythm of the American military band came across from the station. It cut through the German song with its strident tones.

Gühler stopped behind the barbed wire. He had come to the extreme end of the playing field. He raised his hand. Grundmann and Buchwald saw him. They raised their hands and waved. Then they marched into the station to entrain.

Gühler went back. He walked slowly across the soccer field where a couple of players were kicking a ball around. The camp seemed empty and deserted. Böhmer came up to him.

"Well," he said, "have they gone?"

"Yes," said Gühler.

"They were a couple of good fellows."

"Yes, I was at the front with them."

"They should have stayed here."

"It wasn't possible."

"But they weren't Nazis?"

"No, they weren't Nazis," said Gühler.

"We're meeting this evening in Number Six company's kitchen."

"What for?"

"A little get together. I told you about it."

"Oh, yes," said Gühler. "I see."

They went into the barrack. Gühler threw himself wearily on his bed. Buschmann came in with two American officers. "*Achtung!*" shouted Buschmann.

They jumped from their beds and stood at attention.

The American officers saluted and walked slowly along the beds. The prisoners stood in front of their beds. As the officers passed they drew themselves up.

"Inspection," said Böhmer. "Inspection every day, like a training camp."

The officers went out. Buschmann flung open the door and shouted: "At ease!"

Gühler threw himself on his bed again. He felt empty and miserable.

That evening he went over to Number Six company's kitchen. Someone stopped him just in front of the kitchen door.

"Where are you going?"

"To the meeting."

"Who invited you?"

"Böhmer."

"All right."

He went into the kitchen. They were sitting around a table whispering together. Santo was with them.

"You here?" said Gühler.

"Yes. I'm glad you've come."

"What goes on here?"

"The Austrians want to leave the camp."

"Why?"

"They don't want to have anything more to do with the Nazis."

At the other end of the table sat the Austrian with sleek black hair whose bed had been near his in one of the barracks. He said, "We're leaving the camp tonight. The Amis have agreed. They're building a new camp for antifascists, not far from here."

"Why are you leaving?" Gühler asked.

"We're not going to submit to this terror any longer."

"You're making a mistake. Anyone who separates from the main body is just handing influence over to the Nazis."

The man with the sleek hair shook his head and looked at Gühler uncertainly. "What do you think is the right thing to do?"

"Stay here and try to win the camp over to us. Time is on our side."

"But they make it impossible. The pressure on us is unbearable."

"We must adapt ourselves to them and slowly wear them down. Day after day. When the war ends the whole camp must be in our hands."

"Impossible."

"Nothing's impossible," said Gühler. "In politics nothing is impossible."

Böhmer came in and sat down beside Gühler.

"Well," he said, "how's it going?"

"They want to leave the camp."

"Yes, they're right, don't you think?"

"No, they're not right," said Gühler. "They're motivated by nothing but fear and the thought of their own comfort."

The man with the sleek hair jumped up and said, "Just say that again. Say again that we're afraid!"

"You're afraid," said Gühler slowly.

"We don't want anything to do with you, with any of you. We're Austrians, understand?"

"That's what I thought," said Gühler.

"What did you think?"

"That you were Austrians."

"Yes, we're Austrians. You forced us to go with you. You attacked us. We're on the other side."

"We attacked you! *We* did!" said Gühler.

"All of you. You were all in with the Nazis."

Gühler didn't answer. His glance went across to Böhmer and then to Santo. Santo smiled at him. "Let it alone. It's pointless. The whole silly mess is pointless."

"There are a hundred and fifty of us," began the Austrian again. "We're leaving the camp tonight. We don't need you. Anyone who doesn't want to come can stay here."

"I'm staying here," said Gühler.

"With the Nazis?"

"I'm staying where I belong. I'm not an Austrian. I'm staying with the Germans."

"Even if they kill you?"

"Yes, even then."

They both looked at each other in silence. The Austrian sat down again and said, "Well, who's coming? Everybody?"

"Not me," said Böhmer. "I'm staying here."

"You too?"

"Yes, Gühler is right. We must win the camp over from within."

"You'll never do it."

"We'll see."

Santo stood up. He got to his feet with a smile and shook the Austrian by the hand.

"I think we can break it up now."

"You're not coming either?"

"No," said Santo.

They all got up and stood around in the middle of the kitchen.

272

"Is everyone else coming?" said the Austrian.

"Yes," they said.

"Those who are coming put up their hands."

Everyone except Gühler, Böhmer, and Santo put up their hands.

"We'll have a better time over there," said one of the others.

"How do you mean, better?" asked Gühler.

"The Amis will treat us better. More freedom. No guards. Excursions into the town."

"I hope you're not mistaken," said Gühler.

They went out of the kitchen. The Austrian stood by the door and said, "Don't give us away!"

"Don't be silly!" said Böhmer.

"Well, can't be too careful. If they get wind of anything, they might start a brawl tonight yet." They walked away down the camp road. Someone came up to them and said, "Hey, you, what's been going on in Number Six company's kitchen?"

"Soccer meeting," said Gühler.

"Since when do you play soccer?"

Gühler laughed. "How long have you known us?" he said and walked on. The other man stood looking after them.

"They've noticed something," said Böhmer.

"What time are they leaving tonight?"

"At twelve," said Böhmer.

The sound of taps came from the guard tower by the gate. They separated and went to their barracks.

"Have you heard? Two hundred people want to leave the camp," said Konz.

"Where did you hear that?"

"The whole camp's talking about it."

"I haven't heard anything."

"What do you say we go with them? If we lose the war they'll have a much better time and get home quicker."

"We've lost the war already," said Gühler.

In the morning the hundred and fifty were still standing by the gate with their barracks bags. They were being pelted with stones, sworn at, shouted at. More and more prisoners were gathering by the gate. "Traitors! Cowards! Bums!" they shouted.

The Austrians jostled up closer together. They held their barracks bags in front of them as protection against the stones raining down on them. One of them shouted: "You Nazi swine!"

American soldiers stood on the other side of the gate. They rested their rifles on their arms and laughed.

"*Los*, beat them up," someone shouted.

The Austrians looked anxiously around. The prisoners pressed closer and closer upon them. One of the Austrians suddenly let out a yell and put a hand to his back. He fell forward on his knees onto his barracks bag. A brick had hit him in the back. The Americans opened the gate.

They ran out of the gate, panting under the weight of their bags. They ran out like hunted, beaten animals, spat at, pelted with mud. Stones went flying over the barbed wire. A wild howling mob shouted after them: "Rats! Bastards! Swine!" and over and over again: "Traitors! Traitors!"

XXV

THEY drove out to the American hospital which lay almost at the end of the American military camp.

"We'll see some women again today," said Beijerke.

Gühler looked at him. Beijerke's face was fat and puffy from good eating.

"What's the use of seeing them?" he said. Beijerke grinned.

"Ha!" he said. "Legs and hips and if you get good and close you can smell them." He described a female figure in the air with his hands.

"He's snatch-crazy," someone said.

Beijerke didn't answer. He leaned out of the truck and looked down the road. "There," he said suddenly, "do you see her?"

A Negro woman was walking down the road behind them. They all leaned out and looked at the woman.

"A black piece wouldn't be bad either," said one of them.

"Stick to your horsehair mattresses, man," said another.

They drove into the courtyard of the hospital. A smell of disinfectant became noticeable. They climbed down from the truck.

"There's a smell of syphilis here again," said Schmidt, who was the last to get down from the truck.

"Of what?" said Gühler.

Schmidt turned around and laughed. They followed the sentry into the hospital. A nurse passed them in the hall. She nodded to Gühler as she passed.

"Do you know her?" said Schmidt.

"I see her every time I come here."

They both turned around. The nurse went in at one of the doors.

"Out of bounds for us," said Schmidt.

"Yes," said Gühler. "Unfortunately."

They went into the dining room where they were given mops and brooms. Beijerke rolled up his sleeves.

"Well, back to work," he said.

They pushed the tables to one side and began sweeping out the room. They got buckets of water, picked up the mops, dipped them in, and began to wipe the floor. It was oppressively hot in the room.

"This lousy central heating," said Schmidt.

Drops of sweat stood out on his forehead. A fat, elderly nurse brought them some sausages.

"The old girl's all right," said one of them.

Breakfast was brought in. The doctors and the nurses came in and sat down at one of the tables. Gühler looked across at the nurse who had nodded to him.

"She's pretty nice," said Schmidt. "A little fat, but otherwise all right."

276

"Too small for you."

"For me?" said Schmidt. "You mean she's way above us all."

They wiped down the kitchen stove in silence. Gühler looked across at the nurse again. She looked away, bent over her plate, and spoke to one of the doctors.

"Don't keep squinting over at her," said Schmidt. "You know it's out of bounds for us."

"For her too," said Gühler.

They crossed the hall to the sick rooms and began cleaning them out. Gühler was alone in one of the rooms. The door into the hall stood open. He put the bucket down beside him, leaned the mop against the wall, and sat down on the bed. "She looks remarkably like her," he thought.

He closed his eyes for a moment. He saw a woman crossing a street. The houses in the street had been destroyed. The woman turned around. It seemed to him that she looked at him. "If only I could see her again," he thought.

The nurse passed by in the hall outside. She looked casually through the open door into the room. Gühler jumped up, picked up the mop, and dipped it into the bucket. He heard her steps receding down the hall. Then they slowed up. Gühler pushed the mop over the floor. He heard the footsteps coming back again.

"Remember to clean out the ash trays," said the nurse, standing by the open door. Her German sounded as if it had been broken into many little pieces. She went up to the bed and piled the blankets together. Gühler picked up the ash tray, held it out the window and washed it.

"Not out of the window," said the nurse.

He put the ash tray back on the bedside table. He bent

over the bucket and wrung out the mop. The dirty water ran through his fingers back into the bucket. She stood close to the door at the head of the bed. He looked at her legs. He bent lower over the bucket. He watched her foot move toward the door and then come back again. The door shut.

"What does she want?" he thought.

"You shouldn't always throw everything out into the yard," she said.

Gühler stood up. He was standing behind her now. Her white apron gave off a smell of starch and carbolic. He bent over her cap with the hair welling under it. "If only one could smell her," he thought. She turned around and looked at him.

"What do you want?" she said.

"Nothing," he said.

He felt his hands on her arm. "I'm crazy," he thought. She bent forward a little. He could feel her breath on his mouth.

"Go away," she said.

"No."

"You must go."

"No," he said, and squeezed his hands around her arm. She fell onto the bed. Her cap slipped backward. Her hair came down. She was breathing heavily and her mouth was open. "She's got bad breath," he thought.

He opened her frilly collar.

"No," she said.

She tried to push his hands away. But her movements had no strength in them.

"Don't," he said.

She sat up. She propped herself on her elbows but he pushed her back on to the bed again.

278

"No," she said. "No, no."

He pushed her skirt back and under her stockings his hands felt the naked flesh.

"I've gone mad," he thought again.

She cried out and pushed him back. Then she grabbed at his face. He reeled to his feet. "She's scratching," he thought.

His face was burning. A drop of blood ran down into the corner of his mouth. He tasted it on his tongue. She sat up. She pushed her hair back under her cap and smiled. "You're crazy," she said in English.

Her skirt was still pulled up. She stayed sitting there like that looking up at him. He stared at her naked thighs above the tops of her stockings. She smiled again. He fell to the floor and pressed his head between her knees. His hands fumbled around the tops of her stockings. She pushed him away. "Go," she said.

His foot struck the bucket and some water slopped onto the floor.

"You are a German prisoner," she said in English.

He picked up the mop and stood up. He said nothing. He only looked at her. She pulled her skirt down again. Then she stood up. The door opened. Gühler pushed the mop around under the bed. A doctor stood in the doorway. He looked into the room without speaking. Gühler felt the doctor's eyes in his back. "What's the matter?" said the doctor.

"Nothing," said the nurse. She shook her head.

"Keep this door open. There's nobody but you and this German in here."

The doctor left the door open and went down the hall. She turned around. He saw her little squinting eyes. "I hate you," she said slowly. He didn't answer. "She's ugly," he thought. But behind her eyes he again saw the other woman walking down the devastated street. He heard Schmidt laughing in the hall.

"These damned gonococci exterminators," he said.

Someone else laughed. He bent over the bucket and wrung out the mop. She walked past him. He looked at her legs. He was aware of the smell of her body, which had affected him so strongly for a moment, underneath the carbolic smell of her dress. It looked like a uniform with its lieutenant's bars on it. He pulled himself erect. She turned around at the door and looked at him. "Excuse me," he said in English.

She turned the corners of her mouth down a little and smiled. The lipstick on her upper lip had smudged. It reached almost as far as her nose. Gühler pointed with his finger to his upper lip.

"Oh," she said, and pulled a mirror out of her pocket and looked at it. "Oh, excuse me," she said.

She took out a handkerchief and wiped her lips. Then she put on some more lipstick. Gühler dipped the mop into the bucket and slopped it onto the floor without wringing it out. The water splashed on to her stockings, making little black spots on them. She pulled her feet back. Then she went out. He heard her steps going down the hall.

"Not too bad, the little one," said Schmidt in the hall.

Gühler sat down on the bed. The atmosphere seemed oppressively hot. "Much too hot in here again," he thought.

"You're taking forever in there. Aren't you ready yet?" said Schmidt, coming to the door.

"Yes," said Gühler, "I'm coming."

He picked up the bucket and went down the hall with

Schmidt. He saw her again at lunch sitting at the table with the doctors. But she paid no attention to him. When he looked at her, she stared casually past him, as if he wasn't in the room.

"What an old cow," said Schmidt.

They drove back again early in the afternoon. The two prisoners who worked permanently in the laboratory climbed on the truck with them.

"Well, you prisoners," said Schmidt, "cut yourselves off a piece yet?"

The others laughed.

"They've got it good. Women round them all day long," said Beijerke.

"We've got to fall in outside at once," said Konz when they reached the barrack.

"What's the matter now?"

"Ninth of November. *Führer* Day."

"This gets crazier all the time," said Schmidt.

"In uniform. Those are the orders."

"I haven't got one."

"Neither have I," said Gühler.

"Then caps at least," said Buschmann, coming in on his bowlegs. They searched around for their caps and went out to the camp road.

"Speeches aren't allowed. The Americans have forbidden them."

"Attention!" shouted the *Feldwebel* of the various companies.

They stood rigid under the gray November sky.

"Let us think at this moment of our Commander-in-Chief," shouted the battalion commander.

But no one thought about him at all. They stood staring at the roofs of the barracks opposite.

281

"Thank you," said the battalion commander to the *Feldwebel*. The *Feldwebel* dismissed the companies.

That evening Böhmer came into the hut.

"They're doing Egmont this evening. Coming?"

"Yes," said Gühler.

Gerlich was sitting in one of the front rows of the theater. "Two places here," he said.

The camp adjutant was sitting beside him. He turned toward them. He was small and gray haired and peered at them through thick lenses.

"Didn't we manage that well?" he said.

"What?"

"That ninth of November business today. The Amis wouldn't have it at first, but according to the Geneva Convention we're allowed to honor our Commander-in-Chief at any time."

Gühler said nothing. He looked at the stage.

"What a Duchess of Parma!" said Gerlich.

"He should have put on more make-up," said Böhmer.

"It's wonderful though, that falsetto."

The Duchess held herself very stiff and upright. The black stubble of a beard stood out from under the make-up.

"They've cut out all the women except the Duchess," said the adjutant.

"He had to leave her in. Couldn't very well play Egmont with nobody in it but Egmont."

Gerlich leant over to Gühler. "What do you think? Couldn't he have all the women's parts taken by men?"

"He thinks it would be unnatural and offensive," said Gühler.

The drama specialist who was in charge of the camp's cultural welfare appeared on the stage as Egmont.

282

"A first-class Egmont," said Gerlich.

"If everything in this camp was as good as the culture, things might be tolerable," said Gühler.

"What do you mean?"

"You know what I mean. All your political rubbish."

"We're German soldiers," said Gerlich. "We must preserve order and discipline."

Gühler didn't answer. He went out with Böhmer.

"It's damned cold already," said Böhmer.

"What do you think of Gerlich?"

"A Nazi. A real Nazi. A sort of idealist."

"Unshakable?"

"Yes," said Böhmer.

They went over to the canteen. Two men passed them.

"Some opera!" said one of them.

"I went to sleep the minute the violins started," said the other.

They met Beijerke and Schmidt at the long canteen table. They had empty beer bottles in front of them.

"*Prosit!*" said Beijerke.

"Don't get too tight."

"Not a chance," said Beijerke, pushing over the empty beer bottle.

"He's tight already," said Gühler. Schmidt laughed.

"Well, how was the little girl this morning? Did you tear yourself off a piece?" he said.

Gühler looked around the canteen. They were all sitting about on empty beer cases with bottles in their hands, gnawing on chocolate bars and smoking cigarettes. In one corner some of them began to sing.

"They're celebrating the ninth of November. There are always a few crazy ones."

283

They were singing: "Today Germany belongs to us, tomorrow the world."

"Come on," said Böhmer, "let's go." They went out.

"They're like children," said Böhmer. "The whole thing's almost over and they still sing that. Why, tomorrow there won't be as much as a province of Germany that belongs to them."

"Do they really believe in it all?"

"It makes them feel a bit tougher, that's all."

Gühler lit a cigarette. They stood under one of the great arc lamps just beside the gate.

"What's that on your cheek? Someone scratch you?"

"Who could have scratched me?"

"Yes, who?" said Böhmer.

"It's just a pimple I picked during the night."

"Sure," said Böhmer, "with all this rich food."

He shook hands with Gühler and went across to his battalion. Gühler shivered a little. The wind blew cold across the rooftops and swept the smoke from the chimneys down to the road. He walked a little farther and then stopped. The wind blew at him from the direction of the hospital. He seemed to smell carbolic.

"I hate you," he thought in English.

XXVI

LIFE in the camp grew more and more uneventful. There were more transfers to other camps. Buschmann came into the barrack one evening and said, "I'm off tomorrow."

"Where to?"

He stood beside Gühler's bed on his bowlegs and looked at him sadly.

"I don't know," he said, "you never know anything in this lousy country."

"To Oklahoma?"

"I don't know. I think they think I'm a Nazi."

"Aren't you?"

"Never was one, my boy. Never. You know that."

"First I've heard of it."

"Don't be a fool, Gühler. You know me from the old days at the front. I wasn't a Nazi."

"Maybe you weren't. But you did a good job of shooting off your mouth like one."

"Ah, well. One's a soldier, after all. And duty is duty."

"What do you think about the war then?"

"Nothing. Nothing at all. It's lost."

"Oh," said Gühler, "so that's it."

Buschmann took out a cigarette and looked around the barrack. "Can't you do anything for me?" he said.

"What could I do for you?"

"Well, put in a word for me. You're an important person in the camp these days. I'd like to stay here very much."

"I haven't any influence on transfers."

"But you can do something for me."

"I tell you, I don't have any influence on such things," said Gühler.

Buschmann turned around. "Too bad," he said. "I thought you did have some influence."

"Have a good trip to Oklahoma."

"We'll see what happens."

He walked out on his bowlegs. Gühler watched him go. "One after the other," he thought.

The weeks passed. The mood in the camp changed from day to day. Gühler went on giving lectures. The number of people who attended increased by leaps and bounds. He lectured more often. Winter came. It came out of the open plain, almost overnight, driving snow and storm before it. Life receded farther and farther from them. The barbed wire cut them off from reality. Konz came over one night and sat on his bed.

"You must come and see Beijerke."

Gühler sat up. "What's the matter with him?"

"I don't know. He's carrying on like a maniac. I think he's got barbed-wire fever."

Beijerke was sitting on his bed. Gühler said, "What's wrong with you?"

"The whore," he mumbled. "The old tart."

286

He reached for Gühler's hand, felt along Gühler's legs and gripped them.

"Let go of me," said Gühler.

"Come into my bed," he mumbled. "I want you. . . ."

He squeezed Gühler's legs together. Then he fell to the floor and began to weep.

"His old lady ran off with somebody else," said Konz.

"How does he know?"

"His mother wrote and told him."

They picked him up and put him back on his bed. He was muttering to himself.

"We must undress him," said Gühler.

Beijerke jumped up and pulled Konz down with him.

"You whore," he shouted. "You damned tart."

Konz hit him in the face. Beijerke struck his head against the end of the bed and began to howl.

"He can't stop thinking about women," said Konz, hitting him in the face again.

The lights were turned on. Beijerke jumped up and threw Konz to the ground.

"You old sow," he said.

The barrack commander came running up in his shirt.

"What's the matter with him?"

"Can't you see, he's off his rocker," shouted Konz.

He knelt on Beijerke and pinned him to the floor. Gühler squatted beside Beijerke.

"Be reasonable, Beijerke. It's not as bad as all that."

Beijerke began to howl. Foam appeared at his mouth. He grasped at the air and shouted, "Let me at her. I'll fix her. Let me at her."

"We must have him taken away," said the barrack commander.

Konz jumped up. His face was scratched and bleeding.

"Hold him tight. I'll get the doctor."

They lifted Beijerke up and pushed him onto his bed again. He struck out wildly with his feet and arms.

"Tie him up," said the commander. They brought a rope and tied his hands.

"My God, these women!" said the commander.

The doctor came into the barrack. He looked at Beijerke. "There's nothing to be done. We've got to put him away."

They came for him during the night. He was still shouting. "The whore! The dirty slut!"

American soldiers held him firmly and twisted his arms behind his back when he struck at them. They pushed him out of the door. Gühler watched the ambulance drive away, its headlights playing between the darkened barracks.

The next morning Böhmer said, "Heard the latest?"

"No."

"A German offensive has started in the Ardennes."

"It won't last long."

"The Americans have just announced some reverses."

"Well?"

"That means reverses for us too."

"How so?"

"The mood will shift again. They'll get their courage back, and all the floaters will go over to them again. We must look out."

During the afternoon they came through the barracks with the first victory announcements. "Now we'll smash them, the whole pack of them. The Amis can't hang on much longer."

"Don't fool yourselves!" said Schmidt. He stood beside his bed, big and broad shouldered. His companions stood around him laughing.

"Give 'em hell!" said one of them.

"We'll put you guys in your place again. You've got a surprise coming. You'll all wind up in concentration camps. We've got all your names on our lists."

"You can take your concentration camps and stick them!"

They formed up in front of the barracks to be counted. The snow fell on their faces. Schmidt was standing beside Gühler.

"What do you think of all this farce?"

"Not much."

"Do you think they've got a chance?"

"None."

"Do we have to be more careful again?"

"I don't know," said Gühler. "We're still pretty weak."

At his lecture that evening the attendance was about a quarter less than usual. The others sat at the kitchen tables making notes. Gühler walked down between the tables. It was cold in the mess hall. The wind swept the snow through the gap under the door. Gühler said, "So many are missing."

A few people laughed. They looked at each other and laughed. "Perhaps they're afraid," said one of them. It was a fat noncom called Beyer.

"What have they got to be afraid of?"

"Your lectures aren't very highly thought of in certain quarters," said Beyer again.

289

Böhmer and Santo came in. They sat at one of the kitchen tables. Santo nodded to Gühler and laughed.

"Can we begin?" he said.

Gühler walked up and down between the tables. He suddenly started talking about Thomas Mann. "But we're dealing with the romantics," whispered Beyer.

"Just for this evening. By way of comparison. It's a special day," said Gühler.

They all sat and listened. They pushed their notebooks aside and put their arms on the tables. After the lecture Gühler stayed behind with Böhmer, Beyer, and Santo at one of the kitchen tables.

"That was foolish of you," said Böhmer.

"Why?"

"You know very well they send stool pigeons here."

"I was only talking about Thomas Mann."

"Exactly. That's like a red flag to them. It's high treason just to mention his name."

"In the middle of America! It's absolutely crazy," said Gühler.

They went out. The powdery snow blew across the camp road. They walked around the barracks with their coat collars turned up.

"What are you going to do if the Ardennes offensive succeeds? If the Amis give up Europe, and we're handed over?" said Beyer.

"I haven't thought about it."

"We're all on their lists. Everyone who's been to your lectures. They'll report us as traitors."

"I don't care. I've gradually got so I don't care any more. It'll be all up then anyway."

"The Americans won't keep us. They'll send everyone back."

"You're talking nonsense. The Nazis won't win."

"Still," said Beyer, "some people came back from the anti-Nazi camp over there this afternoon. They insisted they'd been sent there by mistake. Now of course everyone mistrusts them. But the Nazis are very pleased about it."

"What do they say about conditions over there?"

"Bad. They have to work more than here. Ten hours a day. On top of that the food's worse. Even the Americans don't think much of them."

"Why not?"

"They're bad boys."

"Haven't they been behaving?"

"Probably not."

"Have you heard that you're supposed to take over the camp newspaper and library?" said Böhmer.

"Who? Me?" said Gühler.

"Yes. The two librarians are being transferred to another camp. A new cultural officer has just arrived at the American headquarters. A Jewish professor from Germany."

"What has that got to do with me?"

"You take over the paper and the library."

"Why me? I don't want to."

"You must," said Böhmer. "Then we'll have control of everything."

The next morning Gühler was called to the *Oberfeldwebel* in command of the third battalion.

"You've been suggested as a successor to the man who used to run the newspaper and the library. He's being transferred."

"I heard something about it."

"There's been a certain amount of resistance to the

idea, but after a conference of the three battalion commanders and the company commanders we've decided on you."

"What sort of resistance, *Herr Feldwebel?*"

"It's said you're not a National Socialist. There's been criticism of your lectures. They're not to everybody's liking."

"I'm not a National Socialist."

"We know that. But they say you're National German."

Gühler didn't answer for a moment. The *Oberfeldwebel* stood in front of him like a giant.

"But that's not right. I'm not National German."

"What are you then?"

"I've told you already."

"Come on, out with it."

"I told you. I'm not a National Socialist."

The *Oberfeldwebel* said nothing but walked once around the table.

"Besides, American headquarters wants you there."

"Yes," said Gühler, "I know."

"I'll tell them you're coming over. They want to speak to you."

"Shall I go at once?"

"Yes. You can go now. I'll tell them you're coming over."

Gühler went slowly down the road to the gate. The sky was gray and lowering. Snow was falling off the roofs of the barracks. A few crows were hopping about in the roadway.

"It's almost a year since they beat up Pips. . . ."

A soldier opened the gate for him and took him to the American headquarters. He stopped at the entrance to the room and gave the Nazi salute. He shot his arm up and clicked his heels. Since the Nazi salute had become compulsory in the German army, all American officers had to be saluted by the raising of the arm.

The Jewish professor from Germany stood behind his desk. He smiled and returned the salute.

"Are you Gühler?"

"Yes."

"We like your lectures. You seem to be a reasonable sort of man."

Gühler didn't answer.

"We want you to take over the camp newspaper and the library."

"So I've heard."

"Good. Well, you can order anything you like. We'll get you everything."

"Yes," said Gühler.

"We don't want any more National Socialists here. We want a peaceful camp with the leadership in the hands of reasonable people."

"Now, all of a sudden, Lieutenant?"

"How do you mean?"

"Up till now nobody's cared about us. Up till now we've been living under a worse terror than anything in Germany."

The lieutenant leaned back and smiled wryly.

"Yes," he said, "I know."

"You know?" said Gühler.

"I heard about it." He smiled again.

"But you must understand," he went on, "every camp is subject to the Geneva Convention. We haven't the right to intervene by force. Every action we take here means that the Nazis can do exactly the same with our prisoners in Germany."

"I see, next-of-kin retaliation."

"What's next-of-kin retaliation?"

"If we desert or give ourselves up, Lieutenant, they take it out on our relations in Germany. They have to pay the penalty for us."

"That's something different."

"It's something similar."

"As you like," said the lieutenant.

"We've got to look after ourselves then."

"Yes, we can't do anything more than give you our support."

Gühler went out of the room. At the door he turned around and gave the Nazi salute.

"You don't need to bother about that with me," said the lieutenant. He smiled wryly again and nodded. "But that only goes when we're alone, understand?"

"Very good, Lieutenant."

Böhmer met him on the camp road.

"Well?" he said.

Gühler looked across the snow-covered rooftops and said, "It's over. It's over at last."

"Thank God," said Böhmer.

He clapped him on the shoulder and laughed. Gühler walked along beside him in silence.

"Well, how do you feel? We've done it at last."

"I don't know," said Gühler. "It all seems absolutely crazy."

The battalion commander came storming out of his barrack. He rushed over to them in agitation.

"God damn it," he said. "What a rotten mess."

"What's the matter, *Herr Oberfeldwebel?*" said Gühler.

"I'm being transferred. Can you imagine? I'm being transferred."

"But you're National German," said Gühler.

"Who, me?" said the *Oberfeldwebel.*

Gühler laughed. The *Oberfeldwebel* looked at him furiously.

"What crap," he said. "I'm nothing, do you understand? Nothing. I'm a soldier, that's all."

"I'm not even a soldier," said Gühler.

"What do you mean? What are you then?"

"I'm a man, just a man. That's all." Gühler laughed.

"Nonsense," said the *Oberfeldwebel.* "Absolute nonsense. Everyone's a man."

He pushed past them and strode down the camp road. They both watched him go. Böhmer laughed and said, "He's not so bad."

"Maybe not," said Gühler.

A few prisoners were standing in the roadway throwing snowballs. Böhmer got one on the nose. He took off his glasses and tried to clean them. "Like a lot of kids," he said.

They bent down, pressed the snow together into balls, and threw them back. The prisoners laughed and shouted. Snowballs flew back and forth.

"It's good to hit back for once," thought Gühler.

XXVII

SOME soccer players were coming from the playing field. They wore red shirts and black shorts.

"Our outside left is lousy," one of them said. "We'll never win with him."

"He's been overeating too long. That's all," said another.

Gühler went past them.

"Have you heard? Hitler's dead?"

"Where did you get that from?" asked Gühler.

"The camp adjutant just told us."

They stopped to talk to him.

"Do you really think we'll lose the war?"

"Yes," said Gühler, "it's all over."

"But it's not possible. What's going to happen to us?"

"I don't know."

"Oh, the hell with it," said a man with the ball under his arm. "It'll all get straightened out again."

They turned and went on.

"That right back now. We ought to change him, too. He lets everybody through," one of them said.

"*Mensch*," said the other, "we can't change the whole team around just before the game."

Gühler walked into the camp adjutant's office.

"Someone told me Hitler was dead. Is it true?"

"Yes," said the adjutant, looking at Gühler through his thick lenses. "It was on the radio."

"What's happening in Berlin?"

"Almost over," said the adjutant.

Gerlich came in. He looked flushed and agitated.

"We must alert the camp at once."

"What do you mean, alert the camp?" said the adjutant.

"Hitler is dead. Every company must parade to honor the *Führer*."

"No," said the adjutant. "I'm through playing along with all that."

"You're through?"

"Yes. You lost the war. You're finished."

"In the name of the whole camp I demand that you go to the Amis and get permission for a memorial to honor the death of the *Führer*."

"I don't want to have anything more to do with you. Go yourself."

"I'm not the adjutant. You must go." Gerlich suddenly began to shout. "I demand that you go to the Amis. Immediately."

"You haven't the right to demand anything. Not in the name of the whole camp by any means. You're not the camp."

"Are you going or not?"

"No," shouted the adjutant. "I was never a Nazi. I don't want to have anything more to do with you."

Gühler looked at both of them. The adjutant's hands were shaking on the desk.

"So you were never a Nazi. That's what you say now," Gerlich leaned forward a little. His mouth was twitching. "So you've been playing ball with the Amis all the time."

"All right," said the adjutant, "I'll go, but only if I can use your name out there."

"A coward, eh? I don't care. Even if they put me in a punishment camp."

"Will you wait here?" said the adjutant.

"Yes, I'll wait," said Gühler.

The adjutant went out.

"Did you ever see such a coward?" said Gerlich. He sat on the chair behind the desk. Gühler turned on the radio.

"There'll be disturbances in the camp," he said slowly.

"What do you mean, disturbances?"

"We're not going to have anything to do with this business of a memorial parade."

"Who isn't?"

"We aren't," said Gühler. "All of us who don't share your opinion."

"So we've reached that point," said Gerlich. Gühler turned around indifferently.

"Yes," he said. "We've reached that point. It's all over, and you people did it. Germany's cities have been destroyed. The war is lost. A hard road lies ahead of the German people. And you, you who brought it all about, you're still screaming your heads off."

Gerlich leaned across the desk. He looked up at Gühler from below. "Didn't you believe in it, then?"

"No," said Gühler. "You knew that all along."

298

"But there was no other way for us."

"There were plenty of ways of avoiding this insanity," said Gühler.

"What's going to happen now?"

"I don't know. We must start all over again."

"No," said Gerlich, "I'm not going to stay in Germany. We'll just become coolies for the others."

"Where do you want to go?"

"I'll emigrate. Canada, or somewhere like that."

They sat there looking at each other.

"Did you really believe in it all?" said Gühler.

Gerlich was silent. He stared at the desk in front of him. He folded his hands.

"Perhaps everything we did was wrong," he said. "But I believed in it."

He raised his head and looked at Gühler.

"Now you must do better," he said suddenly.

"We?" said Gühler.

"Yes, you who were against us. We've been dismissed now."

"You murdered so many. Who is there left? There aren't many of the German intelligentsia left. You did a thorough job with your People's Courts and your gallows."

"Yes, it's damned difficult," said Gerlich.

The adjutant came back. He slammed the door excitedly. "They threw me out," he said.

"I thought they would," said Gühler.

Gerlich jumped up and went to the door.

"We'll do it without permission, then. We owe it to the *Führer*," he said.

"You better get used to the idea that it's all over," said Gühler.

Gerlich turned around at the door. His face looked tired and sunken. "Did you mention my name out there?" he said.

"Yes," said the adjutant. "They asked me for it."

"Well, I might as well prepare for the punishment camp then."

"Maybe," said the adjutant.

Gerlich pulled himself up. He looked at Gühler for a moment. "Well," he said, "I don't care any more now."

He turned and opened the door. Gühler stared in silence at the door as it closed behind him.

"What an ass," said the adjutant. "I'm not going to let myself be pushed around by them any more."

Gühler had propped his head in his hands. He stared at the floor. The triumphant voice of an American announcer came from the radio.

"He really believed it," said Gühler softly.

The adjutant sat down behind his desk again.

"I was never a Nazi," he said. "Never. But they kept putting pressure on you."

Gühler turned the radio off and leaned back in his chair.

"But when all that beating up was going on in camp you didn't do anything about it."

"What could I have done? Nothing. It would have been easier to believe in it oneself."

"Yes," said Gühler, "that's the way it was."

He stood up and went out. As he left the barrack the working parties were marching into the camp. They marched past him with their hats pushed back on their heads and their tunics open. Their faces were red and healthy. They laughed as they marched.

Böhmer came up to him. "The Amis have gone completely crazy out there," he said.

"Victory celebrations?"

"New regulations for us. Everything's being tightened up. We're not allowed to eat anything in the officers' messes any more. And we're not allowed to take anything away with us, either."

"Yes," said Gühler. "We'll be getting a shock or two."

"Come over to my place. We'll go to the movies afterwards," said Böhmer. They went into Böhmer's barrack.

"They've brought in American newspapers again," said Böhmer.

The prisoners were standing around the beds looking at the newspapers.

"All a lot of crap," said one of them. "I don't believe a word of it."

"Why do you read that trash at all?"

"You have to keep informed. There aren't any German newspapers."

An elderly, gray-haired man got up from his bed.

"The war's over, children," he said. "We've lost another one."

"It's not over yet. We'll throw them out of Germany. If we were only there."

"Children," began the old man again, "don't work yourselves up. There's nothing more you can do about it."

Böhmer lay down on his bed. "What if we were home now?" he said. A photograph stood by the bed on the little table beside the window.

"I wonder what she's doing?" he said. "It's so long since I heard from her."

"She'll be all right," said Gühler.

"With all that bombing? Düsseldorf's a heap of ruins. Berlin's a battlefield, and I'm not even sure whether she's in Berlin or Düsseldorf."

"How long since you heard?"

"Three months," said Böhmer.

"You'll hear from her again."

"I don't know," said Böhmer. "Sometimes you lose hope."

They were both silent and listened to the others talking.

"Have you heard?" one of them said. "August's getting a divorce."

"What else could he do?"

"I wouldn't like to be there when he gets home. He'll bash his old lady's skull in."

"Do you know her?" said Böhmer.

"Only from her photograph."

"Here," said Böhmer.

He took some snapshots out of the table drawer and gave them to Gühler. He saw a naked woman walking over some dunes.

"Don't let the others see it."

"Where was that?" said Gühler.

"On the Kurland Peninsula."

"The Russians are there now."

"Yes," said Böhmer. "I wonder if we'll ever go there again."

Neither of them spoke. Gühler looked at the photograph.

"Do you think Hitler's really dead?" said someone from the bed opposite.

Gühler gave the photograph back. "A beautiful woman," he said.

After supper they went over to the cinema. It was crowded. Suddenly Gerlich was standing in front of the screen. "Our *Führer* is dead," he said. "Killed in action. Let us all rise from our seats."

"You're a liar," shouted someone.

A tumult arose. Gerlich turned pale. They jumped up and shouted wildly.

"It's not true," someone shouted.

"Get out," some of them yelled, "get out."

Gühler and Böhmer arose and went to the door. Gerlich came down the center of the hall toward them. He walked slowly, bent slightly forward, paying no attention to the catcalls.

"Who told you that?" shouted someone.

"Get out! Get out!" someone kept roaring in one corner. Gerlich walked slowly past Gühler.

"Did you have to do that?" said Gühler.

Gerlich turned around and looked at Gühler. His eyes were tired. "You tell them," he said.

"No," he said, "it's not necessary. They'll believe it soon enough. When they get home and see the ruined cities."

Gerlich went out.

"He's finished," said Böhmer.

Gühler sat in his seat again. "I think he's responsible for a lot that happened here in the camp."

"Perhaps," said Böhmer, "but nobody knows for sure."

A Mickey Mouse film began to be shown on the screen. The prisoners laughed. They roared with laughter.

"What'll happen to Gerlich?" said Böhmer.

"Punishment camp, probably."

303

"Why punishment camp?"

"He gave himself away this morning," said Gühler.

"Quiet," bellowed a prisoner in front of them turning around resentfully.

"He actually did a lot for the camp," whispered Böhmer.

"Probably an equal amount of good and harm. Who'll bother about the difference now?" said Gühler.

"Shut up. Cut out that jabbering!" someone roared in front of them.

"*Verdammte scheiss!*" said someone else. "Keep your trap shut!"

"They want to have their peace and quiet," said Gühler.

"Yes," said Böhmer, "that's the most important thing for them."

A great burst of laughter came from the rows of seats.

"They still know how to laugh," said Böhmer.

XXVIII

THEY watched the rockets soar above them into the twilit sky.

"Now we ought to let the bastards have it," said Schmidt.

They were sitting on the steps of one of the barracks. From the American camp on the other side of the barbed wire came the uproar of victory celebrations. Double guards had been posted on the platforms of the guard towers. Their machine guns were trained on the camp. Gühler looked at Schmidt and said, "The Amis are alerted. They don't want any trouble in the camp."

"We ought to let the bastards have it just the same," said Schmidt.

"Do you want to be court-martialed by the Americans, now that you've got the whole dirty mess behind you?"

"No," said Schmidt, "not exactly."

"Well, then," said Gühler.

Schmidt looked at a few drunken soldiers who went

bawling past the wire. "Hi ya, boys! The war's over," one of them shouted. They didn't answer.

"*Mensch*," said Schmidt, "what we need is a revolution. A real revolution."

Gühler jerked his head toward the guards on the towers. "They'd stop it," he said. "They'd stop everything."

"*Verfluchte scheiss*," said Schmidt.

He got up and walked off down the camp road. The streets lay empty and deserted in the semitwilight of the May night.

"Let's hope he doesn't make any trouble," said Böhmer.

The rockets were bursting above them. The ragged sounds of a jazz band came across from the American barracks. Böhmer looked at the rockets and said, "It's a strange feeling being on the winning side and the losing side at the same time."

"A very strange feeling," said Gühler.

They fell silent again. A woman's light laugh came across from the station on the other side of the playing field. "What a long time it's been since I saw a woman. It seems an eternity," said Böhmer.

The woman on the other side of the wire let out a shriek. It was followed by a long-drawn-out gurgling laugh that echoed between the barracks. "She's tight," said Gühler.

They got up and walked along the wire. Over the camp lay a benumbed quiet. They walked along slowly with their hands in their pockets.

"You damned Nazis," said one of the guards. He was standing behind his machine gun up on the tower, laughing down at them. They walked on in silence.

"We're all Nazis to them," said Böhmer.

"Yes," said Gühler. "As far as they're concerned, we've all lost the war. You and I and the Nazis who are sitting in the barracks now wanting to see us hung. They don't see any difference."

From far away out on the plain came the sound of a cannon being fired. It rolled dully across the camp. A rocket went hissing up into the sky.

"Victory parade," said Böhmer.

Gühler said nothing. The rocket burst above them sending a shower of red and yellow sparks into the night.

"I imagined it all quite differently," Gühler began again. "Much different. I've waited for this for twelve years, day after day. I hated them like the plague. But I imagined the end would be quite different. We'd have a reckoning with them. We'd celebrate and get tight, we'd be so happy. And now they're over there celebrating while we sit here behind barbed wire."

"Be thankful it's all over at any rate."

"I hope it's all over. My God, it was like a nightmare."

"Yes," said Böhmer, "it was a madman's dream."

They walked down between the barracks. Konz came up to them. "Come quickly," he said. "Schmidt's beginning to raise hell."

"Well, so long," said Böhmer.

"See you tomorrow."

"Tomorrow a new era begins."

They went over to the barrack. Konz said, "When do you think we'll get home now?"

"I don't know. It could take some time."

Schmidt was sitting on his bed. His friends were standing around him. The others were playing skat or lying on their beds staring into space.

"Well," he was saying, "now you feel a little different about things, eh? Now you never were for it, eh? Yes, there's another wind blowing now, I can tell you. If anyone opens his trap from now on I'll knock his teeth in." His friends laughed. The others stared into space and said nothing.

"Well, what do you think, Wilhelm?" he said.

"You're right," said one of his friends.

"You just don't count any more, you Heinies, I tell you."

"Cut it out!" shouted someone, sitting upright in bed.

"Cut it out?" shouted Schmidt. "Now I'm doing the talking, see? It's my turn now and your turn to shut up!"

"Did you win the war, or what? He's acting like he won the war."

Schmidt jumped up, went across to the other man's bed, and held his fist in front of his face.

"Just one more word out of you, just one more word."

The other man was silent. There was a deathly silence in the room. The skat players turned around and looked at Schmidt. Everyone looked at him.

"It's our turn now, understand? In case you make any mistake about it!"

"He's off his head," said one of the skat players.

Gühler went across to Schmidt. "You won't convince them like that," he said.

Schmidt turned round and looked at him in fury. "Good God," he shouted, "it's time someone told them."

"Well," said Gühler, "perhaps it won't do any harm."

They sat down on Schmidt's bed.

"Grand slam," said one of the skat players, "with fours."

"You're right," whispered Gühler. "But that's not the
308

way to do it. If you hit one of them the Amis will come and you'll be years later getting home."

"I don't give a damn."

"Forget it," said Gühler, "it's pointless. They're all outside with their machine guns and they'll soon fix you. It's pointless."

Schmidt lay down on his bed. "*Mensch*," he said, "am I burned up!"

"Forget it. It's senseless. Be reasonable."

"Reasonable! It's always us who have to be reasonable. For twelve years we couldn't do anything. We had to keep our traps shut and put up with all this shit, and now we're supposed to be reasonable again!"

"Yes," said Gühler. "There's nothing else we can do."

He sat down beside Schmidt and looked at him. Schmidt said, "I feel calmer now. Don't worry."

Gühler got up and went out. Konz was standing by the door.

"*Mensch*, but I'd like to go home. If we could only go home now."

"Stop that," said Gühler.

"I'll be going like Beijerke soon. There's something pressing on me inside, I tell you, I can't hold out any longer."

"Pull yourself together."

"Pull yourself together! Christ, that's all I hear. I want to go home, see? I've had enough of this shit. The war's over now and the women are waiting for us."

"They'll have to wait a long time yet," said Gühler.

He went out, slamming the door behind him. He saw two shadows sitting on the bench in front of the barrack. He heard them whispering behind him.

"What's he up to?"

"He's one of the victors now."

"Oh well, if it had gone the other way they would have fixed him good. He'd be a head shorter."

"Now they're acting like big shots."

"We'll cut them down to size again," said the other.

He heard them laughing behind him. He went down the camp road in silence. He stopped in front of the gate and looked out. Drunken soldiers were staggering out of the barracks, singing. Women stood in front of the doors smoking. He could see their red painted lips. They laughed when one of the soldiers came reeling out. He looked at their laughing faces in the half darkness and thought, "To live. My God, to live again."

The rockets rose up into the air. Their spurting sparks fell on the rooftops. He picked up a stone and threw it into the night. "Who will cast the first stone?" he thought, and then, "They all will, all of them."

He was suddenly overcome by a feeling of exhilaration. He laughed to himself. The bugle on the watch tower began to sound. Its notes rose hoarse and shrill into the night. He turned around and walked slowly down the camp road back to his barrack.

"Have you heard?" said Konz from where he lay in the next bed.

"Have I heard what?"

"The people in the kitchen say that the rations are going to be cut from tomorrow. Only fifteen hundred calories a day. Punishment."

"What do you mean, punishment?"

"For losing the war. No more cigarettes or chocolate in the canteen. And the people in the kitchen say that from now on there'll be nothing but dried herring to eat."

310

"Nonsense," said Gühler.

"No, it's true. The Amis say we're all guilty. Guilty for the whole dirty mess."

"Where did you hear that?"

"They're saying it in the orderly room. Our re-education begins tomorrow. American history and English. We're all going to be democrats now. If we all speak English and know American history, we're good democrats. They say that those who don't go to the lectures will never get home."

"That's all nonsense."

"Hell, no. Everybody's signed for the lectures already. They're all going in for this re-education because they want to get home."

"The Nazis too?"

"They were the first to sign."

"My God," said Gühler. "Collective guilt, dried herring, and American history! What lunacy!"

"They're the victors," said Konz.

"But they can't just turn around and repeat the whole dirty mess all over again! It would be insane!"

"Aren't you used to it by now?" said Konz. "We're always the ones who get pissed on, one way or another. First they pushed us around in the training camps. Then we got the dirty end of it at Stalingrad and Cassino. And now we wind up here with dried herring." He laughed. "Herring isn't too bad anyway."

Gühler lay on his back and stared at the ceiling. Slowly the ceiling above him began to revolve.

"You're an idealist," Konz was saying. "Just as goofy as all the rest of them."

Gühler watched the beams of the searchlights from

the guard towers playing on the ceiling above him. The ceiling turned faster and faster like a carousel.

"It can't always go on like this," he said. "Some day we've got to get out of the whole filthy meat grinder."

But Konz just laughed.